THE 4TH REICH

- BOOK FOUR -

Patrick Laughy

The 4th Reich is a work of fiction. Though parts of the book make reference to historical persons, places or events, the characters and the story are all products of the author's imagination

DEDICATION
*This book is dedicated to all Second World War
history buffs out there who, from time to time
wonder...what if?*

ACKNOWLEDGEMENTS

Thanks to Suzy for her long hours of research and editing, David for another great cover and Linette for her continued support.

Patrick Laughy

Nineteen Forty-Two

CHAPTER ONE

- January -

- Hitler -

Hitler often used Walther Hewel as an independent sounding board, someone he could speak to frankly, without having concern that his comments might reach other ears, or that his singular audience had a vested interest in swaying the Fuhrer's own view of whatever topic was raised.

Hewel considered Hitler to be a great man as well as a friend. He had no personal axe to grind and he was an excellent listener.

Due to these facts, reflections from Hewel as to the content of the private conversations he shared with Hitler, tend to provide an honest and unbiased reading on what the Fuhrer really felt and believed at any given moment in time.

These memories delivered by Hewel are likely more unbiased than those of many of the others who spent a good deal of time with the Fuhrer, but saw him through their own eyes and with their own predispositions on the topics being discussed.

Approximately three weeks prior to launching the invasion of Russia on June twenty-second, nineteen forty-one, Hitler had one of those many long discussions with his friend, Walther Hewel. The two men were alone within the confines of the Fuhrer's private bunker and their cloistered conversation went on until late in the evening.

On this occasion, Hitler was expounding on his impression of the Jewish question.

'I feel like a Robert Koch in politics. He found the bacillus and with it showed medical science a new way. I discovered the Jew as a bacillus and the ferment of all social

decomposition...and the one thing I have proven is that a state can live without Jews; that economy, art, culture, etc., can exist even better without Jews, which is the worst blow I could give the Jews.'

* * * * *

- Inner Circle -

Up until nineteen forty-two Hitler had pretty much kept his plans for the Jews to himself. Few around him, secretaries, servants, adjutants, personal staff, knew of his specific intentions in that regard.

A prime reason for Hitler's delay in beginning his campaign to deal with Jewry, which he had envisioned for some time, was his belief that to take such action would bring the US into the war. The attack on Pearl Harbor in December had brought the Americans into the war and for Hitler, any concern as to what Roosevelt might think of his plan to eradicate of the Jews had been negated on that day.

Towards the latter part of nineteen forty-one Hitler had begun to express the odd comment that might have offered a hint as to his inner thoughts. In October during a meal he had rambled on about the necessity of bringing decency into civil life and he'd said: *'But the first thing above all, is to get rid of the Jews. Without that, it will be useless to clean the Augean stables'.*

A couple of days later he suggested that the plan to create a banished, separate, Jewish state would be a dismal failure and reminded his guests: *'From the rostrum of the Reichstag I prophesised to Jewry that, in the event of war's proving invariable, the Jews would disappear from Europe. That race of criminals has on its conscience the two million dead of the Great War, and now already hundreds and thousands more. Let nobody tell me that all the same we can't park them in the marshy parts of Russia! Who's worrying about our troops? It's not a bad idea, by the way, that public rumor attributes to us a plan to exterminate the Jews. Terror is a salutary thing'.*

He then went on to say: *'I have numerous accounts to settle, about which I cannot think today. But that doesn't mean that I forget them. I write them down. The time will come to bring out that big book! Even with regard to the Jews, I've found myself remaining inactive. There's no sense in adding uselessly to the difficulties of the moment. One acts shrewdly when one bides one's time.'*

As previously clearly demonstrated, Hitler believed it was bad policy for him to allow any one person or group to be in a position to take credit or blame for any major decisions. Whatever conundrum he faced, he preferred to delegate to several persons or bodies the responsibility for any individual problem solving. He would then encourage those involved to compete with each other in order to win his praise or displeasure, whatever the individual result should be. With this in mind, he had initially turned over the solving of the *'Jewish question'* to more than one specific agency or arm of his government.

In this case however, one man had quickly taken up the gauntlet and run with it.

Heinrich Himmler saw the solving of the Jewish question, one of Hitler's greatest concerns, as the best way for he and his SS to rise to a place of prime importance within the new Reich and Hitler's inner circle.

His chosen man to head the SS team addressing this pressing question was Reinhard Heydrich.

Just two days after the beginning of *'Operation Barbarossa'*, Heydrich sent a report to his boss stating that the deportation of the Jews, the policy currently in effect, was an impossible undertaking. He specifically referred to the prevailing plan to deport the Jews to the French island of Madagascar as unrealistic, and detailed the impracticability of any such scheme in detail.

Through *'Operation Barbarossa'* the Fuhrer was already dealing with Bolshevism and now he was ready to begin the planning stages for his attack on his, and therefore Germany's, other main enemy, that of the international Jewry.

Heydrich's report had clearly indicated that the current ad-hoc system of isolation and deportation of the Jews could only be considered, at best, as a stop-gap mechanism for dealing with the problem. This report went up the chain of command to the top and only served to confirm Hitler's feelings on the matter.

Keep in mind that the Fuhrer wanted the Jews destroyed; wiped off the face of the earth. He considered himself to be carrying out God's injunction by doing so. It was God's command that he cleanse the world of this vermin.

Hitler was still a member in good standing of the Church of Rome and had clearly and publicly stated: *'I am now as before a Catholic and will always remain so'.*

His church taught that the Jew was the killer of God and he firmly believed that the extermination of the Jewish race could therefore be contemplated without the slightest twinge of conscience. He had been chosen to act as God's instrument and in dealing firmly with the Jews, would be merely acting as the avenging hand of God.

This of course with the proviso that such action was carried out impersonally and without cruelty. Hitler made it abundantly clear to Goering, when he issued his instructions, that the Jews had to be dealt with humanely.

On the thirty-first of July, nineteen forty-one, Heydrich received Goering's cryptic response to his report. This missive had been issued under Goering's signature, but undisputedly, at Hitler's direction.

In part the order commanded that Heydrich was: *'to make all necessary preparations regarding organizations and financial matters to bring about the complete solution of the Jewish question in the German sphere of influence in Europe.'*

Himmler took this response as an answer to his prayers.

He was delighted...obviously he and his SS had won the political gamesmanship over the others who had been involved in seeking to find a way to deal with the *'Jewish Question'*.

The SS and therefore Himmler, had been ordered to make plans that would efficiently have all Jews humanely eliminated.

In view of his personal experience of the executions at Minsk, Himmler had then turned to his chief SS physician to ask what method would serve to best manage this aim both humanely and efficiently.

The answer he'd received was - gas chambers.

Himmler had then arranged for gassing tests to be run at Auschwitz.

He'd summoned the commandant, Rudolf Hoess to Berlin where he'd gave him secret oral instructions to arrange such tests after explaining what he intended to do and justifying this action with words to the effect that: *'the Fuhrer has given the order for the final solution of the Jewish question. We, the SS, must carry out that order. If it is not carried out now the Jews will later on destroy the German people.'*

Absolute secrecy was a top priority regarding any plans for the Jews at this point. Hoess was ordered not to discuss the matter with anyone including his superior, the inspector of concentration camps.

Hoess followed these instructions to the letter. He did not even tell his wife what he was doing.

These directives about secrecy had come down the line orally from Hitler, who still fervently believed that he had been destined by God to save the world from the Jews but understood that his people were not yet ready to easily embrace the manner in which that was to be accomplished.

The Fuhrer had carefully taken into consideration several facts before deciding to turn the SS loose to fulfill the need for the cleansing.

When he'd come to power Hitler had recognized that the majority of his countrymen were solidly behind him, that they supported his racist crusade and the persecution his government had quickly initiated against the Jews.

At this point in the war he was convinced, not unjustly, that the majority of his countrymen favoured the continuation of these harsh policies and just as importantly, on the international scale, that Germany's achievements in this regard had also received the tacit support of millions of Westerners.

He was now ready to give the SS, through Goering, the authority to take the next step and begin planning for the organized elimination of the Jews. He instructed that, in its initial stages, this process was to be carried out with complete secrecy. However, over time, it was his intention to publicly reveal more of the truth in stages, with the expectation that his crusade to cleanse Europe of Jewry would have, by then, become a national mission, with the entire population of the expanded Reich fully aware and in complete support of, his plan.

* * * * *

- Wannsee Conference -

The Wannsee Conference was a meeting of several senior officials of Nazi Germany, held in the Berlin suburb of Wannsee on January twentieth, nineteen forty-two. This meeting was called by the director of the *'SS-Reichssicherheitshauptamt'* (Reich Main Security Office), or RSHA, Obergruppenfuhrer Reinhard Heydrich. Its purpose was to ensure the cooperation of administrative leaders of the various government departments in the implementation of the *'final solution to the Jewish question'*.

Those Heydrich invited to attend the meeting included representatives from several government ministries, including state secretaries from the Foreign Office, Justice, Interior and State Ministries as well as representatives from the SS.

As a result of Goering's order, Heydrich had prepared an overall plan for the *'total solution to the Jewish question'*. This plan followed the principles outlined in *'Generalplan Ost'* which called for the deportation of the Jewish population of occupied Eastern Europe and the Soviet Union to Siberia where they would be used as slave labour on road building or other projects for the betterment of the Reich or, if incapable of work, be exterminated.

For the purposes of the meeting it was envisioned that an

estimated five million Jews from the Soviet Union as well as an additional three million from the Ukraine would be dealt with in this manner.

The Nazis also planned to reduce the population of the conquered territories by thirty million additional sub-humans through starvation in an action called the *'Hunger Plan'*. In the case of these individuals, it was intended that food supplies would be removed from the areas in which they were living. The food would then be transported elsewhere to provide provisions for the German army and German citizens.

This would solve two problems.

Firstly, it would deprive the sub-humans within newly captured territory from sustenance, leading to starvation and death and thereby the reduction of *'useless mouths'*. Secondly, it would serve to help deal with the situation brought about by Germany having had poor harvests in both nineteen forty and nineteen, forty-one. Goering was therefore now finding it difficult to feed its own citizens as well as the massive numbers of forced labourers which had been brought into the country to work in the armaments industry.

In preparation for the Wannsee meeting, SS-Obersturmbannfuhrer (Lieutenant Colonel) Adolf Eichmann, head of *'Referat IV B4'* of the Gestapo, prepared a list of the numbers of Jews to be found in the various European countries. These were listed in two groups, 'A' and 'B'.

Those in group 'A' were to be found in the countries currently under direct Reich control or occupation, or under puppet regimes. 'B' countries were those allied, client states, neutral or at war with Germany. The total number of Jews still remaining to be dealt with in these countries was estimated by Eichmann to be eleven million.

This list was on a single sheet of paper and copies were provided to those in attendance at the meeting.

Eichmann had prepared briefing notes for Heydrich a week prior to the conference and Heydrich followed these as he spoke. He opened the conference with a rundown of the anti-Jewish measures that had been taken by Germany since nineteen thirty-three, telling his audience that between that year and October of nineteen forty-one, five hundred and thirty-seven thousand German, Austrian and Czech Jews had emigrated.

He went on to explain that there were approximately eleven million Jews left in the whole of Europe and that half of those resided in countries which were not as yet under direct German control. He then informed those in attendance that Himmler was prohibiting further Jewish emigration. A new solution was now to be followed, that of *'evacuation'* of the Jews to the east. He went on to explain that this was to be only a temporary answer, a step toward the final solution of the *'Jewish question'*.

As was always the case when references were made with regard to those who would require *'special handling'*, the words used during the *'official'* part of this meeting (that which would be recorded in the minutes of the conference) were loaded with euphemisms that, to those in the know, had double meanings.

For example, *'resettlements to the east'* at the time of the meeting meant transport to concentration camps and shortly after the meeting, it also signified a one way trip to an extermination center.

The minutes of the *'Wannsee Protocol'* indicate that, among other things, Heydrich said the following:

'Under proper guidance, in the course of the final solution the Jews are to be allocated for appropriate labour in the East. Able-bodied Jews, separated according to sex, will be taken in large work columns to these areas for work on roads, in the core of which action doubtless a large portion will be eliminated by natural causes. The possible final remnant will, since it will undoubtedly consist of the most resistant portion, have to be treated accordingly, because it is the product of natural selections and would, if released, act as the seed of a new Jewish revival.'

The minutes for the meeting were carefully prepared by Eichmann with instructions from Heydrich as to what was to appear in them. They were definitely not to be verbatim.

Eichmann ensured that nothing too explicit appeared in them. He condensed his records of the meeting into a document outlining the purpose of the meeting and the intentions of the regime moving forward. The minutes were personal edited by Heydrich and thus reflected the message that he intended the participants to take away from the conference.

When asked about them, Eichmann later stated:

'How shall I put it - certain over-plain talk and jargon expressions, had to be rendered into office language by me.'

Heydrich did not call the meeting to make fundamental new decisions on the Jewish question. Massive killing of Jews in the conquered territories of the Soviet Union and Poland were ongoing and a new extermination camp was already under construction at Belzec at the time of the conference. Others were under construction or in the planning stages.

The decision to exterminate the Jews had already been made and Heydrich, as Himmler's emissary, only held this meeting to ensure the cooperation of the various departments in providing the infrastructure and mechanics needed to conduct the deportations.

This conference was being held so that Heydrich could impose his own SS authority on the various ministries and agencies involved in Jewish policy matters and to avoid any chance of disputes arising about the, already determined, campaign against the Jews. He intended to assert his total control over the fate of the Jews in the Reich and the East by using this venue to oversee and intimidate all other interested parties and to ensure that they toed the line set by the SS.

The primary aim of the Wannsee Conference was to emphasise that once the deportations had been completed, the implementation of the *'Final Solution'* would become an internal matter for the SS and at that point would be totally outside the purview of any other agency.

A second goal was to determine the scope of the deportations and arrive at specific definitions of who was Jewish, who was *'Mischling'* (crossbreed), and who, if anyone, should be spared.

Heydrich spoke for nearly an hour. When he had finished he opened up the floor for about thirty minutes of questions and comments. The official meeting was then brought to a close and cognac was served during a period of less formal conversation.

Eichmann later indicated that during that less formal time: *'the gentlemen were standing together, or sitting together and were discussing the subject quite bluntly, quite differently from the language which I had to use later in the official record. During the conversations they minced no words about it all - they spoke about methods of killing, about liquidation, about extermination'.*

Later that day Eichmann recorded that Heydrich was pleased with the outcome of the meeting - that he had expected a lot of resistance, but instead he had found: *'an atmosphere not only of agreement on the part of the participants, but more than that, one could feel an agreement which had assumed a form which had not been expected'.*

Heydrich had never in his wildest dreams anticipated that these men would share Hitler's determination of what the fate of the Jews would be. He had not even asked them to. All he had asked was that they do their part in fulfilling the mechanics of getting the Jews into the hands of the SS, arrange train schedules, see to Jewish registrations in their areas of responsibility etc. To his surprise, he not only got what he was hoping for, he also got a very firmly-applied rubber stamp of approval.

Much historical importance has repeatedly been attached to the Wannsee Conference by those who study Nazi Germany. This meeting is often alluded to it as the forum for taking major decisions regarding how Nazi Germany was going to deal with the Jews and others who they considered as sub-human, as to the determination of their fate.

In fact, in the Nazi Germany of January nineteen-forty-two, all decisions in that regard had already been made long before this gathering.

Heydrich's meeting was called in order for him to advise,

and to smooth the logistics of the processes and determinations needed to ensure that the Jews would be handled efficiently by an organized system that would efficiently ship them to the SS camps.

These men had not been called together to make any decisions as to the future of the Jews. That had already been determined by others, long before these Nazi appointed officials and officers sat down, listened, accepted and then pleasantly enjoyed their cognac and cigars.

* * * * *

- Concentration Camps -

Those undesirables now being arrested were told that they were to be taken to *'resettlement in the east'.*

They were led to believe they were being taken to labour camps, but in reality, from nineteen forty-two onward, deportation meant being sent via a transit to a camp where they would be put through a selection process. Here an SS officer, often a doctor, would decide whether they went right or left; one path lead to forced-labour and the other to a gas chamber. Those predetermined to be of a danger to, or who were considered to be unsuitable for work for the Reich, did not even have that option when they arrived at their destinations. Extermination camps were not constructed to offer options. If one de-trained at one of these, there was only a single path and it led directly to a gas chamber.

As these individuals had to travel by rail to the camps in occupied Poland, the European rail network played a very important role in managing the deportations. On occasion, passenger cars were used for the job but it was primarily done through the use of freight cars.

Once full, the freight cars were sealed and those crammed inside often suffered from intense heat during the summer and freezing temperatures during the winter.

The deportees were rarely provided with food or water

for their journey and often had to wait for days on railroad spurs to allow other trains to pass. Aside from a bucket, there was no provision for sanitary requirements and many died well before the trains reached their destinations.

These trains carried armed guards who rode on the top and anyone aboard trying to escape was instantly shot.

* * * * *

- Count von Stauffer -

Karl had been pacing the length of his office restlessly. He paused at the edge of his desk and selected yet another cigarette from the silver box and lit it, exhaling strongly and adding to the general blue haze floating above his head.

Call, for Christ's sake...this suspense is too much!

For what seemed to him like the tenth time over the last hour, he turned slightly and glanced over at the clock on the far wall.

He should have heard by now...the last group should have arrived at a safe house in Bordeaux an hour ago. Had something gone wrong? They were running out of time. Had he misjudged, tried to take out too many? His sources had kept him apprised of Himmler's ongoing plans for dealing with the Jews. He had known that the time for a change in policy in regard to exit visas was imminent.

He'd done his best to speed up his underground escape route while recognizing that he had been pushing his luck for the last few weeks. There were more still within the Reich of course. Some had been determined to stay and ride the Nazi policies out - still hoping for a reprieve, but time for them had now run out, as it had for the part he'd played in saving those already safely ensconced in Brazil.

So much expertise and talent lost. What a waste!

But in order to keep below the Party radar he would have to distance himself from any future public tie to Jewish migration.

He had done what he could.

* * * * *

- Eric -

As was usually the case after they had breakfasted together, Eric and Klaus von Stauffer, the Brazilian family patriarch, had retired to the elder's study and over coffee, discussed the plans for the day and shared their common concerns.

Eric had been advised the night before that Hans would be picking him up shortly to take him on a complete tour of the mining complex and the facilities nestled below, and that this was likely to occupy his time for the rest of the day.

As yet Eric had not been able to find an opportunity to get Heidi on her own and although nothing had been said to indicate it, he had high hopes that she would be accompanying him and Hans for the day. It was therefore with some anticipation and inattention that he settled into the large leather covered armchair across from Klaus and raised the cup of excellent coffee to his lips.

He had brought a sealed, thick manila envelope from his father with him this trip, as had become the norm, and had just delivered it to Klaus at breakfast. The elder von Stauffer was opening the envelope now and slipping on glasses as he shifted to a more comfortable position in his chair to read.

Eric's thoughts drifted back to Heidi while he sat quietly savouring his coffee and a fresh cigarillo.

It seemed that his thoughts were never far from her of late.

Understandable enough, she was definitely eye candy and he had considered her as such from the first time he'd laid eyes on her. And, yes he was physically attracted to her without doubt; what man wouldn't be? Still, now the whole concept had changed somehow.

Previously he had been appreciative, and very much

aware of her whenever he was in her presence and had enjoyed the warm electric-like sensations that infused him whenever she was present.

But that had not prevented him from dismissing her from his mind when she hadn't been physically present and turning his thoughts to other matters. Since he'd arrived this time however, it seemed that he could think of nothing else but Heidi, present or not. His considerable experience with women told him that the change in the relationship had been initiated on her side of the equation, not his.

His own feelings for her had not changed since the last voyage and when he had come ashore on this trip he had been looking forward to seeing her for sure, and he could not deny that it had been his intention to do his level best to take the relationship a step further on this visit. Before his arrival, he'd definitely intended to take her to bed before he left Brazil for the return trip to France.

The change in her demeanour had been subtle, but powerful nonetheless. He couldn't really pin down what it was.

She was definitely not snubbing him, nor was she particularly playing hard to get. No, the change was more understated than that, less definitive. Since his arrival this time she had been attentive, almost coy when with him. It seemed though that, for whatever reason and unlike on the previous trips, he was now never presented with an opportunity to be alone with her.

It was almost as if she were on show somehow, taking great care with the impression she was presenting, dressed simply and appealingly but not provocatively, well-groomed and definitely exuding an extremely feminine presence regardless of the circumstances...but always accompanied by someone, never on her own.

His thoughts were interrupted as Klaus shifted forward in his chair, removed his glasses and placed them and the letter on the table beside him before looking across to Eric. The older man gently rubbed the bridge of his nose where his glasses had rested and lowered his voice conspiratorially.

"I have an important personal family matter to speak to you about before we discuss the Rio Conference and its complications, if that's all right."

Eric took a moment to clear his head of his Heidi musings before answering.

"Of course sir."

* * * * *

- Erika -

"Well I never!"

The Countess returned the telephone hand unit to its base none too gently and Ursula, who had joined her mother for coffee in the morning-room after breakfast, looked up from her cup questioningly.

"What is it Mother?"

A look of deep displeasure filling her face, a disgruntled Erika shook her head, then sighed and shrugged her shoulders.

"I have been trying to get your father to organize this Oslo trip for several days now he keeps putting me off, and I have just been informed that Karl is unavailable to take my call and advised, by some self-important secretary, that he will return my call at his first opportunity.

Really, who do these people think they are?"

Ursula stifled a laugh.

"Yes Mother I completely agree. Why you'd think there was a war going on or something, wouldn't you?"

* * * * *

- The Count -

The sound of the intercom buzzing broke the silence and Carl quickly stepped to his desk and impatiently pressed the button. The hollow voice of his secretary filled the room.

"The call you were expecting from France, Herr General,

and your wife called a few moments ago."

The earlier sense of foreboding was immediately replaced by one of relief.

The call could mean only one thing. The last shipment of human cargo had reached the safe house in Bordeaux.

* * * * *

- Eric -

Klaus von Stauffer was obviously a little uncomfortable in broaching the topic and the pregnant pause lengthened. Eric found himself wondering what it could possibly be that the normally outwardly confident Brazilian patriarch was finding so difficult to raise with him.

Finally Klaus spoke.

"In my letter to your father that you carried back to Europe for me on your last voyage I raised a family matter with him and asked for his advice. He has been good enough to respond to me. "There was another lengthy pause while the old man shifted about uncomfortably in his chair and seemingly searched for the words he wanted.

"As this matter concerns you, I not only asked for you father's advice; I also asked for his permission to raise the matter with you in order to clarify the situation we are now facing."

Eric could read the concern written on the other man's face and his mind began to race.

Something to do with the family? Something he had done. What could it be?

He opened his mouth to respond but Klaus raised his arms and shook his head.

"I am not doing this very well I'm afraid."

He continued to shake his head as he lowered his hands.

"There is no sense in my beating about the bush…It's this thing between you and Heidi. The girl is head over heels in love with you, and unless these old eyes are completely blind, you seem to be attracted to her as well."

He paused in his head shaking and looked Eric straight in the eyes.

"Neither I, nor your father, have any desire to place any pressure upon either of you, but he and I agree that the current situation is unacceptable. We here, are perhaps a little less sophisticated and more old fashioned than those of our family who still reside in Europe, but be that as it may, after discussing this with your father, he assures me that you will understand and accept our position on the matter.

Heidi is young…just turning twenty next month, and she has no shortage of admirers here. To be blunt, she is ripe for marriage and while you have displayed an obvious interest in her, there has been no commitment. Your father agrees with me that it would not be in the interest of either of our immediate families to have a serious complication arise between us and I'm sure that you would concur in that assessment.

It is unfair to both of you to ignore the situation. Heidi has eyes for no other and frankly she makes life hell for us here when you leave, moaning and mooning about until you return to us. "

Eric was dumbstruck.

Klaus settled back into his chair obviously waiting for a response and then, taking in the expression of surprise registered on Eric's face, he continued.

"Please do not misunderstand me Eric. I look upon you as a son and Heidi is the apple of my eye. Whatever you decide, that is not going to change.

Neither I nor your father wish to autocratically chart the courses of your lives, but we both know that this current situation is unhealthy for both of you and has to be dealt with one way or other before it goes badly off track. I am not asking you to make a decision as to your future if you are uncomfortable doing so at this point in your life, but I am asking that you specifically and clearly state your future intentions with regard to Heidi so that everyone in the family will know where we stand and can breathe easily again."

CHAPTER TWO

- January -

- British Air Operations -

Bomber Command hits numerous targets this month including Bremen, Hamburg and Emden. Sorties are also sent to the port of Brest targeting the *'Scharnhorst'*, *'Gneisenau'* and *'Prinz Eugen'*.

* * * * *

- Maritime Warfare -

The operational U-boat fleet has now reached ninety-one. An additional one hundred and fifty-eight are on sea trials or training missions.

Of these, sixty-four are operating in the Atlantic, twenty-three in the Mediterranean and four in the Artic.

One hundred and six ships, for a total tonnage of four hundred and nineteen thousand tons, are sunk by Axis submarines.

* * * * *

- Mediterranean -

The transfer of Fliegerkorps II into this theatre from the Eastern Front has ensured that the Germans have been able to maintain heavy attacks on Malta, pinning down both British naval and air forces. This allows Axis supply convoys from North Africa to pass with little chance of interference. Additionally, the Italians have begun to provide much stronger escorts for all the Axis convoys involved in plying the Mediterranean.

* * * * *

- January First -

- Washington -

The initial step toward the organization which will be later known as the United Nations is taken when twenty-six allied countries meet in Washington for the *'Arcadia Conference'* to endorse the principles of the Atlantic Charter.

* * * * *

- Eastern Front -

German forces near Kerch in the Crimea counterattack. The attacks against the Kalinin front retake Staritza.

* * * * *

- January Second -

- Philippines -

Manila is taken by the Japanese, who also occupy the Cavite naval base. The American and Filipino defenders retreat and establish a defensive line on the approaches to the Bataan Peninsula.

* * * * *

- Eastern Front -
South of Moscow, the Soviets retake Malayaroslavets from the Germans.

* * * * *

- North Africa -

The besieged Axis garrison of Bardia on the Egyptian border surrenders.

* * * * *

- Malaya -

The 15th Indian Brigade is driven back from Kampar as all British and Empire forces are forced to retreat southward
.

* * * * *

- January Third -

By authority provided through the members of the Arcadia Conference, Chiang Kai-shek is appointed Commander in Chief of Allied forces in China. General Wavell is appointed to the newly created ABDA (American/British/Dutch/Australian) Command. He is promptly given the task of holding against the Japanese at, what is designated as, the *'Malay Barrier'*, which is a line drawn from Malay through the Dutch East Indies to Borneo.

* * * * *

- January Fourth -

- New Britain -

Japanese air attacks are launched against Rabaul.

* * * * *

- Malaya -

Suffering increasingly severe Japanese air attacks from bases newly established in Thailand, the 11th Indian Division digs in to hold the line of the River Slim.

* * * * *

- January Fifth -

- Eastern Front -

Ignoring advice from General Zhukov and the majority of his military advisors, Stalin orders offensives to be initiated on all fronts rather than concentrating the majority of his forces against the Nazi's Army Group Center. Zhukov argues that such action will drain resources and while it may have short-lived gains will result in obliteration of reserves to break through German fortified lines of defense. However, he follows his orders as issued.

* * * * *

- Philippines -

Under continued Japanese attack, Allied forces begin to withdraw to the main Bataan defensive position.

* * * * *

- January Sixth -

- North Africa -

The British 1st Armoured Division comes on line in Cyrenaica as the German retreat through Cyrenaica comes to a halt.

Advancing British forces have now reached Mersa Brega and El Agheila.

* * * * *

- USA -

In his State of the Union speech, Roosevelt promises to deliver more aid to Britain, including planes and troops.

* * * * *

- January Seventh -

- Malaya -

Japanese attacks around Trolak and Kampong Slim inflict serious damage on the defenders.

* * * * *

- USA -

Roosevelt delivers his budget for nineteen forty-three to congress. He is asking for fifty-nine billion dollars.

Production targets for nineteen forty-two are listed at sixty thousand planes, forty-five thousand tanks and eight million tons of shipping.

This it to increase to one hundred and twenty-five thousand planes, seventy-five thousand tanks and eleven million tons of shipping in nineteen forty-three.

* * * * *

- Philippines -

The Japanese siege of Bataan begins.

* * * * *

- Malta -

Malta is hit by extremely heavy Axis bombing attacks.

* * * * *

- January Eighth -

- Malaya -

General Wavell orders the withdrawal of Allied forces to positions south of the Muar River.

Japanese troops penetrate the outer defences at Kuala Lumpur.

* * * * *

- Eastern Front -

Soviet forces begin an assault on Mozhaysk.

* * * * *

- January Ninth -

- Borneo -

The Japanese invasion onslaught meets little resistance.

* * * * *

- Eastern Front -

The Soviets launch large-scale attacks against the Volkhov and Kalinin fronts. The Germans put up strong resistance but the Russians advance rapidly.

* * * * *

- Philippines -

The Japanese begin their attack against besieged Bataan.

* * * * *

- January Tenth -

- War Declaration -

Japan declares war on the Netherlands.

* * * * *

- January Eleventh -

- Pacific -

Near Hawaii the carrier USS *'Saratoga'* is severely damaged by torpedoes from the Japanese submarine I-6.

* * * * *

- Dutch East Indies -

The Japanese make landings on the small islands of Tarakan and Minahassa.

* * * * *

- Malaya -

Kuala Lumpur is taken by the Japanese.

* * * * *

- January Twelfth -

- North Africa -

With improved protection for Axis convoys Rommel has been receiving replacement equipment and tanks while the British have had their forces reduced by the withdrawal of two of their Australian divisions and the 7th armoured Brigade , who have been transferred to the Pacific Theatre of war. Additionally, replacement and support forces which had been destined for the Eighth Army have been diverted, while in transit, for the same purpose.

Sensing a change in the balance of power, Rommel orders planning for counteroffensive strikes.

* * * * *

- East Indies -

Tarakan is take by the Japanese invading forces and they immediately begin constructing airbases on both Tarakan and Manado in the Celebes to provide air support for their advance.

* * * * *

- Yugoslavia -

Professor Yovanovic replaces General Simovic as Premier and Colonel Mihajljovic is appointed as Minister of War.

* * * * *

- January Thirteenth -

- Eastern Front -

Russian counter-offensive forces take Kirov and Medya.

* * * * *

- Atlantic -

Admiral Doenitz unleashes *'Operation Paukenschlag'* (Drum Roll), turning his U-boats loose against commercial traffic on the US east coast. He uses his larger seven hundred and forty ton, ocean-going submarines for this task. He has eleven of these in position and an additional ten more en route.

These patrolling U-boats off the US coastline have great success during the month. Spotting and sinking ships which are cruising brightly lit at night, practicing no radio discipline, sailing under peacetime conditions and unescorted, is like shooting fish in a barrel.

They sink one hundred and fifty thousand tons before the end of the month.

* * * * *

- Philippines -

The Japanese attack on Bataan continues furiously, making slow progress on the east side of the peninsula.

* * * * *

- London -

Representatives of the Allied powers publicly announce their intention to prosecute those involved in war crimes, after the war.

* * * * *

- January Fifteenth -

- Artic -

In response to the recent Allied actions in Norway, Hitler, who has already ordered four U-boats into the area, now sends the battleship *'Tirpitz'* into Norwegian waters.

* * * * *

- Occupied Poland -

The SS begins to deport the Jews from the Lodz Ghettos to the Chelmno Concentration Camp.

* * * * *

- Burma -

Units from the Japanese 55th Division begin their move into Burma just north of Mergui.

* * * * *

- Malaya -

Japanese forces attack south of Malacca. The 5th Division is now heavily engaged with Australian troops at Batu Anam on the River Muar. On the coast, the Imperial Guards Division attacks against the 45th Indian Brigade.

* * * * *

- January Sixteenth -

- Eastern Front -

A displeased Hitler replaces Field Marshal Leeb with General Kuchler as commander of Army Group North. The Fuhrer has now replaced the commanders of all three Groups fighting on this front.

Two of the Panzer Group leaders, Guderian and Hoeppner have also been replaced as have thirty-three of the senior officers commanding divisions or higher ranked formations.

There is absolutely no doubt that Hitler and Hitler alone, now makes all planning and battle decisions on this front.

* * * * *

- Washington -

Donald Nelson is appointed to head the newly created War Production Board.

* * * * *

- Malaya -

The fighting in Muar becomes more intense as the Japanese forces begin to make headway.

* * * * *

- January Seventeenth -

- Artic -

The first attack on a convoy in the Artic is launched by U-454. She sinks one destroyer and one merchantman.

* * * * *

- Eastern Front -

Field Marshal von Reichenau dies of a stroke while returning to Germany.

* * * * *

- North Africa -

British forces take Halfaya, capturing five thousand, five hundred Axis troops.

* * * * *

- South Africa -

General Smuts is given a vote of confidence when the South African Parliament rejects a motion calling for independence from Great Britain.

* * * * *

- January Nineteenth -

- Eastern Front -

Hitler appoints von Bock to succeed von Reichenau as commander of Army Group South. Soviet forces take Mozhaysk in the central sector. Soviet paratroops drop south of Smolensk.

* * * * *

- Singapore -

Japanese forces capture large numbers of British and Empire troops north of Singapore.

* * * * *

- January Twentieth -

- Berlin -

Heydrich chairs the *'Wannsee Conference'*, sealing the fate of the Jews.

* * * * *

- New Britain -

Four Japanese carriers launch their planes in a major attack on Rabaul.

* * * * *

- Singapore -

Japanese bombers hit Singapore to soften it up as their troops near the city.

* * * * *

- January Twenty-First -

- North Africa -

Rommel goes back on the offensive, using his new reinforcements and equipment to launch a surprise counter-offensive at El Agheila. He captures Agedabia, then pushes north to Beda Fomm.

* * * * *

- China -

General Stillwell is named as Chief of Staff to Chiang Kai-shek.

* * * * *

- Malaya -

Allied forces begin a retreat south of Muar after taking heavy losses. The 45th and 215th Brigades have been practically wiped out. Japanese planes continue to harass Singapore and what is left of the Allied fighters are badly outmatched by the attacking Japanese Mitsubishi long-range Zero fighters.

* * * * *

- January Twenty-Second -

- North Africa -

Rommel's attack is picking up steam and his forces take Antelat and Agedabia. His Axis troops fighting in North Africa are renamed *'Panzer Army Africa'*.

* * * * *

- January Twenty-Third -

- Pacific -

Japanese forces land at Rabaul in New Britain and at Balikpapan in Borneo near Kavieng on New Ireland and on

Bougainville in the Solomon Islands. Rabaul is quickly adopted as a forward Japanese naval base.

* * * * *

- January Twenty-Fourth -

- Eastern Front -

South of Kharkov the Russian counter-offensive has crossed the Donets and Barvenkovo is taken.

* * * * *

- East Indies -

Four Dutch and American destroyers attack Japanese troop transports off Balikpapan and sink five ships. The Japanese make landings at Kendairi in the Celebes and capture the airfield.

* * * * *

- January Twenty-Fifth -

- Declaration of War -

Thailand declares war on the US and Great Britain.

* * * * *

- North Africa -

Rommel's advance continues and the German forces decimate the British 2nd armoured Brigade near Msus.

* * * * *

- Malaya -

Wavell is given the order to retreat to Singapore as he is forced to retire from Batu Pahat near the Muar River.

* * * * *

- Burma -

While in Rangoon, Wavell orders the defense of Moulmein despite the slim chance of holding the position against the Japanese onslaught.

* * * * *

- Solomon Islands -

Japanese troops make their first landing on the islands.

- January Twenty-Sixth -

* * * * *

The first US troops destined for Europe arrive in Northern Ireland.

* * * * *

- North Africa -

Rommel takes Msus.

* * * * *

- January Twenty-Seventh -

- Eastern Front -

The Soviet counter offensive enters the Ukraine and takes Lozvaya and begins to advance on Dnepropetrovsk where the main supply depot for Army Group South has been set up. German defensive lines are solidifying however, and the Russian successes are now coming at much higher cost and begin to rumble to a crawl.

* * * * *

- Malaysia -

The carrier HMS *'Indomitable'* delivers forty-eight fighters to Java, from which they will hope to take up defensive positions for Singapore. The Indian 22nd Brigade is cut off from its supply lines near Layang-Layang just south of Kluang.

* * * * *

- January Twenty-Eighth -

- Brazil -

As a result of the *'Rio Conference'* Brazil breaks off relations with the Axis powers.

* * * * *

- January Twenty-Ninth -

- North Africa -

Rommel's forces take Benghazi in Libya. Both sides in the conflict now enter a period of licking their wounds and regrouping.

Patrick Laughy

* * * * *

- Iran -

Russia and Great Britain sign a treaty of alliance with Iran. This will allow them to move supplies through the country, from the Western Allies to Russia.

* * * * *

- January Thirtieth -

- Berlin -

Hitler makes his *'Sportpalast'* speech in which he expounds on his plans for the annihilation of the Jews and blames the lack of an immediate victory over the Russians as a fluke brought about by horrendous weather conditions.

* * * * *

- Burma -

The 55th Japanese Division begins its assault on Moulmein.

* * * * *

- Philippines -

The Japanese add to the fury of the siege of Bataan by making amphibious landings along the coastline.
Amboina, a large naval base in the Dutch East Indies is attacked by Japanese forces.

* * * * *

- January Thirty-First -

- Burma -

The Japanese take the port of Moulmein in Burma, and now are in a position to threaten both Rangoon and Singapore.

* * * * *

- Malaya -

The last organized Allied forces abandon Malaya. The fifty-four day battle to defend the country from the Japanese onslaught is over.

* * * * *

- Eastern Front -

German forces have been forced to organize a controlled retreat in several areas, but the wild Russian rout is grinding to a halt.

CHAPTER THREE

- February -

- Hitler -

During his meals over this month Hitler has made little reference to the situation on the Eastern Front. He clearly prefers to discuss other, more mundane, topics.

On those rare occasions when he does raise the issue, he chooses to make only brief and generally optimistic comments about it, framing these dispassionately and seemingly without serious concern as to the eventual outcome.

For example, on one occasion he pontificates that no struggle should ever be considered as hopeless, provided leadership stands firm: *'As long as there is one stouthearted man to hold up the banner, nothing has been lost. Faith moves mountains. In this respect, I am ice cold. If the German people are not prepared to give everything for the sake of their self-preservation - very well - then let them disappear!'*

Hewel's evaluation of Hitler's mood at this time in the war belied the impression that the Fuhrer was currently providing those who attended him at mealtime. He believed that this outward expression of ambivalence on the part of Hitler over the state of affairs on the Russian Front was a façade created to camouflage Hitler's lagging confidence; *'He is not the man he was. He has grown gloomy and obdurate. He will shrink from no sacrifice and show no mercy or forgiveness. You would not recognize him if you saw him.'*

* * * * *

- Inner Circle -

- Fritz Todt -

On February eighth news was received at Wolfsschanze shortly before ten in the morning that Major General Fritz Todt, Hitler's Reich Minister of Armaments and Munitions, and one of the Fuhrer's most trusted administrators, had been killed in an air crash.

An already generally depressed Hitler, was visibly shaken by the accident and the resulting loss of the man who had arguably held the most crucial position in the Nazi civil hierarchy.

Now that the man was gone, Hitler was not alone in realizing that Todt, builder of the Siegfried Line and Germany's greatest military engineer, was likely irreplaceable.

Who, in all of Germany could the Fuhrer realistically call upon to fill the shoes of a man who had played such an important part in the delivery of Hitler's promises to his people, who had among other accomplishments, built the Autobahn and effectively taken the leadership in the shepherding of Germany's war production?

* * * * *

- Albert Speer -

Albert happened to be at *'Wolfsschanze'* when the news of the crash taking Todt's life was received.

He'd recently finished a tour of the Russian occupied territories by airplane with a view to effectively applying his staff to the tasks of railway and road construction in the newly occupied territories. That completed, he had then taken the opportunity to make a brief stop at *'Wolfsschanze'* to spend some personal time with Hitler to discuss their favorite topic, the ongoing work on the plans for the future reconstruction building projects planned for Berlin and Nuremberg.

The evening prior to the receipt of news of Todt's death, he and Hitler, who thoroughly enjoyed these planning sessions and had them whenever they had an opportunity to get together, had discussed plans and designs for new buildings for the two cities well into the evening of the eighth.

The next day Speer was advised of the fatal crash while breakfasting and was later summoned by Hitler as his first caller of the day at an unusually late hour, close to one in the afternoon.

In delivering the summons, Hitler's Chief Adjutant at the time, Julius Schaub, expressed to Speer the importance of the meeting with the Fuhrer and Speer surmised that he was probably going to be asked to take up some lesser part of Todt's duties on an interim basis for the sake of continuity. Upon Speer's arrival at Hitler's bunker he was ushered in to Hitler's presence and immediately sensed a change in demeanour on the part of the Fuhrer. Unlike the evening before, when they had informally discussed their future building projects, Hitler greeted him now in a very official manner, standing and posed in an earnest and formal fashion.

Speer responded in kind, adopting a subordinate attitude, appropriate to the situation. He greeted Hitler officially and then delivered his personal condolences over Todt's passing. Hitler received these and made a brief reply and then changed topic without further ado.

'Herr Speer. I appoint you the successor to Minister Todt in all his capacities.'

Speer was dumbfounded.

Hitler crossed to him and solemnly shook his hand and then turned and walked away, obviously a sign of dismissal.

Speer, thinking that Hitler had probably misspoke, replied.

'I will try my best to be an adequate replacement for Todt in his construction assignments.'

Hitler immediately turned and corrected him.

'No, in all his capacities, including that of Minister of Armaments.'

Speer began to protest.

'But I don't know anything about...'

Hitler cut him off brusquely.

'I have confidence in you. I know you will manage it. Besides, I have no one else. Get in touch with the ministry at once and take over!'

Speer responded.

'Then, Mein Fuhrer, you must put that as a command, for I cannot vouch for my ability to master this assignment.'

Hitler tersely complied and then turned away from him again and picked up some papers from his desk, obviously turning his attention to other matters. His aloofness was nothing like the previous norm between the two men, which had been a type of fellowship for their mutual love of design and architecture.

Speer sensed this and took it as a firm notification that from this point on his relationship with Hitler was to be one of leader of the Reich to his subordinate.

Speer's importance within Hitler's expanded inner circle had skyrocketed overnight - from the reasonably unthreatening position as Hitler's pet architect, to that of one of the most powerful positions in the Reich.

He turned and moved toward the door to leave.

* * * * *

- Herman Goering -

Schaub entered the door to Hitler's private quarters just as Albert Speer was reaching for the handle to leave.

'The Reich Minister is here and urgently wishes to speak to you, Mein Fuhrer. He has no appointment.'

Hitler's expression dulled and when he spoke his words seemed to Speer as both sulky and displeased.

'Send him in.'

He then turned to address Speer.

'Stay here a moment longer.'

Goering bustled through the door.

Without acknowledging Speer's presence, he immediately

expressed to Hitler his condolences over Todt's death. He then switched topics abruptly to state the purpose of his visit..

'Best if I take over Dr. Todt's assignments within the framework of the Four Year Plan. This would avoid the frictions and difficulties we had in the past as a result of overlapping responsibilities.'

It occurred to Speer that Goering must have come by his special train from his hunting lodge in Rominten which was located approximately sixty miles from *'Wolfsschanze'* and that the Reich Marshal had wasted no time in making the trip once he had been advised of the plane crash.

Hitler responded.

'I have already appointed Todt's successor. Reich Minister Speer here has assumed all of Dr. Todt's offices as of this moment.'

Goering was very much aware of the unequivocal tone and delivery of the Fuhrer's statement. He knew better than to argue; however, he could not hide that fact that the news both stunned and alarmed him. As a long-time member of Hitler's inner circle, Goering was used to rolling with the punches and quickly recovered his equilibrium, although on this occasion when he spoke, his words were cold and expressed with ill-humour.

'I hope you will understand Mein Fuhrer, if I do not attend Dr. Todt's funeral. You know what battles I had with him. It would hardly do for me to be present.'

Speer, up until now at best only a fringe member of the inner circle, had no previous knowledge of any animosity between Goering and Todt. Certainly it was common knowledge that there was some rivalry between Goering's Four Year Plan organization and that of Todt's ability to directly order industry with the Fuhrer's authority. As well, Goering had seen to it that Todt wore the uniform of a Luftwaffe General and was therefore subordinate to himself and often publicly browbeat the engineer at meetings.

Hitler, as was so often the case, had set up both organizations in such a manner that ensured their responsibilities and authority overlapped, pitting them against each other; thereby guaranteeing that they would not find common cause to unite against his leadership.

Lost in his own thoughts, Speer paid little attention to the remaining exchange between Hitler and The Reich Marshal, but the end result was that Hitler instructed Goering that, for the sake of appearances, he would not only attend Todt's funeral, but was to see to it that no word as to his various disagreements with Todt were to ever reach the ears of the German public.

Albert Speer, the fly on the wall, left Hitler's bunker that day with one very clear thought.

Herman Goering was never going to be one of his allies.

It was a fact that would be driven home again within a matter of days.

Field Marshal Erhard Milch, State secretary of the Air Ministry, invited Speer to attend a conference to be held in the great hall of the Air Ministry on Friday February thirteenth, advising that armaments questions were to be discussed with the three branches of the services and representatives of industry.

New to his job, Speer suggested that he would need some time to familiarize himself before taking up his duties.

Milch, who had a good relationship with Speer, smiled and took a deep breath before responding.

'The top industrialists from all over the Reich are already on their way to the conference, and you going to beg off?'

Speer then graciously accepted Milch's invitation.

On the day before the big conference Goering summed Speer to his office. This would be the first time he had seen Goering since his new appointment.

When Speer arrived he was swiftly shown into the great man's office where Goering met him, all smiles and with a great deal of charm, if somewhat condescendingly. The Reichsmarschall then immediately launched into a review of the harmony that had flowed between the two of them when Speer had been his architect.

He then expressed the hope that the qualities of this previous relationship could continue under this new set of circumstances.

Formalities out of the way Goering got down to the business at hand. He informed Speer that he'd had a written working agreement with his predecessor, Todt, and would be drawing up a similar document for Speer to sign. He further advised him that the agreement would stipulate that in Speer's future procurement efforts for the army he could not infringe on areas covered by Goering's Four Year Plan. He then told Albert that he would learn more about the arrangement during the upcoming conference.

Speer made no comment, leaving Goering's office cordially but definitely under no allusions.

If he signed such a document he would be placing himself squarely under the Reichsmarschall's thumb. Obviously Goering had no intention of allowing him to infringe in any way on his own authority and intended to use this conference to ensure that Speer would emerge from it with little or no real power.

Hitler, who had travelled from *'Wolfsschanze'* to Berlin for Todt's funeral where he had delivered a long and heartfelt eulogy, was still in the city when Albert left Goering's Ministry.

Speer went directly from the Air Ministry to the Fuhrer's office.

Hitler had supported him the last time the three men had been together and Albert felt sure that if he explained to the Fuhrer what he thought was going to happen at the conference, he could count on the Fuhrer's support to derail Goering's plans.

Hitler heard him out without comment and then nodded.

'Very well, if any steps are taken against you, or if you have difficulties, interrupt the conference and invite the participants to the Cabinet Room. Then I will tell those gentlemen whatever is necessary.'

* * * * *

- The Meeting -

The large conference hall of Goering's Air Ministry was packed. Thirty men were present.

In attendance, General Manager Albert Vogler, head of the German Industry association; Wilhelm Zangen, Chief of the Reserve Army; General Ernst Fromm accompanied by his subordinate, Chief of the army Ordinance Office, Lieutenant General Leeb; Admiral Witzell, armaments chief of the navy; Chief of the OKW War Economy and Armaments Office and Walther Funk, Reich Minister of Economics.

Additionally, several officials representing Goering's Four Year Plan and several of the Reich Marshal's closest associates were also present. As the representative of the conference host, Milch took the chair. He asked Funk to sit to his right and invited Speer to sit on his left.

Milch then concisely delivered his introductory address.

He specifically belaboured the difficulties that had arisen in armaments production due to the conflicting demands of the three armed forces.

Vogler then took up the topic and quickly and succinctly explained how orders and disputes over priority level and the constant shifting of individual priorities interfered with industrial production. He proved his point by pointing out there were currently unused reserves available, but due to the conflicts between services these were sitting in stagnation. In wrapping up, he blatantly told those present that in his opinion it was time to establish clear relationships and then took that a step further by demanding that one man and only one man, be in a position to make all decisions and expressed the view that neither he nor the rest of industry particularly cared who that man was, as long as he had absolute authority.

Fromm then spoke for the army, followed by Witzell for the navy. Each had some reservations but expressed agreement with Vogler's view of the situation.

There was then an open discussion about the problem before Economics Minister, Funk, took the floor. He turned to face Milch as he spoke.

'We are all in essential agreement, the course of the meeting has revealed that. The only remaining question, therefore, is who the man should be. Who would be better suited for the purpose than you, my dear Milch. Since you have the confidence of Goering, our revered Reich Marshal, I therefore believe I am speaking in the name of all when I ask you to take over this office!'

Speer hadn't taken long to realize that the entire proceeding had been carefully scripted. Before Funk had finished speaking, Albert leaned over and whispered into Milch's ear.

'The conference is to be continued in the Cabinet Room. The Fuhrer wants to speak about my tasks.'

Nobody's fool, Milch graciously thanked Funk for his vote of confidence, but declined to accept.

Albert then spoke to the gathering for the first time, advising those in attendance that, at Hitler's direction, the meeting was to be moved immediately to the Cabinet Room as the Fuhrer wished to speak to them. He further advised them that a continuation of the discussion currently being held would be picked up in a meeting at Speer's ministry to be held on February eighteenth, since it obviously dealt specifically with his recent assignment from the Fuhrer.

Albert got up and headed directly for Hitler's office. The others, obviously taken aback, looked around at each other briefly and then got up and began to make their way to the Cabinet Room.

Hitler listened carefully to what Speer had to tell him about the content of the meeting. He made several notes as Speer spoke and then the two of them entered the Cabinet Room together, where Hitler immediately took the floor.

The Fuhrer spoke for nearly an hour. For the majority of that time, he provided his personal overview of war industries and expressed concern that the expected acceleration in production anticipated with the setup of the Four Year Plan had not reached its goal.

He made specific reference to Goering.

'This man cannot look after armaments within the framework of the Four Year Plan. It is essential to separate this task from the Four Year Plan and turn it over to Speer. A function was given to a man and then taken from him again; such things happen. The capacity for increased production was available, but things had been mismanaged.'

He then praised Speer for his work in construction, and made it clear that this new job was not something Speer had sought, quite the contrary, but was an appointment that he, the Fuhrer, had determined was necessary. He asked for their full support for his selection, made it clear that he expected their full cooperation and ended by saying.

'Behave toward him like gentlemen.'

No one in the room was left in doubt as to who was now in charge of armaments production and allocation.

Goering had lost this battle.

* * * * *

- Rio Conference -

President Roosevelt sponsored the third conference of Latin American Foreign Ministers that had taken place at Rio de Janeiro, Brazil from the fifteenth to the twenty-eighth of January, nineteen forty-two.

The US President's aim in calling the conference was to win the unanimous approval from the participants for a resolution recommending a complete severance of all diplomatic and economic ties between the South American countries and those of the Axis powers. The US hoped that this would be a first step toward these countries eventually joining the Allied side and declare war against the Axis powers.

The countries of South America were currently neutral

and not eager to buy into such an agreement. They all had their own reasons for this outlook. Many of them had strong diplomatic and trading ties to the Axis, particularity with the Germans, and their sympathies did not necessarily lie with those of the Allied nations.

Brazil for instance, was very interested in getting new military hardware for her armed forces and had an order in with Germany's Krupp Corporation for the supply of one thousand and eighty coastal and antiaircraft guns. The country had very strong economic and diplomatic ties with Germany and a large expatriate German population. Brazil was currently benefiting greatly by the increased trade in raw materials with Germany that the war had initiated and had every reason to maintain it's position of neutrality which would allow this trade to proceed unimpeded.

It was only by offering direct *'Lend-Lease'* military aid to the country that the US was able to convince Brazil to sign on to a final, much diluted, and less severe agreement, and they were only able to achieve that through intense negotiation which had taken place right up to the very last day of the conference.

By the end of the conference those in attendance, with the exception of Chile and Argentina, had agreed on a watered-down resolution, one which went only so far as to recommend the breaking off of diplomatic relations with the Axis. The US had made some progress in bringing the South American countries onside but had been forced to settle for far less than they wanted.

* * * * *

- Bangka Island Massacre -

Just before the fall of Singapore to the Japanese, a merchant ship, the *'Vyner Brooke'* had left the harbour. The ship was carrying injured troops and sixty-four Australian nurses.

Japanese aircraft bombed the ship and sank it. Two of the nurses were killed in the attack and nine were last seen drifting away from the ship on a raft. The remainder of the nurses reached shore at Bangka Island in the Dutch East Indies.

That island was in the hands of the Japanese.

The nurses joined up with a group of men and injured personnel from the ship. An officer from the ship, accompanied by a small group of women and children, went to the authorities in Muntok to surrender the party to the Japanese.

The Australian nurses remained behind on the beach to care for the wounded, setting up a shelter displaying a large Red Cross sign on it.

At midmorning the ship's officer returned accompanied by approximately twenty Japanese soldiers who promptly ordered all the wounded men capable of walking to accompany a party of them.

This splinter group then disappeared around a small headland. The nurses gathered on the beach then heard a series of shots before the Japanese soldiers returned to where they were waiting to join the remaining troops who then sat down as a group in front of the women and cleaned their bloodied bayonets and rifles.

Once they had finished their task, a Japanese officer ordered the remaining twenty-two nurses and one civilian woman to walk into the surf. A heavy machine gun was then set up on the beach and as soon as the women were waist deep in the water they were systematically machine gunned.

Only one nurse survived the massacre, Sister, Lt. Vivian Bullwinkle. Hit in the diaphragm by a single machine gun bullet she was unconscious when she washed up on the beach and the Japanese left her for dead. This nurse managed to evade capture for ten days but was eventually picked up and imprisoned.

She survived the war and lived to tell her story of what is now known as the *Bangka Island Massacre*.

* * * * *

- Eric -

Eight days into the return voyage to Bordeaux, Eric was having trouble sleeping and tossed restlessly on his bunk which was tucked away in the corner of the relatively large Captain's cabin afforded on the massive U-boat. So far the trip had been uneventful with the exception of the fact that rough seas had meant that there had been only a single occasion so far, when he'd found it practical to travel on the surface at night.

Since the advanced engines with which the vessel had been fitted meant that the U-boat was capable of moving just as quickly submerged as on the surface, this inclement weather would make little or no difference in the time it would take to reach port. It did however mean that he and the crew would have less opportunity to enjoy the freedom and exercise that a few daily evening hours of fresh air taken on the substantial deck of the big craft could offer.

It also meant that he had a fair amount of additional downtime to kill and that gave him lots of opportunity to review the activities of the last few days of his recent time ashore in Brazil.

He had the responsibilities of the command of the U-boat of course, but he was now functioning with a seasoned crew, who were more than comfortable with their duties and very familiar with the operation and capabilities of the vessel itself.

He had used previous return trips to France to prepare a written record for his father of what he had seen and done while ashore, and so far on this voyage he'd spend part of his free time accomplishing that. In addition to the progress of construction on the facilities, he had detailed the discussions he'd had with Klaus with regard to the outcome of the Reo Conference. He and his father had of course been aware of the US intentions when the conference had been initiated and had been awaiting the outcome with some concern. The longer Brazil remained neutral, the easier it would be for them to transport their ore from the new mine to Germany and thereby maintain the cover it provided for the *'Operation Fatherland'* facilities buried below it.

His father had predicted the likelihood of some form of a Brazilian agreement with the US as a result of the conference, as he knew the Americans would put a great deal of pressure on the Brazilians by way of offering to provide them with the military hardware that they strongly desired. He had therefore taken pre-emptive steps, in conjunction with Klaus von Stauffer through his upper echelon Brazilian military partners, to arrange for guarantees from the Brazilian government to the effect that they would allow the transport of ore from the mine by rail to Argentinean ports, if, as they believed, the Argentinians intended to reject US pressure and hold to their neutrality.

From the Argentinian ports the raw materials could then be safely shipped to Germany using neutral registered Argentine ships. Ruling government palms had now been greased on both sides of the Brazilian and Argentine border and the shipment of the ore could be reasonably expected to flow smoothly, if and when Brazil broke off relations with the Axis powers and even in the eventuality of Brazil declaring war on the Axis powers.

But it wasn't the responsibility for these tasks that were keeping Eric from a good night's sleep.

Heidi....Heidi...Heidi!

Why hadn't he seen that one coming?

From a family viewpoint it was a natural. Eric was the eldest son. It was he who would inherit the title when his father passed. Heidi was the granddaughter of the Brazilian family patriarch. What better way for the extended family to solidify their distant relationship than for the two of them to marry. Any doubts that he may have ever, however briefly, harboured as to the correctness and necessity of the families' joint participation in 'Operation Fatherland' had dissipated long ago....Germany was going to lose this war. The future of his family and that of Germany herself, depended on what was being built in Brazil.

His birthright determined he would be the next Count von Stauffer. It also determined that, unlike his younger brother, he had a well-defined responsibility and obligation to his immediate family. His marriage could only be based on what was best for the entire family. Other concerns could, and no doubt had been taken into consideration certainly, but he had played no part in that.

The decision had been made for him and in hindsight that too should not have surprised him.

Initially, when Klaus had hit him with it, the very idea of any commitment to marriage had blindsided him.

He'd wondered where in hell it had come from, but almost immediately he'd been able to see the sense in it and in so doing, he'd easily dismissed his surprise and irritation at the way it had been broached and instead taken a step back to give the whole idea a few moments of sober second thought.

In doing so he quickly accepted that it was a good move for both his immediate and extended family and boded well for the future of everything he believed in. Germany's future...his predetermined part in leading the von Stauffer clan into the aftermath of a German defeat...fulfillment of the need for him to produce at least one male heir at a reasonably early age.

Then he came to the core of it.

Was it something that he personally wanted? Was he ready to settle down with a family of his own? Did he feel the depth of commitment for Heidi that marriage would require of him? Did the thought of a future together with Heidi excite and please him? Was he mature and responsible enough to make the commitment now? How would it work in practice? Once the official engagement had been announced, would she then join him in Germany or were they to suffer through a long-distance relationship until the end of the war?

Everything else aside, it felt right. He was in love with her, had been since he'd first set eyes on her.

The night before he'd sailed from Brazil, he had dined with Klaus and the members of Heidi's immediate family and it was then that he had publicly shared his commitment to her.

He'd entered a brand new era in his life and had done so sincerely and with his eyes wide open.

And had been unable to think about little but Heidi and their eventual nuptials, ever since.

CHAPTER FOUR

- February -

- British Air Operations -

Kiel, Mannheim and Cologne are targeted by Bomber Command.

* * * * *

- Maritime Warfare -

On the first of the month the Germans begin to use a new cipher code-named *'Triton'* for their U-boat radio traffic. The British will not be able to break this new encoding system until the end of the year.

This inability to read U-boat traffic greatly diminishes the ability of the British to wage effective war against Germany's submarine fleet, although it is offset somewhat by the fact that they have improved their radio direction finding techniques and photo reconnaissance abilities.

The U-boat campaign against shipping off the US coast continues with great success and is extended to the Caribbean.

* * * * *

- Mediterranean -

The bombing of Malta continues, often occurring both day and night. This and the fact that the Germans now have airfields in Cyrenaica is making it very difficult for the British to bring in convoys of replacement troops and equipment. In general terms, resupply for Malta is becoming very difficult.

Having lost the Cyrenaica airfields to the Germans, the RAF is also finding it extremely challenging to effectively strike out at the Axis convoys steaming to resupply Rommel.

* * * * *

- February First -

- Norway -

The German occupational forces appoint Vidkun Quisling as a puppet Minister-President.

* * * * *

- North Africa -

Rommel forces the British to retreat and digs in at El Gazala in Libya close to the Egyptian border.

* * * * *

- Pacific -

US naval forces under the command of Halsey and Fletcher attack air bases in the Marshall and Gilbert Islands. In these attacks the carrier USS *'Enterprise'* is damaged.

* * * * *

- February Third -

- East Indies -

Japanese air attacks on Java increase. The naval base at Surabaya and other Dutch bases are targeted and all defending aircraft are destroyed.

Port Moresby in New Guinea is bombed.

* * * * *

- North Africa -

The British abandon Derna.

* * * * *

- February Fourth -

- Malaya -

The British reject Japanese demands for the surrender of Singapore and continue to rush in reinforcements.

* * * * *

- Washington -

The first meeting of the Combined American and British Chiefs of Staff is held.

* * * * *

- East Indies -

Japanese aircraft target a joint American and Dutch naval force in the Makassar Straits damaging two of the US cruisers, and land forces take Amboina despite strong resistance from the mixed Dutch and Australian forces garrisoned in defense.

* * * * *

- Philippines -
Japanese reinforcements land on Luzon.

* * * * *

- February Seventh -

- Eastern Front -

To this point in the war, the average German citizen has seen no real cuts to his standard of living and production has remained similar to that of peace time. Germany's stalled blitzkrieg against the Russians brings about a reassessment of wartime production priorities and Fritz Todt, the outstanding German engineer, has recently been appointed to the position of German Minister of Armaments and Munitions. Todt is killed in an air crash on this date. In his short tenure in the position, Todt has tackled the problem of the general inefficiency of the German war industries and established more sensible priorities. Hitler appoints Albert Speer to replace Todt.

* * * * *

While fighting west of Moscow, Soviet forces attack the German positions in Rzhev.

* * * * *

- North Africa -

Having disrupted the British 1st Armoured Division and dealt a damaging and morale-shattering blow to the forces of the Eighth Army while retaking almost all of the ground won by the British toward the end of nineteen forty-one, Rommel decides to pause to regroup and reequip near Gazala.

* * * * *

- February Eighth -

- Malaya -

After a heavy bombardment Japanese troops land at Singapore northwest of the island in an area defended by the 22nd Australian Brigade. The invaders are considerably outnumbered. Guns of the Singapore fortress can do little to assist in the defence of the city, in that they have been placed in fixed positions and supplied with ammunition specifically designed for a seaborne attack.

* * * * *

- Eastern Front -

The Russians drive the German forces out of Kursk.

* * * * *

- February Tenth -

- Burma -

Japanese troops begin to advance, crossing the Salween at Martaban and Pa-an. Reinforcements are now in position to bolster the move.

* * * * *

- London -

The first meeting of the Pacific War Council is held. Representatives from Holland, Australia, New Zealand and Britain attend.

* * * * *

- Malaya -

Allied defensive forces are in disarray after the initial Japanese landings. They fall back from their positions, unnecessarily abandoning good defensive stands and retire to the Jurong Line.

* * * * *

- February Eleventh -

- Brest -

In what becomes known as the 'Channel Dash', the battleships 'Scharnhorst' and 'Gneisenau' join the cruiser 'Prinz Eugen' in the start of a high speed run out of the French port, slicing though the English Channel and steaming at top speed for northern German ports.

The British are caught with their pants down and all three major ships-of-the-line, although receiving some damage, slip through to the safety of German and Norwegian waters.

* * * * *

- Malaya -

A hastily organized Allied counterattack on Singapore Island is driven off with heavy losses and the defending forces lick their wounds and retreat to their final perimeter positions around the city.

* * * * *

- February Thirteenth -

- Berlin -

The long postponed invasion of Great Britain codenamed *'Operation Sea Lion'* is officially canceled by the German High Command.

* * * * *

- Eastern Front -

Resistance from dug-in German forces becomes stronger and while some advance Russian units have reached the territory of *'White Russia'* their effectiveness has begun to pall.

* * * * *

- February Fourteenth -

- London -

There is a major shift in the mandate of Bomber Command. The force is now ordered to shift their targets from the actual manufacturing plants of Germany to the inflammable residential districts surrounding them, with the aim of destroying the worker's houses and damaging morale rather than concentrating on the actual means of production itself.

* * * * *

- East Indies -

Japanese paratroops land at Palembang on Sumatra. Reinforcements for support are already on the way by ship.

* * * * *

- February Fifteenth -

- Malaya -

Japanese fighting the Malayan campaign have now confined the defenders around Singapore.

In a struggle that was scheduled to take one hundred days to complete, the Japanese have completed their goal in seventy.

Demonstrably better trained and led, holding supremacy in the air and using small numbers of tanks to back up infantry, the Japanese have lost a total of just under ten thousand men during this fight while the British have lost one hundred and thirty-eight thousand troops.

The Allied defending forces are suffering ammunition shortages and they have been cut off from a source of water as the Japanese troops now hold the reservoir area.

General Percival surrenders Singapore to General Yamashita, bringing to a close the worst disaster to date ever suffered in British military history.

* * * * *

- Burma -

Outpost units of the defending Indian 17th Division retreat as the invading Japanese forces pour over the Salween in strength.

* * * * *

- East Indies -

Reinforcements arrive by ship and the strengthened Japanese immediately attack the garrison at Palembang, forcing them to abandon the area before they can complete the destruction of the massive oil refinery located there.

* * * * *

- February Sixteenth -

- US -

Discussions begin for plans to intern Japanese Americans living primarily in the western United States.

* * * * *

- Japan -

General Tojo delivers the Japanese war aims to the members of the Diet.

* * * * *

- Atlantic -

U-boats shell oil installations at Aruba.

* * * * *

- Dutch East Indies -

The Bangka Island massacre takes place.

- February Seventeenth -

- Rangoon -

The city is evacuated as the invading Japanese forces approach.

* * * * *

- February Nineteenth -

- Washington -

General Dwight Eisenhower is appointed Chief of the War Plans Division of the US Army General Staff.

* * * * *

- Australia -

Carrier born Japanese aircraft attack Darwin. Harbour installations are damaged and several warships are sunk.

* * * * *

- Washington -

Roosevelt signs Executive Order 9066 ordering the US military to define areas as exclusionary zones. This will affect the Japanese on the west coast and Germans and Italians on the east coast of the USA.

* * * * *

- Ottawa -

The Government of Canada passes a conscription law.

* * * * *

- Vichy France -

General Gamelin and two former prime ministers, Reynaud and Blum are put on trial at Riom charged with the responsibility for the French defeat in nineteen-forty.

* * * * *

- February Twentieth -

- Bali and Timor -

Using both paratroops and amphibious troops, the Japanese invade.

* * * * *

- East Indies -

The carrier USS *'Lexington'* with an escort of cruisers and destroyers attempts to launch an attack against Rabaul but are repelled by the Japanese defenders.

* * * * *

- February Twenty-First -

- Britain -

American Air Corps personnel are now firmly established in their bases in the United Kingdom.

* * * * *

- Artic -

The pocket-battleship *'Admiral Scheer'* and the cruiser *'Prinz Eugen'* sail from Germany for ports in Norway.

* * * * *

- Burma -

The 17th Indian Division begins to retreat to the Sittang through Kyaikto.

---

* * * * *

- February Twenty-Second -

- London -

Air Marshal Harris is appointed to head RAF Bomber Command.

* * * * *

- Philippines -

General MacArthur is ordered by the President to leave the Philippines and re-establish his headquarters in Australia.

* * * * *

- Burma -

The 17th Indian Division struggles to hold its positions defending the bridge on the River Sittang near Mokpalin.

* * * * *

- February Twenty-Third -

- Burma -

The single accessible bridge over the Sittang River is destroyed. A large part of the defending Indian Division is cut off and left on the east bank of the river. The majority of the troops are able to make their way across but all heavy equipment is lost.

* * * * *

- February Twenty-Fourth -

- Eastern Front -

German resistance has firmed up. The Russians manage to encircle II Corps of the German Sixteenth Army south of Lake Ilmen in the Demyansk area. The Germans will have to supply this force from the air until a relief force is able to break the circle.

* * * * *

- February Twenty-Fifth -

- USA -

The internment of Japanese-American citizens begins in the Western United States.

* * * * *

- London -

Princess Elizabeth registers for war service.

* * * * *

- Burma and the East Indies -

The ABDA Command is dissolved. General Wavell takes up his old position of Commander in Chief of India. The Dutch General, Ter Poorten, takes command in Java.

* * * * *

- February Twenty-Sixth -

- Eastern Front -

Russian troops in strength attack the German Sixteenth Army at Staraya, inflicting heavy casualties.

* * * * *

- Washington -

Litvinov, the Soviet Ambassador demands more direct assistance from the Allies. He wants them to open a second front in Europe against the Germans immediately.

* * * * *

- Burma -

Japanese troops infiltrate west of the Sittang and instantly threaten the Rangoon-Mandalay railroad.

* * * * *

- February Twenty-Seventh -

- Java -

A naval force under the command of the Dutch Admiral Doorman, consisting of five cruisers and eleven destroyers and made up of four nationalities, attempts to intercept a Japanese invasion force headed for Java.

The Japanese invasion force is made up of four cruisers and fourteen destroyers.

The Japanese take good advantage of their experience in night fighting and are aided by virtue of their superior torpedo equipment. They virtually eliminate the Allied force, sinking one aircraft tender, the USS 'Langley', six destroyers, and five cruisers.

In the confrontation the Japanese fleet suffers only slight damage.

* * * * *

- February Twenty-Eighth -

- Occupied France -

British commandos land at Bruneval and slip into the German radar station situated high on the shoreline. They remove some of the equipment and successfully spirit it back to England for examination and evaluation.

CHAPTER FIVE

- March -

- Hitler -

Toward the end of February Hitler's spirits began to rebound.

He starts to speak confidently at meals with a renewed assessment of the terrible winter situation as an ordeal, which has been successfully and miraculously, endured. He suggests that the fate that Napoleon's troops had faced under a similar set of circumstances, had been held at bay due to the superiority of German troops and as a direct result of good leadership.

Unlike France, Germany had not been driven out of Russia.

At dinner one evening toward the end of the month he gave a sigh of relief that the upcoming Sunday would be the first of March, then said.

'Boys, you can't imagine what that means to me...how much the last three months have worn out my strength, tested my nervous resistance.'

He went on.

'Now that January and February are past, our enemies can give up the hope of our suffering the fate of Napoleon - Now we are about to switch over to the squaring of the account. What a relief!'

Warmed to his topic, he continued.

'I've noticed, on the occasion of such events, that when everybody loses his nerve, I'm the only one who keeps calm. It was the same thing at the time of the struggled for power.'

* * * * *

- Inner Circle -

- Einsatzgruppen -

The preparations for the *'Final Solution'* were maturing and SS Einsatzgruppen forces now began a renewed sweep through the occupied territories. Well-coordinated in the areas under military control, progress in civilian territories was proceeding less satisfactorily.

* * * * *

- Rosenberg -

The activities of the Einsatzgruppen could not slip by without notice and members of Rosenberg's staff were very much aware of what was going on. These bureaucrats firmly supported their boss's relatively liberal concept of setting up separate states with varying degrees of self-government and they strongly petitioned him to urge Hitler to treat the peoples of the occupied areas as allies, not enemies.

Rosenberg was still in awe of Hitler. He found it very difficult to speak in the Fuhrer's presence. What was of more importance was the fact that Bormann now firmly dominated the setting of Hitler's meeting agendas.

Rosenberg's liaison man at *'Wolfsschanze'*, Koeppen, was now finding it nearly impossible to provide to Hitler the true story of what was going on in the East. Prior to Hess's flight this had not been the case. Then he had simply passed on memoranda directly to Hitler, but now that avenue was no longer available to him.

Everything now went through Bormann and Bormann had, by this point in time, solidly aligned himself with Himmler and Heydrich when it came to the manner of dealing with those in newly conquered territories.

Hitler had his personal vision of what needed to be done

in occupied territory. He neither asked for nor needed advice in this matter. It had been settled as far as he was concerned, clearly and publicly stating in late February: *'My prophecy, shall be fulfilled that this war will not vestry the Aryan humanity but it will exterminate the Jew. Whatever the battle may bring in its course or however long it may last, that will be its final course.'*

* * * * *

- Goebbels -

Despite Hitler's repeated private and public utterances in relation to the Jews, very few individuals, even in the upper echelon of the Nazi party, who were not members of the SS and of necessity personally involved, were aware of the extent of what the Einsatzgruppen was doing in that regard.

For example, In February, one of Goebbels' employees was notified about the activities undertaken by the Einsatzgruppen, as a result of a letter being forwarded from an SS member of the unit which had followed the victorious army into the Ukraine.

The originator of that letter claimed that he had suffered a nervous breakdown after being ordered to liquidate Jews and members of the Ukrainian intelligentsia. He claimed that he was unable to complain about the order through normal channels and was asking for help in thwarting future official instructions of a similar nature.

The Propaganda Ministry employee, Hans Fritzsche, went directly to Heydrich and asked him: *'Is the SS there for the purpose of committing mass murders?'*

Heydrich indignantly denied that any such thing was taking place, inferring that collateral damage must be expected at a time of war and that it must have been an isolated incident. He promised to immediately order a full investigation into the occurrence.

Heydrich reported back to Fritzsche the next day

explaining that the order inciting the action had originated from Gauleiter Koch, who had acted without the Fuhrer's knowledge: *'Believe me Herr Fritzsche, anyone who has the reputation of being cruel does not have to be cruel; he can act humanely.'*

It was not until March that Hitler saw fit to bring Goebbels fully into the picture, informing him that Europe must be cleansed of all Jews; *'If necessary by applying the most brutal methods.'*

We know that on this occasion Hitler did not dance around the facts as to what that meant. Goebbels later wrote in his diary: *'...A judgement is being visited upon the Jews that, while barbaric, is fully deserved...One must not be sentimental in these matters. If we do not fight the Jew, they will destroy us. It's a life and death struggle between the Aryan race and the Jewish bacillus. No other government and no other regime would have the strength for such a global solution of this question.'*

* * * * *

- Speer -

By the time of his next meeting with those involved in war production which was held on February the eighteenth, Albert had drawn up a plan that he was confident would provide the organization needed to put armament production on the rails to success.

He spent an hour explaining the plan and when he'd finished and had received general acceptance, he passed around the table a document which endorsed his new position and gave him complete authority over all future war production. In an unusual move, he asked all present to put their signatures to this agreement.

Milch had taken to heart Hitler's admonitions and wishes at the end of the previous conference. He knew what Hitler wanted and he was not about to second guess the Fuhrer. He instantly signed his name to the document when Speer passed it to him and it began to move from there, around the table.

As it made its way, each man signed on the dotted line. Some raised questions but Milch quickly used his position to dismiss any concern and it was only Admiral Witzell who slowed its progress for any length of time. The Admiral was not pleased and it was only under protest and the unity of pressure from all the others who had already signed the document, that he affixed his name.

The next day Albert went to see Hitler, accompanied by Field Marshal Milch and General Olbricht, (General Fromm's representative) to report to him the results of the latest conference.

Hitler approved of everything that had taken place.

Upon his return to his office Speer found a summons from Goering waiting for him. He was to come to Goering's lavish hunting lodge, Karinhall, some forty-five miles north of Berlin for a meeting with the Reichsmarschall. Speer left Berlin and arrived at the appointed time of eleven. Goering was famous for his tardiness in attending meetings and Albert found himself spending the next hour wandering about in Goering's reception hall looking at the priceless artworks and tapestries draped on the walls.

Shortly after noon, the Reichsmarschall, dressed in a large green-velvet dressing gown, made his way down the stairs from his upper living quarters and coldly greeted Albert before preceding Speer into the interior of his luxuriously appointed home office.

Goering promptly settled his bulk into the oversized chair behind the massive desk that dominated the room.

He immediately expressed his strong displeasure at not having been invited to attend the latest conference and began to berate his deputies in a long tirade, calling them spineless wretches who had, by providing their signatures to Speer's document, made themselves Speer's underlings for all time and berating those in attendance for not even having the decency to consult him beforehand.

Albert took some comfort in the fact that the Reichsmarschall was not openly attacking him, other than indirectly. It meant Goering was somewhat unsure of his ground and taking care not to unleash his obvious wrath straight at him.

It was however, just as obvious to him that Goering held him responsible and had no intention of letting the matter go.

Speer let the man rant with no response and when the Reichsmarschall had run out of steam, waited silently for the conclusion of the one-sided conversation. Goering ended with the statement that he could not accept such interference in his power and that he would therefore go immediately to Hitler and resign his offices as the head of the Four Year Plan.

Albert carefully considered the threat before commenting.

As did Goering, Speer knew full well that Hitler, if actually presented with such a threat, would in all probability forestall such action by dreaming up some type of compromise that would satisfy Goering enough to keep him on board. Albert knew that this would only bring about some sort of administrative interrelationship between the two that would result in nothing but yet another bureaucratic nightmare.

Hitler would do this, not because the removal of Goering from the position would bring about any loss in production. Almost everyone in the Nazi hierarchy was aware that after initially pushing hard and with great energy over the promotion of the project, Goering had grown ambivalent. Goering had generally lost interest and was currently doing little in the way of work to further its goals.

Hitler would do it to keep peace and avoid any political backlash that the removal of Goering as head of the plan might cause.

Speer had to forestall any such step.

He did this by dismissing such a suggestion and pandering to Goering by indicating that this new arrangement, determined by Hitler and approved by the representatives of both industry and the armed forces, would in no way infringe upon his position as head of the Four Year Plan. He told

Goering that he was prepared to become his subordinate and carry out his new responsibilities within the framework of the Four Year Plan.

The staunchly-egocentric Reichsmarschall, was mollified by these remarks, seemingly unaware that the fawning words delivered by Speer were simply a ploy created to remove his threat to take the matter back to Hitler.

Speer managed to leave Karinhall on somewhat shaky but reasonably good terms with Goering.

Knowing he would have to take steps to ensure that he had closed every loophole, Speer returned to see the Reichsmarschall three days later and showed him a draft decree appointing him *'Chief Representative for Armaments'* within the Four Year Plan.

On March first, nineteen forty-two Goering signed the decree and in so doing gave his stamp of approval in writing and removed any chance of later realistically disputing the arrangement with Hitler without looking a complete fool.

Speer took the decree to Hitler and the Fuhrer, more than pleased to find that the squabble with Goering had been put to rest, agreed fully with Speer's adeptness at bringing the Reichsmarschall on board and putting an end to the gossip over the matter which was currently making its way around Berlin.

On March the sixteenth Speer apprised the German media of his new appointment.

Goering, ever petty over matters relating to his prestige, complained, by way of his press agency, that the release should have come from him and not Speer. A short time later there was a further complaint with regard to the foreign press coverage of Speer's new position which Goering felt gave the impression that his position within the Reich had been downgraded and he felt that this would weaken his prestige within German industry.

It was common knowledge among those of Hitler's inner circle that Goering's princely lifestyle was primarily financed by *'gifts'* provided to him by the elite of the Reich's Industrialists.

Speer correctly assessed that these recent niggling complaints on the part of the Reichsmarschall, with regard to any public perception of a loss of his power over German Industry; was primarily a reflection of Goering's concern that any indication of a reduction in his power over the industries might well lead to a reduction in the funds routinely being provided to him by the leaders of these manufacturing companies.

The Reichsmarschall wanted no part of that scenario. Speer met with Goering yet again and sympathized with his concern and suggested that perhaps the Reichsmarschall should invite the industrialists to a conference in Berlin where Speer could make an appearance during which he would formally declare his subordination to Goering.

Goering was extremely pleased with this suggestion and immediately recovered his good humour.

The conference, attended by over fifty of the most important Industrialists took place a short time later and Speer spoke briefly, doing what he had promised Goering that he would. Goering then took the floor and in a long rambling speech rallied everyone present to make maximum effort to support armaments output. He made absolutely no direct reference to Speer or his new position, ignoring it completely. Taking advantage of that situation, Speer asked Hitler for another decree on March twenty-first, this one designed to give him full dictatorial powers over Industry. In part it read: *'The requirements of the German economy as a whole must be subordinated to the necessity of armaments production.'*

From then on things went smoothly for Speer, Goering's indolence ensured that the Reichsmarschall very rarely interfered with Speer's future activities.

* * * * *

- Extermination Camps -

The first extermination camp established in occupied

Polish territory was at Chemo in Warthegau. This camp was designed to deal with the Lodz ghetto Jews as well as additional deportees from Germany, Austria, Bohemia and Moravia and Luxemburg, in addition to approximately five thousand Gypsies and several hundred Polish and Soviet prisoners of war.

Gassing operations, using hermetically sealed trucks, had begun there in December of nineteen forty-one and had been in continual operation until March of nineteen forty-two.

As part of *'Operation Reinhard'*, three additional camps were on the drawing board for use in the Polish occupied territories to deal with the masses of Polish Jews the Reich had inherited with the takeover of the country. These were named Belzec, Sobibor and Treblinka.

Belzec was the first of these to come on stream, beginning operation in March of nineteen forty-two. Its task was to deal with the Jews from southern Poland. The deportation of Jews from the Lvov Ghetto to Belzec began.

Auschwitz, located near the prewar German-Polish border in Eastern Upper Silesia which Germany had annexed after the invasion of Poland had been operating as a concentration and forced labour camp up to this point, but had now, under the administration of the *'Generalgouvernement'*, been expanded to become Auschwitz-Birkenau. It began to function as an extermination camp in March of nineteen forty-two.

From that point on trains from all over German occupied territory arrived at the camp almost daily.

Newly arrived deportees at the much enlarged camp now underwent a selection process upon arrival. Those deemed fit for work were held for forced labour use while the vast majority were now sent directly to the newly constructed gas chambers which were designed to use *'Zyklon B'* (crystalline hydrogen cyanide).

The Drancy internment camp that had been established in the Parisian suburb of Drancy in August of nineteen-forty-one had now morphed into a major transit center for the deportation of French Jews. The systematic deportation of the French Jews to Auschwitz-Birkenau began in March of nineteen forty-two.

* * * * *

- Ghettos -

By the end of March nineteen forty-two, the two ghettos that had been created in Lublin to hold approximately thirty thousand Jews, had been emptied by way of deportations to Belzec.

* * * * *

- Erika -

The Countess was not one to be put off and she had persevered relentlessly toward the achievement of her two latest pet peeves. Finally it appeared that her labours had occasioned what she considered, very positive results She, Karl, and Wilhelm were now traveling comfortably from Berlin to Oslo aboard the family's' private railcars which had been attached to the rear of a resupply train.

They were on their way to meet her new granddaughter.

Ursula had only managed to beg off the trip by way of giving in to her mother about getting pregnant.

She'd actually made her decision to do so after Friedrich had begun to vocally support his mother-in-law in urging her to have a child and only after having discussed it with him over several weeks. It wasn't until then that she had announced the news to her mother.

After doing so she had promptly pointed out to Erika that, since Friedrich could not get leave to join them on the trip north, and if she intended to keep faith with her marriage vows which she did, the possibility of delivering on her promise to get pregnant anytime in the near future would be quite unattainable if she was expected to leave him at the castle and accompany them to Norway.

Erika had immediately seen the logic in that view and Ursula, who was now privately quite pleased with the prospect of pending motherhood, was off the hook for the trip and very much looking forward to she and Freidrick being on their own in the castle and getting started on the task at hand.

CHAPTER SIX

- March -

- British Air Operations -

The British had finished testing on their new radio navigation system, code-named *'GEE'*, which was now put into operation for Bomber Command. This system measured the time delay between two radio signals to produce a fix and had been initially designed as a short-range blind landing system to improve safety during night operations but had now been further developed into a long-range navigation method. *'GEE'* provided much greater accuracy for large fixed targets such as cities.

Bomber Command strikes Essen, Lubbock, Cologne and Kiel.

* * * * *

-Maritime Warfare -

Operational U-boat strength reaches one hundred and eleven. Eighty of these are deployed in the Atlantic and the operations off the shores of the United States had been increased. Axis subs sink a total of ninety-five ships, thirty-five of these in U.S. or West Indian waters, half of which are large tankers. Two U-boats sink eleven ships off Freetown.

The first of the *'Milch Cows'* leaves the port of Lorient to join the U-boat fleet.

These large German Type XIV U-boats had been developed from the Type IXD with the length reduced to that of the Type VIIC and were specifically designed for use as resupply craft for the operational submarine fleets. Their only armament consisted of anti-aircraft guns. The use of *'Milch Cows'*, two or three of which were to be on station at all times, served to double the time the operational time U-boats could remain on patrol. A total Allied tonnage of eight hundred and thirty-four thousand, two hundred tons, consisting of two hundred and seventy-three ships is lost, five hundred and thirty-four thousand in the Atlantic.

In the Pacific two hundred and fifty-two thousand tons of Allied shipping goes to the bottom.

German air attacks continue against Malta and the British are struggling to supply the island.

* * * * *

- March First -

- Eastern Front -

A new Russian offensive begins in the Crimea. General Halder estimates that the German losses on this front to date have reached one and a half million.

* * * * *

- Burma -

The Chinese Fifth Army is being concentrated one hundred and fifty miles from Rangoon and Chennault's *'Flying Tigers'*, who have shone in their defence of Rangoon, now move to the RAF air base at Magwe.

* * * * *

- East Indies -

The Remainder of Doorman's fleet, in retreat from Java, engages Japanese forces in the Sunda Straight suffering the loss of three cruisers and four destroyers.

The Japanese successfully land troops at Kragan, Merak and Eretenwetan on Java. They find little opposition.

* * * * *

- March Second -

- Philippines -

Japanese come ashore on Mindanao and carry out naval bombardments on targets on Mindanao, Cebu and Negros.

* * * * *

- East Indies -

On Java, the capital of the Dutch East Indies, Batavia, is taken by the Japanese.

* * * * *

- March Third -

- Western Australia -

Japanese aircraft carry out a surprise raid on the airfield and harbour at Broome.

* * * * *

- March Fourth -

- China -

General Stillwell sets up the US Headquarters at Chungking.

* * * * *

- Pacific -

Halsey's task force attacks Marcus Island.

* * * * *

- March Fifth -

- London -

New conscription laws now include women and men up to the age of forty-five.

General Brooke replaces Admiral Pound as Chairman of the British Chiefs of Staff Committee.

* * * * *

- Burma -

General Alexander arrives in Rangoon to take command and immediately orders a counter-attack.

* * * * *

- New Guinea -

A Japanese invasion force leaves Rabaul headed for New Guinea.

* * * * *

- March Sixth -

- Malta -

An additional eighteen Spitfire fighters, delivered by the carrier HMS *'Eagle',* arrive to beef up the defence.

* * * * *

- Burma -

Counter-attacks fail to relieve Pegu and Alexander orders the evacuation of Rangoon.

* * * * *

- March Seventh -

- East Indies -

Japanese troops take Surabaya and Lembang on Java.

* * * * *

- Burma -

Rangoon is evacuated by British troops. Japanese troops march into and occupy Rangoon. With the loss of this, the only significant port in Burma, all Allied supplies will now have to come in overland from India.

* * * * *

- New Guinea -

The Japanese invasion fleet begins its landings in the Salamaua region.

* * * * *

- March Eighth -

- New Guinea -

The Japanese land in strength at Lae and Salamaua on Huon Bay and begin their push toward Port Moresby.

* * * * *

- March Ninth -

- East Indies -

The Dutch government is evacuated and General Ter Poorten surrenders one hundred thousand troops. The Japanese now control Java.

* * * * *

- March Tenth -

- New Guinea -

Aircraft launched by the carriers USS *'Lexington'* and *'Yorktown'* attack Japanese naval units near Lae.

* * * * *

- March Eleventh -

- Philippine's -

Japanese troops land on the most southern island of the Philippines at Mindanao.

General MacArthur leaves Luzon, declaring: *'I shall return!'*

* * * * *

- Mediterranean -

U-565 sinks the cruiser HMS *'Naiad'* north of Sollum.

* * * * *

- March Twelfth -

- Pacific -

American troops begin to land in Noumea, New Caledonia, garrisoning the island and building a base.

The Japanese consolidate their hold on the Solomon Islands.

* * * * *

- East Indies -

Units of the Japanese Imperial Guards Division land in northern Sumatra.

* * * * *

- March Fourteenth -

- Australia -

Large numbers of US troops begin to arrive in Australia.

* * * * *

- March Fifteenth -

- Eastern Front -

Despite the fact that German casualties have reached two hundred and fifty thousand men since the beginning of the year, Hitler publicly announces that the Russians will be: *'annihilatingly defeated'* in the coming summer campaign.

* * * * *

- March Seventeenth -

- Australia -

General MacArthur arrives in Australia.

* * * * *

- London -

The British institute rationing of electricity, coal and gas as well as a decrease in the clothing ration.

* * * * *

- March Nineteenth -

- Burma -

General Slim arrives to take command of British forces now to be designated as *'1 Burma Corps'*.

* * * * *

- March Twentieth -

- London -

The British launch *'Operation Outward'*, a plan to attack

Germany with the launch of free-flying balloons filled with hydrogen. Two types are dispatched, one with a long steel wire hanging from it with the intention of damaging high voltage power lines and the other carrying three small incendiary devices.

* * * * *

- March Twenty-First -

- Eastern Front -

The encircled German Sixteenth Army at Demyansk begins breakout attempts.

* * * * *

- March Twenty-Second -

- Malta -

A heavily mauled British convoy trying to resupply Malta arrives after being targeted by both the Luftwaffe and a large Italian fleet and with little support from the overtaxed RAF. Only five thousand tons of cargo is safely landed by the three cargo ships that manage to succeed in reaching port.

* * * * *

- March Twenty-Fourth -

- Burma -

Japanese troops attacking near Toungoo, gain a successful beachhead.

* * * * *

- Philippines -

Japanese artillery and aircraft attacks on the American positions on Bataan intensify.

* * * * *

- March Twenty-Sixth -

- Berlin -

By law, Jews residing in Berlin must now identify their houses.

* * * * *

- March Twenty-Seventh -

- Australia -

General Blamey arrives in Australia accompanied by some troops from North Africa. He is appointed to command the Allied land forces in Australia,

* * * * *

- Burma -

RAF aircraft and the volunteer American squadrons are withdrawn from Burma. Japanese attacks on the Chinese Two Hundredth Division continue at Toungoo.

* * * * *

- Ceylon -

British Admiral Somerville takes command of the British Far East Fleet.

* * * * *

- March Twenty-Eighth -

- Lubeck -

RAF Bomber Command sends a raid to this northern German city. This air attack destroys over thirty percent of the city and eighty percent of the medieval center. Hitler is infuriated.

* * * * *

- Occupied France -

British commandos aboard the HMS *'Campbeltown'*, which is filled with explosives on a time-delay fuse attack the port of St. Nazaire, ramming the dock gates. Suffering terrific loses, the commandos demolish other parts of the navel service area while they wait for the ship to *'go up'* and succeed in completely destroying the port.

CHAPTER SEVEN

- April -

- Hitler -

The Russian counter-offensive had spent its strength and a hiatus had set in all along the Eastern Front. This breather in the fighting serves to help revitalize the German Fuhrer and, coupled with the onslaught of spring, combine to improve both his health and spirits.

On the twenty-fourth of April he reaches Goebbels by phone and informs the Propaganda Minister that he wishes to deliver a major speech before the Reichstag.

On the following Sunday at three in the afternoon, he appears before this body and denounces Bolshevism as *'the dictatorship of Jews'*, labelling the Jew as *'a parasitic germ'*.

He makes no attempt to lessen the seriousness of the situation now facing German forces on the Russian front. He does however, leave no doubt in their minds that he is extremely confident in their eventual victory, falling back yet again on a comparison between himself and Napoleon.

'We have mastered destiny which broke another man a hundred and thirty years ago'.

The Russian winter had destroyed Napoleon, but he, Adolph Hitler, had persevered. Winter was over and German forces remained entrenched deeply into Russian territory.

He then demanded that he now be given unlimited powers to ensure that Napoleon's French debacle did not repeat itself.

The terms of these powers were all-encompassing. They required upon every German an obligation to follow his personal orders. Failure to do so would in future doom any individual to serious consequences. This placed the Fuhrer personally above the law and gave him the power over life and death.

This speech recalled the early oratory that had brought Hitler to power. It was hard-hitting and steeped in German pride and accomplishment. His demand for absolute power was not only enthusiastically applauded by those in attendance, it was unanimously approved.

* * * * *

- Inner Circle -

- Albert Speer -

In December of nineteen forty-one, Todt had taken the first steps toward organizing a central planning system for military production. On April fourth of nineteen forty-two, Speer, using an overview of these initial ideas, presented to Hitler a plan for the establishment of an *'amt fur zentrale Planung'* (bureau for central Planning).

The group envisioned would consist of Speer as Chairman and include Field Marshal Milch, Goering's deputy, Paul Koerner and Walther Funk, Minster of Economic Affairs.

Hitler authorized the creation of this new Bureau.

From that time on the Wehrmacht received top priority in the fulfillment of orders, which Speer's ministry took over and then promptly assigned which companies were to carry them out and what production methods were to be used.

With Hitler's full backing and by taking a firm hand at the helm Speer quickly turned production around and brought about an increase of sixty percent over the next three months.

* * * * *

- Extermination Camps -

Sobibor began operation in April of nineteen forty-two,

primarily receiving deportees from the ghettos of eastern Poland, especially from the Lublin area. Sobibor also accepted deportees from German occupied Russian territory, Bohemia and Moravia, Austria, the Netherlands, Belgium and France.

* * * * *

- Ghettos -

In April of nineteen forty-two a new ghetto was established in Majdan Tatarski, near the Majdanek camp to house the remaining Jewish population of Lublin, which numbered five thousand.

* * * * *

- Medical Experiments -

Beginning in early nineteen forty-two, a series of medical experiments on humans were undertaken by Nazi doctors.

These experiments were conducted at the concentration camps of Birkenau, Dachau and Auschwitz under the supervision of SS-Dr. Sigmund Rascher, who reported directly to Himmler.

The first of these experiments were conducted at Dachau to investigate high-altitude, low-pressure problems experienced by German pilots during high altitude flight. Using a portable pressure chamber supplied by the Luftwaffe, selected camp prisoners were locked in the chamber.

The interior pressure was then lowered to a level corresponding to that suffered at very high altitudes. The pressure within the chamber could be adjusted very swiftly. This allowed Rascher to simulate the condition which would be experienced by a pilot freefalling from altitude without the benefit of oxygen.

Himmler's comment upon reading a report of the experiments, was to suggest that any subject who might survive such treatment (a very unlikely outcome) should be *'pardoned'* to life imprisonment. Rascher replied, that as all the victims to date had been merely Poles and Russians, he believed that no amnesty of any sort should be considered.

The next in this series of experiments involved research into the circumstances of freezing and hypothermia, and looked for answers to the problems facing the German soldiers serving in the severe weather conditions of the Russian winter and those of Luftwaffe pilots who had been forced to bail out into the freezing temperatures of the North Sea.

This next experiment also took place at Dachau. Three hundred inmates were used in this research. One third of them died. Rascher was looking to find the best way to warm a human who was suffering from Hypothermia.

Those selected were forced to remain naked outside in freezing weather for up to fourteen hours or kept in a tank of ice water for three hours. Their pulse and internal temperature was measured through a series of electrodes. Warming of the subjects was then attempted by different methods.

Himmler was very interested in these experiments and he attended some of them. He then told Rascher that he should go to the North Sea and find out how the ordinary people there warmed victims of extreme cold as he thought that *'a fisherwoman would well take her half-frozen husband into her bed and revive him in that manner'.* He thought it probable that *'animal warmth had a different effect than artificial warmth'.*

Rascher then brought four women from Ravensbruck concentration camp to Dachau and experimented by placing the naked test subjects between two of the naked women.

In the end Rascher decided immersion in hot water was the best revival method.

* * * * *

- Eric -

When Eric's U-boat entered the port in Bordeaux he learned that his brother and parents had already left for Oslo.

In anticipation of at least a two week layover for minor repairs and resupply, he had seriously considered taking leave and making the journey by train to join them but a letter from his father was waiting for him at the dockyard and any such thought was dismissed by its contents.

Although the short letter made no direct reference to Himmler's decision to halt all Jewish emigration from German territories, it in fact, skirted the matter, while at the same time making it clear to Eric that he must return to sea as soon as was practicable in order that the safe houses in Bordeaux could be emptied of the last of their inhabitants before someone took note of their presence.

Eric gave immediate orders to rush the resupply and in four days' time he was at the helm of the massive U-boat as it once again sailed out of Bordeaux harbour.

* * * * *

- The Count -

Karl von Stauffer sat to the right of the fire in a large leather wingchair in the comfortably appointed library of his daughter and son-in-law's mansion in Oslo.

Konrad sat to the other side of the hearth in a matching chair puffing on his cigar as his aide moved to refill their glasses with port, and Wilhelm stood in front of them, resting with one arm against the mantelpiece as he stared into the flames of the crackling fire.

The three of them had just left Gabriella and her mother to enjoy tea after an excellent meal and the Count and Wilhelm had been listening to his son-in-law expound on the topic of the expansion of the Lebensborn project into the captured German territories.

As the Count lit his own cigar and once Wilhelm had accepted port from the aid, Konrad advised the man that he would not be further needed, and could retire for the remainder of the evening.

As soon as the door had closed behind the man Karl spoke.

He turned to face his son-in-law squarely.

"Konrad, would I be correct in saying that you are ambivalent when it comes to politics?"

Wilhelm, aware of where his father was headed with this line of questioning, shifted position in front of the fire, turning his attention to take in the reactions of both men.

Konrad, obviously taken aback at the question, frowned and in the midst of raising his glass to his lips, reconsidered and set it down on the table between him and Karl before he spoke.

"Politics... I don't understand. I am a doctor."

Wilhelm smiled at the response and shook his head.

"Father, I think you will have to be a little more specific if you want Konrad to understand your question."

The count looked at Wilhelm briefly and then turned his attention back to his son-in-law.

"Konrad do you have strong political views? I know you are not a member of the party, but, are you committed to Nazi doctrine?"

Relieved at finally grasping what the Count was trying get across to him, Konrad shook his head and shrugged.

"Not particularly, but as I said, I am a doctor and my duty is to serve the sick and improve the health of my nation. I'm not interested in the politics, other than perhaps in how and if it affects my ability to serve in my chosen profession. My country is at war and I wear a uniform because of that fact. However my wearing of this uniform should not be construed as loyalty to a specific political regime as it is simply a demonstration of my loyalty to my country."

Wilhelm grinned broadly and the Count nodded solemnly before continuing.

"That being the case, I believe it's time for me to make you aware of *'Operation Fatherland'* and the part I would like to offer you in the furthering of its aims."

CHAPTER EIGHT

- April -

- British Air Operations -

RAF Bomber Command attacks expand. Targets include the industrial areas of both France and Germany as well as ports in France and Norway. Hamburg, Cologne and Rostock are heavily hit in Germany.

In addition, fighter sweeps are made over occupied France, almost daily.

In the Mediterranean the RAF make sorties against the Sicilian airfields. In spite of these, Malta takes a beating from Axis aircraft.

The situation there is worsening for the military forces and by the end of the month the British submarines are forced to leave the harbour when one destroyer is sunk, virtually blocking it. The dockyards are heavily damaged and few minesweepers remain fit for duty.

The RAF lose one hundred and twenty-six planes on the ground and another twenty in air defense battles. Due to the deterioration of Malta's defences Rommel loses very few of his supplies through Allied action against his convoys and receives a full one hundred and fifty thousand tons of resupply.

* * * * *

- Maritime Warfare -

In the Atlantic the expanded U-boat campaign off the coast of the US continues to bear fruit. Oil tankers are a prime target. The tremendous toll of lost ships forces the Americans to find a way to beef up their escort duties and British and Canadian convoy forces move in to assist. They take this action even though doing so will cause them to reduce the number of convoys leaving Halifax, on Canada's east coast for the United Kingdom. There is really no option as they move to assist the Americans in their battle against the marauding U-boats.

The allies lose one hundred and thirty-two ships for a total of six hundred and seventy-four thousand five hundred tons. Axis submarines account for seventy-four of these sinkings.

In the pacific only seven allied ships are sunk.

In the Indian Ocean the allies lose a total of one hundred and fifty thousand tons, primarily due to attacks from a Japanese carrier force.

* * * * *

- Eastern Front -

During this month the German troops receive considerable reinforcement from their allies. Italy, Rumania, Hungary, Slovakia and Spain all send units to bolster the German positions.

* * * * *

- April First -

- New Guinea -

The Japanese land on New Guinea at Hollandia and Sorong. They encounter very little opposition and begin a buildup of their beachheads.

* * * * *

- Philippines -

The remaining American and Philippine troops on Bataan are succumbing to disease as their rations fall far short of demand. The Japanese attack their positions mercilessly.

* * * * *

- Mediterranean -

A British submarine sinks the Italian cruiser *'Band Nere'*.

* * * * *

- Burma -

Japanese attacks continue and the Chinese troops at Toungoo are forced to retreat while the British forces at Prome take a beating.

* * * * *

- April Second -

- Burma -

Under the risk of encirclement, the British troops are forced to evacuate Prome.

* * * * *

- April Third -

- Burma -

The Japanese bomb Mandalay.

* * * * *

- Philippines -

After a long bombardment the Japanese launch a ferocious attack on the Allied forces hold up in Bataan.

* * * * *

- April Fourth -

- England -

On Hitler's direct order, the Luftwaffe begins the *'Baedeker Blitz'*. He classifies these air attacks against militarily unimportant targets against picturesque cities in England as *'Vergeltungsangriffe'* (retaliatory attacks) for the RAF attack that were made earlier against the German city of Lubeck on the night of March twenty-eighth of nineteen forty-two and which had resulted in outrage within the German leadership.

These bombing raids are to be directed against targets selected from the German *'Baedeker Tourist Guide to Britain'*, from those cities which have been awarded at least three stars for their historical significance.

* * * * *

- Indian Ocean -

On a patrol out of Ceylon, a British Catalina seaplane sights Admiral Kondo's fleet containing their main carrier forces, including Akagi, Soryu, Hiryu, Shokaku and Zuikaku as well as four battleships of the Kongo Class.

The British have no forces available to take on a Japanese naval force of this magnitude and order all shipping to disperse from Colombo.

* * * * *

- April Fifth -

- Indian Ocean -

In the expectation of finding the British fleet in port at Colombo in Ceylon, the Japanese launch a force of one hundred and thirty planes against the anchorage. The British are able to send a small force of fighters against the Japanese planes but they are ineffectual. The Japanese, frustrated by the lack of targets found in the port, send out scout planes and manage to locate the heavy cruisers HMS *'Dorsetshire'* and *'Cornwall'* which they quickly send to the bottom.

* * * * *

- Philippines -

The Japanese take Mt. Samat on Bataan destroying a strongpoint on the allied defensive line. Japanese forces leave Luzon, headed for Cebu Island.

* * * * *

- Berlin -

Hitler issues Directive Forty-one, his plans for the coming summer offensive against the Russians. The main thrust of these attacks is to be directed at the seizure of the Soviet oil fields in the Caucasus while a secondary thrust is to take Stalingrad, while protecting the flank of the main advance.

* * * * *

- Scapa Flow -

The US Task Force Thirty-Nine, including the aircraft carrier USS *'Wasp'* and the battleship *'Washington'* arrives to bolster the British Home Fleet.

* * * * *

- April Sixth -

- Solomon Islands -

Japanese forces land at Bougainville.

* * * * *

- Indian Ocean -

A Japanese naval force, which includes a small carrier supported by cruisers, attacks shipping anchored in the Bay of Bengal. They sink approximately eighty-three thousand tons of shipping, made up largely of vessels that had earlier been ordered to disperse from Colombo.

* * * * *

- Papua New Guinea -

A Japanese naval force lands troops on Manus Island in the Bismarck Archipelago.

* * * * *

- April Seventh -

- Philippines -

Japanese attacks have now pushed the allied defenders behind a line running inland from Limao. Washington orders the commanders to take whatever steps they deem necessary and Wainwright begins to withdraw as much of his force as possible to the fortress island of Corregidor on Manila Bay.

* * * * *

- April Ninth -

- Ceylon -

An air raid by Japanese naval forces is launched against Trincomalee and the aircraft carrier HMS *'Hermes'* and the Australian destroyer HMAS *'Vampire'* are sunk off the east coast.

* * * * *

- Philippines -

Bataan capitulates to the Japanese and they take seventy-five thousand prisoners. The captured allied force is immediately marched one hundred miles to detention camps in the north as the *'Bataan Death March'* begins. Thousands of men die due to this forced march as those who cannot keep up are slaughtered out of hand.

Corregidor in the middle of Manila Bay remains as the final point of resistance.

* * * * *

- Eastern Front -

German initiatives to relieve units of the Sixteenth Army encircled around Demyansk have limited success. New attacks by the Russians in the Crimea accomplish little.

* * * * *

- Burma -

British and Japanese troops dig in between Taungdwingyi and Minhla on the Irrawaddy. Both sides are planning offensive moves while they regroup. The Japanese are receiving far more reinforcements than the British defenders.

* * * * *

- April Tenth -

- Philippines -

Japanese troops land on Cebu Island, forcing the small group of American defenders to retreat inland.

* * * * *

- April Twelfth -

- Burma -

The Japanese take Migyaungye.

* * * * *

- April Thirteenth -

- Burma -

The Japanese launch a new offensive pushing the British forces back to Magwe and the Chinese Sixth Army leaves the Shan States to take up new positions in Mandalay.

* * * * *

- April Fourteenth -

- North Carolina -

USS *'Roper'* becomes the first US warship to sink a U-boat after spotting U-85 on the surface off the US coast. The destroyer pursues the German submarine and sinks it with artillery fire.

* * * * *

- Burma -

Destruction of oil installations at Yenangyaung begin as the threat of Japanese capture increases.

* * * * *

- London -

The American plan codenamed *'Bolero'* outlining the buildup of American troops in Great Britain in preparation for the opening of a second front against the Germans is adopted by the British.

* * * * *

- April Sixteenth -

- Philippines -

Four thousand Japanese troops land on Panay.

* * * * *

- April Eighteenth -

- Doolittle Raid -

The USS *'Hornet'* launches the B-25 raid which strikes targets in Nagoya, Tokyo and Yokohama Japan. The costly effort accomplishes little but succeeds as a morale booster in that it demonstrates that the US can strike Japan at will.

* * * * *

- Eastern Front -

Hitler relieves von Leeb from command of Army Group North which is attacking Leningrad.

* * * * *

- Burma -

The Japanese 56th Division wipes out the Chinese 55th Division, opening the road to Lashio, the terminus of the Brume Road, which is now left undefended.

* * * * *

- April Twentieth -

- Malta -

The USS *'Wasp'* escorted by British warships delivers forty-seven Spitfire Mk V fighters to the RAF, thirty of which are destroyed on the ground shortly after delivery.

Governor General and Commander-in-Chief , General Dobbie, sends Churchill a message, part of which reads: *'it is obvious that the very worst may happen if we cannot replenish our vital needs, especially flour and ammunition, and that very soon...'*

Churchill is not impressed and decides to replace him

with Lord Gort.

* * * * *

- April Twenty-First -

- Eastern Front -

German forces successfully relieve the German Pocket trapped at Demyansk, which has been successfully supported by resupply from the air for almost three months.

* * * * *

- April Twenty-Third -

- England -

In the first of Hitler's ordered *'Baedeker Raids'* the vengeance attacks begin with the Luftwaffe striking non-military targets in provincial towns. Exeter is the first target. In the next few days Norwich, York and Hull will be hit.

* * * * *

- April Twenty-Seventh -

- Canada -

A national plebiscite is held on the issue of conscription and it passes.

* * * * *

- April Twenty-Eighth -

- Burma -

The Chinese 28th Division is dispatched from Mandalay with orders to defend Lashio.

* * * * *

- South Africa -

The bulk of British assault troops depart from Durban headed for Madagascar. Days previously, the large and slower cargo ships carrying transport and heavy weapons needed for the invasion left port in great secrecy.

* * * * *

- April Twenty-Ninth -

- New Guinea -

The Japanese ready forces in preparation for their amphibious attack on Port Moresby code named *'Operation Mo'*.

* * * * *

- Philippines -

Heavy Japanese bombardment of Corregidor and on Mindanao continues to batter defenders.

* * * * *

- Burma -

The Japanese take Lashio, cutting off the supply lines to the Chinese who will now require all supply to be made by air. General Alexander withdraws his troops to new positions in the

Chindwin and Irrawaddy Valleys.

* * * * *

- Salzburg -

Hitler calls Mussolini to a summit conference with the intention of securing an increased Italian military commitment on the Eastern Front. Il Duce agrees to send seven divisions in addition to the two he has already promised.

* * * * *

- April Thirtieth -

- Southwest Pacific -

The Japanese carriers Shokaku, Zuikaku and Shoho leave Truk for the Coral Sea to join upcoming *'Operation MO'*.

* * * * *

- Burma -

After withdrawing north of the Irrawaddy, retreating British troops destroy the bridge at Ava.

CHAPTER NINE

- May -

- Hitler -

Having achieved his demand for God-like power over all Germans by the vote from the Reichstag in April, Hitler's confidence and outlook for the future, as well as his general health had improved considerably.

Prior to this point he had held very strong dictatorial powers and control over any form of criticism or dissent, now he was above the law and held the power of life and death.

Open disparagement with the Fuhrer's wishes, no matter how slight or well intentioned and uttered from any level of the hierarchy was now unthinkable.

You do not argue with, nor do you question, God.

* * * * *

- Inner Circle -

- Reinhard Heydrich -

Although Heydrich was Himmler's subordinate and chosen star in the SD (civilian foreign intelligence agency), the Reichsfuhrer-SS had no illusions about the man.

SS-Obergruppenfuhrer, Chief of the Reich Main Security Office (Gestapo, Kirpo, and SD), Heydrich was feared much more than he was trusted by his contemporaries.

This was primarily due to the fact that, using his positions over the years, Reinhard had amassed vast secret files on everyone within the party, including Hitler. If any important individual in Germany had a skeleton of any kind in his closet,

Heydrich held the key to that closet.

He was therefore not a man anyone in Germany, without a death wish, wanted to alienate. Hitler held Heydrich in good stead.

In addition to his other high offices, the Fuhrer had appointed him *'Acting Protector of Moravia and Bohemia'* on the twenty-fourth of September in nineteen forty-one. At this time in the war Hitler was actively considering selecting Reinhard to succeed him upon his death. Officially, that position was currently held by Goering, who was the authorized number two in the Nazi leadership order. However, the dismal performance of the Reichsmarschall's Luftwaffe against the English, coupled with his many and well known self-indulgences and poor performance as head of the Four Year Plan, had caused him to lose favour with the Fuhrer.

In Hitler's view, Heydrich was proving to be an excellent administrator in his position as the *'Acting Protector of Moravia and Bohemia'.*

Upon his arrival in the conquered territory Heydrich had initiated an autocratic reign of terror that had very rapidly destroyed the existing resistance movement.

That accomplished Reinhard quickly went about winning the support of the citizenry of the occupied territory by immediately changing direction and adopting the guise of sincere benefactor.

He gave particular attention to improving the lot of all workers and peasants.

He did this by introducing several measures, including to all intents and purposes eliminating the black market, raising the fat ration for industrial labourers, improving the social security system and turning luxury hotels into dedicated holiday destinations for the working class.

Despite his public displays of goodwill towards the populace, in private Heydrich left no illusions as to his eventual goal for the Czechs.

'This entire area will one day be definitely German, and the Czechs have nothing to expect here'.

Eventually up to two-thirds of the populace were to be either removed to regions of Russia or exterminated after Nazi Germany had won the war. Bohemia and Moravia were to face annexation directly into the German Reich.

Heydrich saw to it that the Czech workforce was exploited to serve as slave labour.

More than one hundred thousand workers were removed from so called, *'unsuitable'* jobs and conscripted by the Ministry of Labour. By the end of nineteen forty-one, Czechs could expect to be called to work anywhere within the Reich and beginning in April of nineteen forty-two, over seventy-nine thousand Czechs were sent off to work within the new Reich.

In February of forty-two, the eight hour work day for these forced labourers had been raised to twelve hours per day.

Heydrich was in fact, the military dictator of Bohemia and Moravia and the changes he made to the government structure of President Emil Hacha, left him and his cabinet powerless.

* * * * *

- Operation Anthropoid -

Reich Protector Heydrich's ability to subjugate the Czech territory and prevent the organized resistance the Nazis were suffering in other occupied territories, was significant. Territory under his control remained relatively calm and its people were now involved in manufacturing significant amounts of military material for use by the Third Reich.

In Berlin it appeared that the Czech population was beginning to passively accept the domination by the Nazi's. The exiled Czech government in England was under considerable pressure by the British to do something about the situation. The Allies wanted a strong and organized resistance toward the German occupiers and concerned that the now benevolent Heydrich was preventing that to occur, reached the decision that he should be assassinated. This needed to be done in order to demonstrate that the exiled Government was the legitimate representative of the Czech people as well as to show the world that the occupied Czech people were fighting against, and not supporting the German occupation.

The assassination plan was code-named *'Operation Anthropoid'*.

Two Czech non-commissioned officers, Jan Kubis and Josef Gabcik were selected for the job and went into training at a school for sabotage situated in Scotland. Having completed their training they were parachuted into the protectorate by the RAF.

On the morning of May twenty-seventh, nineteen forty-two, accompanied by two compatriots, these two men hid at a curve on the road Reinhard used for his daily travel between his country villa and his office at Hradschin Castle in Prague.

As the Protector's green Mercedes 320 convertible B approached with the top down, Gabcik jumped into the road and attempted to open fire with his British-issued Sten submachine gun. Instead of pouring out automatic fire, the gun jammed and he frantically cocked it again trying to free the mechanism.

The gun would not fire.

From behind Gabcik, Kubis tossed a grenade at the car, which by this point was slowing to a halt. Heydrich could see what was going on and he shouted at the driver, SS-*'Oberscharfuhrer'* (Sergeant) Klein, a last minute replacement for the drive, to: *'Step on it man!'*

Unfortunately the confused driver kept his foot on the brake.

Heydrich stood up in the rear of the car and drew and aimed his Luger pistol at Gabcik, as Kubis standing behind him threw a modified anti-tank grenade at the vehicle and it exploded sending fragments ripping through the car's right rear bumper and embedding shrapnel and fibers from the upholstery in Heydrich's body.

Kubis was also injured by the flying shrapnel.

Both Gabcik and Kubis began to fire at Heydrich with

handguns, but suffering the aftershock from the blast, failed to hit their target. Heydrich, seemingly oblivious of his injuries staggered out of the car and returned fire before trying to chase down Gabcik.

He then collapsed and Klein, who had recovered from the initial shock and had unsuccessfully given chase to Kubis, who had fled the scene on a bicycle, returned to his boss's side.

Bleeding profusely, Heydrich ordered the sergeant to chase Gabcik on foot.

Klein did as he was told and chased the man into a butcher shop, where Gabcik shot him twice with his revolver, severely wounding him in the leg. Gabcik then made his escape via tram to a local safe house.

Based on Heydrich's actions at the time of the incident, both Gabcik and Kubis were convinced that the attack had failed miserably.

A Czech woman rushed in to help Heydrich and flagged down a delivery van.

Heydrich was helped into the passenger seat but complained that the vehicles movement was causing him pain. He was then shifted into the back of the truck and placed on his stomach for the trip to the emergency room at the hospital at Na Bolovce.

Upon arrival Heydrich, who was suffering from severe injuries to his left side, with major diaphragm, spleen and lung damage, refused to be examined by any doctor who was not German. Doctor Slanina packed the chest wound then Dr. Walter Diek, the Sudeten German chief of surgery tried unsuccessfully to remove the splinters. Professor Hollbaum, a Silesian German who was chairman of surgery at Charles University in Prague, then operated on Heydrich with the support of Diek and Slanina. The surgeons re-inflated the collapsed left lung, removed the tip of the fractured eleventh rib, sutured the torn diaphragm and removed the spleen, which contained both grenade fragments and shredded upholstery material.

When Himmler, who was at his quarters in *'Wolfs-*

schanze' at the time of the attack, was notified of the seriousness of the situation faced by his second in command, he wept and immediately dispatched his personal physician, Karl Gebhardt to the scene. Gebhardt arrived at the hospital that evening and from that point on, Heydrich was under the care of SS doctors only.

Heydrich seemed to respond well to the treatment, however seven days later while sitting up eating his noon meal, he collapsed and went into shock. He died at four-thirty the next morning.

The official cause of death was blood poisoning.

Hitler's reaction to the attack was predictable. Heydrich had been his current golden haired boy and he was furious at the audacity of the incident. On the day of the attack he ordered an investigation and reprisals. He told Himmler to send SS-General Erich von dem Bach-Zelewski to Prague. Bach-Zelewski had a reputation as being even more hard-lined than Heydrich.

The Fuhrer was also of the opinion that a random selection of ten thousand politically unreliable Czechs should be executed in reprisal.

Hitler and Himmler then discussed the Fuhrer's plan for reprisals over the assassination and as a result of that discussion it was decided that because of the fact that the Czech territory was an important industrial zone for the German military, the concept of indiscriminate executions, might have a negative effect on the productivity of the region, and should be reconsidered.

They agreed to leave the reaching of a final decision as to what was to be done until the investigation into the incident had been completed.

Himmler may have publically shed tears upon learning of the attack, however those of his immediate staff believed that the SS-Reichsfuhrer was in reality, at least privately satisfied, if not pleased by the turn of events.

Himmler did not like to have others within his organization outshine him and the Fuhrer had, of late, been extremely enamoured of Heydrich's administrative abilities.

Heydrich's assassins hid in a safe house and eventually took refuge in an Orthodox church in Prague. A member of the Czech resistance betrayed their location and the church was promptly surrounded by eight hundred members of the SS and Gestapo. Several of the Czech were killed as the Germans moved in and the remainder hid in the church's crypt. The Germans attempted to flush them out with gunfire, tear gas and by flooding the crypt and eventually an entrance was blasted through using explosives.

The men inside took their own lives rather than be taken alive.

The SS saw to it that any and all supporters of the assassins were killed in the wake of these events, including Bishop Gorazd.

More than thirteen thousand Czechs were arrested in the immediate aftermath of the assassination.

* * * * *

- Jewish Councils -

One of the reasons often used by those who deny that the Jewish Holocaust ever took place, or question its extent, is the statement that it would have been physically impossible for so few members of the SS to control and ensure the cooperation of so many potential victims.

The answer to that question is not surprising if we weigh it against the political situation, within Germany and her captured territories at this point in the war.

Nazi Germany was an absolute dictatorship. It was a police state.

These facts allowed the SS to register and then round up the Jews and herd them, like so many sheep, into transit camps, concentration camps and Ghettos.

Nazi camps and ghettos were sold to the demoralized Jews as steps toward deportation and resettlement to eastern locations. In fact this was initially the German plan.

However as the war progressed, these institutions morphed into workhouses and prisons in which conditions were abysmal and the administrators held absolute power over life and death.

Add these things together and couple them with inherent German organizational skills and efficiency and it soon becomes easy to understand how it was all accomplished.

* * * * *

- Ghettos -

In each Ghetto the Nazis appointed a puppet *'Judenrat'* (Council of Elders).

These were made up of members who were chosen from within the Ghetto's own ranks and would then be ordered to act as a quasi-mini-government within the confines of the Ghetto, taking up the task as administrators of their own people.

They even had their own police.

Once ghettoized, more often than not in the most run-down areas of a given city, they were surrounded by barbed wire or high walls patrolled by guards on the outside.

The Jews held inside were thereby isolated from the general population and their rights could then be safely restricted to the required level. This could be accomplished while being unobserved by the outside world.

With the appointment of their own governing councils, the responsibility of the administration of the day to day running of a Ghetto was then, for the most part, no longer of particular concern to the Germans.

Put simply, it didn't take very many Germans to manage a ghetto.

When the determination was made to begin a large scale liquidation of the ghettos, it wasn't the Germans who administered and organized the inmate's deportations to the new camps which had been set up for this purpose. They simply provided the *'Judenrat'* with the desired number of inmates required for each outgoing transport and the job of selection and roundup was done for them by their puppets.

It has been said often and in various forms, that power corrupts and absolute power corrupts absolutely. That these *'Judenrat'* councils were corrupted to varying degrees by the power they held over those in the Ghettos goes without saying.

The German overseer's pulled the strings and the job got done.

The leader of one such council, all of whom believed that cooperation with the Germans was the best policy is quoted as saying.

'I will not be afraid to sacrifice fifty thousand of our community in order to save the other fifty thousand.'

Suffice to say that if one served as a leader or member of the *'Judenrat'*, he valued the perks associated with his position and wished to hold on to them. It was therefore paramount that he did what his SS masters ordered him to do and he did it quickly and efficiently. And, if you lived in a Ghetto and valued your life, it was a very good idea to impress the members of your *'Judenrat'* with the extent of your personal loyalty.

If one of them asked something of you, you complied without question. If you found your name or the name of a family member on a list, there was always the possibility of negotiation, providing of course, that you had something of value to negotiate with.

The concentration camps and extermination camps were run under a similar system. The Germans supervised from above; chosen inmates from within the establishments ran the day to day operations.

No German ever had to carry bodies from the gas chambers to the crematoria, tear out gold teeth from the mouths of the bodies, and no German ever emptied the ashes from the ovens.

Once again, practically speaking, it didn't take very many Germans to manage these institutions.

The question remains today however. What would your personal decision be if you were presented with the choice of becoming a puppet, versus a trip to the deportation train?

* * * * *

- Argus AS 292 -

Originally developed in nineteen thirty-nine by the *'Argus Motoren Company'*, the AS 292 was a small remote-controlled, unmanned, anti-aircraft target drone.

The initial unguided flight was made on June ninth of that year, with the first remotely-controlled flight taking place on May fourteenth of nineteen thirty-nine.

Testing of an *'Aufkalarungsgerat'* (reconnaissance device) version of the machine, started in early nineteen thirty-nine and the first aerial photography by the machine was accomplished in October of that year.

After demonstrations, the AS 292 received an initial production order for 100 machines, the first of which was delivered to the German military in nineteen forty-two.

In late nineteen thirty-six, while employed with the Argus Motoren company, Fritz Gossalau began work on the further development of the remote-controlled aircraft concept of the successful AS 292.

He did this with a goal of designing a full-sized machine that would be capable of carrying a payload of twenty-two hundred pounds over a distance of three hundred and ten miles.

Argus joined with *'Lorentz AG'* and *'Arado Flugeugwerke'* to develop such a project as a private enterprise and they forwarded a proposal to manufacture such a craft to the RLM (German Air Ministry).

In April of nineteen-forty, Gossalau presented an improved study of the original concept, named *'Project Femfeuer'* to the RLM under a new designation as *'Project P 35 Erfurt'*.

On May thirty-first, nineteen-forty Gossalau received a

response from Rudolf Bree of the RLM in which he indicated that he saw no chance that the projectile envisioned could be deployed under combat conditions, indicating that he saw the remote-control system as a design weakness.

Heinrich Koppenberg, an Argus director, met with Ernst Udet, a Luftwaffe Colonel General, on January sixth of nineteen forty-one to push him toward continuing the development of the conceived craft but Udet opted to cancel it. Disappointed but believing that the basic idea was sound, Gossalau determined to improve and simplify the design.

Argus was an engine manufacturer and it lacked the capability to produce a fuselage for the project, so Koppenberg approached Robert Lusser, chief designer and technical director at *'Heinkel Flugzeugweke'* the German aircraft manufacturer, to discuss the problem.

On January twenty-second nineteen forty-two, Lusser left *'Heinkel'* for a position with the *'Fieseler Aircraft Company'*.

In February Lusser met with Koppenberg who then informed him fully on the design of Gosslau's projected craft.

Lusser then evaluated the project and suggested, among other changes, that the original design to use two pulse-jet engines, be changed to a single engine.

* * * * *

- The Count -

Karl von Stauffer's advisory reports as to advances in the various fields of scientific development, which he still made directly to Hitler on a regular basis, had been received without comment for several months.

He put this down primarily to the Fuhrer's now direct involvement in commanding military operations on the Easter Front coupled with Bormann's strengthened position and his tendency to involve himself more often in what the Fuhrer now saw on a day to day basis.

Under the current circumstances the Count was not

particularly displeased about this turn of events. Flying beneath the Fuhrer's radar by this point in the war was not necessarily a bad thing in his estimation.

He was therefore somewhat surprised and a little concerned when he received a telegram from Bormann, while he was with the family in Oslo, summoning him to a meeting with Hitler at *'Wolfsschanze'*.

The communique was brief, providing no specifics but there was obviously some urgency in view of the fact that the Fuhrer had ordered a plane placed at the Count's disposal for transport early in the next week.

Using his contacts, Karl was able to discern the reason for the meeting.

The week before, in one of his regular reports, among other research developments, he had advised Hitler of the progress being made in the design of the remote-controlled aircraft based on the earlier developed AS 292 and the Fuhrer, upon reading of it, had ordered the meeting.

Karl advised Wilhelm that he would be accompanying him to the scheduled meeting and suggested he brush up on the facts with regard to the newly designed craft, as he would need him to supply the answers to any specific question about its development on the project, while he, himself, concentrated on setting up the proper responses tailored to satisfying Hitler's impression of the significance of the proposed new weapon.

Konrad was now fully apprised of the aims of *'Operation Fatherland'*, which he admittedly didn't fully understand but was willing to be a part of if it allowed him to resume his involvement in research projects in conjunction with his earlier mentor Dr. Baron Heinrich von Kliest.

It was decided that he should join Karl and Wilhelm on the plane in order to avail himself of the opportunity it presented for him to meet with the good doctor on a one to one basis.

Karl informed Erika of the command to attend the Fuhrer at *'Wolfsschanze'* and it was decided that in view of the fact that Konrad would be away for a few days, she would spend a few more days keeping Gabriella company in Norway and then make her way back separately by rail.

CHAPTER TEN

- May -

- British Air Operations -

Bomber Command hit Mannheim and Stuttgart in addition to critical installations in France. A major mission was also launched against Cologne toward the end of the month.

* * * * *

- Maritime Warfare -

In the Atlantic the introduction of the German `Milch Cow' program of supply support subs has made it possible to maintain a much larger U-boat force, of between sixteen and eighteen craft on active patrol off the US coast.

The upgraded presence of allied convoy patrol ships being provided by the Canadian and British Navies along the northern coast has made it more difficult for the Germans to find easy targets along the northern reaches in this area however, and the largest Nazi successes would be off the southern coast of Florida.

As a result the German U-boat fleet begins to move further south to the Caribbean and the Gulf of Mexico where commercial ships are still operating outside of the protection of escorted convoys and thereby provide much easier targets.

In response, the rapidly expanding Royal Canadian Navy responds with the provision of additional escort craft to assist in protecting its American neighbour's merchant ships along their northern coast. This move allows the US to transfer the bulk of its own escort forces south to meet the new German U-boat threat. Axis submarines sink one hundred and twenty-five ships for a tonnage of six hundred and seven thousand, two hundred tons out of the total seven hundred and five thousand tons lost by the Allies.

In the Mediterranean the axis air attacks on Malta are still severe, but the defensive forces have been substantially strengthened and the RAF actively attacks airfields in Sicily at Catalina and Augusta.

* * * * *

- May First -

- Philippines -

Japanese reinforcements land on Mindanao and Corregidor is bombed and shelled by their naval forces. Despite these efforts they gain little headway.

- Burma -

The Japanese take Mandalay and Monywa securing the western terminus of the Burma Road.

* * * * *

- The Battle of the Coral Sea -

A large Japanese force consisting of five groups sets in motion their intent to take Port Moresby. Their first step is a plan to invade the island of Tulagi and set up a seaplane base.

The Americans have been successful at breaking the Japanese codes and they have advance knowledge of the plan of attack. In order to encourage the Japanese in this aim by feigning weakness, the Australian garrison from the Island of Tulagi is evacuated.

The US then plans to meet the Japanese offensive with a

naval offensive of their own, using three separate task forces, two of which include carriers.

The Japanese believe that there is only a single aircraft carrier in the area.

The stage is now set for the massive naval battle to come.

* * * * *

- Artic -

The British cruiser HMS *'Edinburgh'*, which has previously been damaged by U-456 while escorting convoy QP-11, is sunk by destroyers in the Barents Sea.

* * * * *

- May Third -

- Tulagi Island -

In the initial move to take Port Moresby, the Japanese make an un-opposed landing on Tulagi.

* * * * *

- Burma -

US General Stillwell decides the battle for Burma is over and the time has come to evacuate his troops to India.

* * * * *

- May Fourth -

- Battle of the Coral Sea -

The first of the US naval Task Forces, Force 17, which includes the carrier USS *'Yorktown',* makes the first carrier strike in the battle, attacking Japanese naval targets near Tulagi. The carrier's planes fail to locate the large Japanese covering force, which had accompanied the invasion of the island as hoped, because it has moved on toward Port Moresby; but they do locate and sink a few smaller targets.

* * * * *

- Burma -

The British evacuate Akyab and the Chinese troops are defeated at Wanting on the Burma Road and at Bhamo on the Irrawaddy.

* * * * *

- May Fifth -

- Madagascar -

British forces begin *'Operation Ironclad'*, the invasion of Madagascar, to prevent the Vichy French territory from being taken by a probable Japanese invasion.

* * * * *

- Philippines -

The Japanese land on Corregidor, where the majority of the gun implements have been destroyed by their naval bombardment. They eventually make a beachhead but suffer serious losses to the defending forces before they can hold it.

* * * * *

- England -

In another of their Hitler-ordered reprisal attacks against non-military targets, codenamed the *'Baedeker Raids'*, the Luftwaffe bombs Exeter.

* * * * *

- Tokyo -

Imperial Headquarters orders the Japanese navy to prepare a plan of attack for a landing on Midway Island.

* * * * *

- May Sixth -

- Philippines -

General Wainwright surrenders his remaining fifteen thousand troops to the Japanese. Additional Japanese attacks are made against Mindanao.

* * * * *

- May Seventh -

- Madagascar -

'Operation Ironclad' forces the surrender the major port city of Diego Suarez as the retiring Vichy troops withdraw in good order.

* * * * *

- Battle of the Coral Sea -

One of the three US naval Task Forces, number 44, is sent to attack the Japanese transports bound for Port Moresby.

Japanese recognisance aircraft sight these ships and the Japanese bring land-based aircraft into play against them with heavy attacks, but these cause little damage.

The USS *'Neosho'* a refuelling ship and the destroyer USS *'Sims',* which have broken off from Task Force 17 to seek a safe spot for the first to refuel the second, are also spotted and the Japanese, erroneously identify them as an aircraft carrier and cruiser.

Admiral Takagi, who subsequently believes that Task Force 17's main fleet has been located in this sighting, orders a full out attack by the carriers *'Shokaku'* and *'Zuikaku'.*

His carrier-born planes quickly sink both ships.

The American naval forces are also led astray by way of an aerial recognisance spotting of two Japanese cruisers and two destroyers which are mistakenly reported as two carriers and four cruisers. In response, Fletcher of Force 17 dispatches from the USS *'Lexington'* and *'Yorktown'* and by chance these aircraft stumble across the path of the Japanese light carrier *'Shoho'* and promptly sink her.

This successful sinking by the Americans alarms Admiral Inoue to such a degree that he halts the Port Moresby invasion group north of the Louisiades, until the American carriers can be found and destroyed by his forces.

* * * * *

- Crimea -

The first of the German summer offensives begins with an attack by the 22nd Panzer Division of the Eleventh Army. They take the Kerch peninsula.

* * * * *

- May Ninth -

- Ceylon -

Overnight the gunners of the Ceylon Garrison Artillery on Horsburgh Island in the Cocos, rebel. Their mutiny is promptly put down and three men are executed. These men are the only British Commonwealth soldiers to be executed for mutiny during the entire war.

* * * * *

- Malta -

USS *'Wasp'* joins forces with HMS *'Eagle'* to deliver sixty-four more Spitfires. Churchill is jubilant and signals the *'Wasp'* with one of his famous, brief, but poignant, comments: *'Who says a Wasp can't sting twice?'*

These new Spits are immediately put to aggressive work and over the next few days the Axis air forces are quickly forced to abandon their daylight bombing and strafing runs against Malta, giving it a chance to breathe for the first time in the onerous siege.

* * * * *

- May Tenth -

- Malta -

Misreading the turning tide, General Field Marshal Kesselring, repots to Hitler that Malta has been effectively neutralized.

Churchill, never known as a particularly patient man and growing more frustrated each day with General Auchinleck's inactivity, sends him a telegram with a clear order: *'Attack in time to cover for the Harpoon/Vigorous convoys sailings to Malta during the dark of the moon in early June'.*

By so doing, he has placed the General in the position of either complying with the order or resigning. Auchinleck fails to immediately reply to the command, leaving both the Prime Minister and his War Cabinet in virtual limbo.

* * * * *

- Philippines -

General Sharp, in command of the remaining American forces, gives the order to surrender to the Japanese.

* * * * *

- May Eleventh -

- Ottawa -

With the support of the April referendum behind them, the Canadian Parliament passes legislation introducing full conscription.

* * * * *

- Mediterranean -

A specially trained force of aircraft based in Crete successfully sink the British destroyers HMS *'Jackal'*, *'Kipling'* and *'Lively'*.

* * * * *

- May Twelfth -

- Canada -

The German sub U-553 sinks the British freighter *'Nicoya'* near the mouth of the St. Lawrence River, opening the *'Battle of the St. Lawrence'*.

* * * * *

- Easter Front -

The Russians unleash a renewal of their attempts made in January, to trap German forces against the Sea of Azov.

* * * * *

- May Thirteenth -

- Burma -

Pursuing the Chinese Sixth Army, Japanese troops cross the Salween River on the way to Kengtung.

* * * * *

- Eastern Front -

Russian troops begin to retreat from Kerch in the face of strong German attacks.

* * * * *

- May Fourteenth -

- Midway -

American code-breakers provide the US with warning of a proposed Japanese attack against the island.

* * * * *

- Eastern Front -

Hitler orders elements of Richthofen's Fliegerkorps VIII north to provide ground support for German forces dealing with the Russian offensive in the area of Kharkov. By the end of the day the Germans have established a small air superiority in the air above the battle lines. The Fuhrer then orders General Kleist, who is commanding forces opposite and to the south of the Russian's left flank, to prepare to launch a strong armoured counter-offensive.

* * * * *

- May Fifteenth -

- India -

The first British forces from Burma reach India.

The British have suffered some thirty thousand casualties from the Burmese campaign, out of their force of forty-five thousand, many of these being Burmese deserters.

Chinese losses from the campaign are enormous. Out of ninety-five thousand troops, only one Chinese formation, the 38th Division, still remains as a viable fighting unit, while Japanese losses of only eight thousand reflect the superior training and experience of their forces.

* * * * *

- Artic -

While on active convoy escort duty, the British cruiser HMS *'Trinidad'* is sunk by German bombers.

* * * * *

- New Guinea -

Australian troops, destined to reinforce the defenders at

Port Moresby, board transports.

* * * * *

- Eastern Front -

Manstein's Eleventh Army takes Kerch, killing or capturing one hundred and fifty thousand Russians.

* * * * *

- USA -

Rationing of gasoline begins in eighteen states.

* * * * *

- May Sixteenth -

- Ireland -

The US 1st Armoured Division arrives in Northern Ireland.

* * * * *

- May Seventeenth -

- Malta -

General Auchinleck has still made no reply to Churchill's earlier telegram.

The Prime Minister sends a terse follow-up; *'It is necessary for me to have some account of your general intentions in light of our recent telegrams'.*

He receives no immediate reply

* * * * *

- Eastern Front -

The 28th and 57th Russian Armies fighting in the salient north of Kharkov are experiencing difficulty in making any progress against German General Paulus's 6th Army, which is largely up to strength and fully equipped in preparation for the coming drive to Stalingrad. This is also one of the rare areas of command to which Hitler has not chosen to issue a strict *'no-retreat'* order, freeing Paulus to conduct efficient delaying actions.

In the south salient Kharitonov's Russian Ninth Army has managed to rout the Romanian troops facing them, capture Krasnograd and begin a push toward Poltava, and Gorodnyanski's Sixth Army has made its planned turn to the north to link up with the Twenty-Eighth and Fifty-Seventh Armies.

The Ninth Army's offensive had now stretched its armoured units out over a seventy-mile track, weakening it, and all its attempts to cover its left flank by driving the Germans back, have been unsuccessful.

The Ninth has managed to take a few prisoners along this left flank, and its commander, Timoshenko, is surprised and somewhat intimidated by the extent and variety of the equipment captured with these German prisoners, which includes armour due to the German buildup for the summer offensive.

As a result, the Russian Marshal has his Political Officer, Nikita Khrushchev, request that he be allowed to hold his offensive thrust until he is able to secure his left flank. This request is denied by the 'Stavka' (Russian High Command).

* * * * *

- May Eighteenth -

- Mediterranean -

The Force H carriers HMS *'Argus'* and *'Eagle'* deliver seventeen Spitfires to Malta. Admiral Harwood is appointed to command of the British Mediterranean Fleet.

$$* \ * \ * \ * \ *$$

- Eastern Front -

The Russians are in full retreat from Kerch. Many prisoners are taken by the Germans.

The Soviet offensive in the salient north of Kharkov has bogged down and in the southern salient, Kleist has launched his counter-offensive which is instantly successful. By the end of the day his advancing German units have reached the confluence of the Oksol and Donetz rivers, greatly narrowing the base of the salient.

In so doing, the German forces have captured or disrupted the majority of the lines of communication for Kharitonov's Ninth Army which rapidly becomes ineffective in its aim of protecting Gorodnyanski's Sixth Army which, due to its shift north, is poorly positioned to defend against the frenzied German attack striking at it from the south.

$$* \ * \ * \ * \ *$$

- May Nineteenth -

With the effectiveness of Kleist's counter-offensive at Kharkov underway, Paulus launches a second counter-attack from the north with the intention of joining up with Kleist to encircle and destroy as many Russian forces as possible.

The Russian Stavka, beginning to perceive the danger implied by German troop movements, issues orders to Gorodnyanski's Sixth Army to halt their advance; while in the field, Timoshenko has abandoned his position and is already doing to his best to save whatever forces he can before the

Germans can complete their planned encirclement.

* * * * *

- Malta -

General Auchinleck finally replies to Churchill indicating that he will have an attack ready by the sailing of the Harpoon/Vigorous convoys for Malta.

* * * * *

- May Twentieth -

- London -

The Russian foreign Minister, Vyacheslav Molotov, arrives for high-level talks.

* * * * *

- Burma -

The Japanese conquest of Burma is complete.

* * * * *

- Eastern Front -

The German encircling armies are rapidly closing the pincer movement around the Russians at Kharkov.

* * * * *

- May Twenty-First -

- Malta -

Hitler indefinitely postpones the German code-named plan to invade Malta, *'Operation Herkules'*.

* * * * *

- London -

Molotov, in discussions with Churchill and Anthony Eden, the British Foreign Secretary, presses Russian demands for territorial acquisitions earlier made during the run-up to the war.

These include the Baltic States, Eastern Poland and Bessarabia.

Churchill will not acquiesce to these demands and the talks quickly become deadlocked.

* * * * *

- May Twenty-Second -

- Declaration of War-

Mexico declares war on the Axis.

* * * * *

- May Twenty-Third -

- Eastern Front -

Units from Kleist's and Paulus's forces meet at Balakleya, southeast of Kharkov, having now encircled most of the Russian Sixth and Ninth Armies.

* * * * *

- London -

Anthony Eden attempts to reopen the stalled talks with Molotov by suggesting that the attempts to reach territorial understandings should be abandoned and offers to instead work to conclude a twenty year alliance between their two countries.

In view of the deteriorating situation on the Eastern Front, Molotov deigns to express interest in such a move.

* * * * *

- May Twenty-Fifth -

- Tokyo -

The Japanese send two light carriers and two cruisers out from Hokkaido with the intention of carrying out diversionary raids in the Aleutian Islands in preparation for the attack on Midway.

* * * * *

- US -

The Americans send submarines out from Hawaii to begin patrols against the enemy's Midway operation.

* * * * *

- India -

Part of the Chinese 38th Division has managed to escape from Burma and safely reaches India.

* * * * *

- May Twenty-Sixth -

- London -

The talks with Molotov end by reaching an agreement. The Anglo/Soviet Treaty is signed. It falls far below Molotov's demands, specifying only that no peace will be signed with the Axis powers by one, without the approval of the other.

* * * * *

- North Africa -

Rommel begins his spring offensive against the Gazala line just west of Tobruk.

Opening with what becomes known as *'Rommel's Moonlight Ride',* a ferocious mechanized thrust around the First Free French Brigade Group positions at Bir Hakeim, on the British left flank.

The Desert Fox's forces shatter the 3rd Indian Motorized Brigade, taking six hundred prisoners, who he promptly releases in the desert.

* * * * *

- Midway -

On route to Midway, the Japanese First Carrier Fleet under Admiral Nagumo, leaves the Japanese Inland Sea. This fleet consists of the carriers *'Akagi', 'Kaga', 'Soryu'* and *'Hiryu'* with two battleships plus cruisers and destroyers as escort.

* * * * *

- Pearl Harbour -

US naval Task Force Sixteen, which includes the carriers USS *'Enterprise'* and *'Hornet'* returns from the south and sails into Pearl.

* * * * *

- May Twenty-Seventh -

- Czechoslovakia -

Reinhard Heydrich is mortally wounded as a result of *'Operation Anthropoid'*.

* * * * *

- Midway -

The Japanese invasion fleet sails from Saipan and Guam with five thousand men aboard transports being escorted by cruisers and destroyers.

* * * * *

- Pearl Harbour -

The USS *'Yorktown'*, damaged during the Battle of the Coral Sea limps into Pearl and is put directly into repair and refit in preparation for the impending battle.

* * * * *

- Belgium -

The German occupation forces order all Jews to forthwith wear the identifying Star of David *'Yellow Badge'* prominently displayed on their outer clothing.

* * * * *

- May Twenty-Eighth -

- North Afrika -

Some of Rommel's panzers literally run out of gas, on Rigel Ridge. Other units, though in short supply, continue onward toward Acroma.

* * * * *

- Midway -

The remaining Japanese fleet sets out with Admiral Yamamoto in supreme command. He has seven battleships, one small carrier, cruisers and destroyers. He will take this fleet out and join Admiral Kondo's Second Fleet consisting of two battleships, one light carrier and two seaplane carriers plus escorts and eventually they will joined by Kakuta's fleet with his two light carriers and escorts.

Kakuta will become part of the battle plan to take Midway once he has finished covering the landing on the Aleutians.

The amassing of these forces is expected to assure a surprise attack and allow for the occupation of Midway before the defenders on the island can be reinforced.

The Japanese then believe that the Americans will be obliged to come in force to dispute the taking of the island. The massive Japanese naval force will then be able to wipe the Americans out completely and thereafter their prime enemy will have to rely on an extensive building program to replace their naval force in the Pacific, giving the Japanese the time they need for victory before the US can again effectively challenge them in those waters.

Having broken Japanese codes the US is aware of the complex Japanese plan of attack and is rapidly moving to counter it. Task Force Sixteen sails from Oahu with the carriers USS *'Enterprise'* and *'Hornet'* and escorts while

Fletcher's Task Force Seventeen, after a herculean repair program makes USS *'Yorktown'* seaworthy, quickly follows.

* * * * *

- May Twenty-Ninth -

- Occupied France -

The Jews are ordered to wear the yellow star.

* * * * *

- Eastern Front -

The Russians have badly underestimated the German forces at Kharkov. Their moves against the Nazi forces in place have in fact simplified a German plan to pinch out the salient and played into the Germans hands, in that, as the Germans complete their encirclement west of the Donets, they take even more Russian forces than anticipated and end up by eliminating or capturing two hundred and fifty thousand men.

* * * * *

- North Africa -

There is heavy fighting around the Knightsbridge road junction.

The British seem unable to develop a coordinated counter-attack, while German anti-tank guns are applied with great success. The Italian Trieste Division which had gotten itself lost earlier has subsequently managed to run into the British 150th Brigade. They manage to clear a path through the brigade and therein preserve a lifeline for the remainder of Rommel's Africa Korps.

* * * * *

- Shanghai -

South of the city, Japanese forces are making strong gains.

* * * * *

- May Thirtieth -

- Midway -

Four Japanese submarines sent to patrol off Pearl Harbour arrive as part of the plan to prevent reinforcements reaching midway during the attack planned against the Island. They are too late to intercept the American fleets. who have already sailed.

Two additional subs have been sent with supplies to the French Frigate Shoals to aid in the construction of a seaplane base but arrive to find that the Americans have beaten them to the punch.

* * * * *

- North Africa -

The Desert Fox draws his tanks into the *'Cauldron'* in a tight semicircle backing onto minefields and while holding the main British attack here, he works to eliminate the British 150th Brigade and ensure his supply lines stayed open.

* * * * *

- Cologne -

British Bomber Command unleashes an attack against the German city using in excess of one thousand planes. Only forty craft are lost. The massive raid is as much a propaganda success as it is militarily.

* * * * *

- May Thirty-First -

- San Francisco -

In a desperate attempt to strengthen the Pacific fleet, the battleships USS *'Colorado'* and *'Maryland'* sail for Hawaii.

* * * * *

- North Africa -

Rommel manages to overrun the British 150th Brigade to keep his lines open, but his offensive against Tobruk has stalled well short of target. Here he faces the British 1st Armoured and 7th Armoured Divisions, which are now partially equipped with the new American built Sherman Tanks.

He also finds himself forced to rely upon on a very long supply line which must circle around and is under constant threat from the 1st Free French Brigade Group of the British 50th Infantry Division, which is located at Bir Hakeim.

* * * * *

- Sydney -

Japanese mini-subs enter the harbour and manage to sink one support ship. Concerns over an impending invasion are heightened.

* * * * *

- Malta -

The expanded numbers of Spitfire fighters now based in Malta have turned the tide.

Kesselring is left with only eighty-three serviceable aircraft, down from the peak of the four hundred the Axis had achieved earlier in the spring.

CHAPTER ELEVEN

- June -

- Hitler -

Over the past few weeks little had changed with regard to the battle on the Eastern Front. The Germans were gearing up for a summer offensive but only minor heartening reports have reached Hitler.

The steady reports of Japanese victories help to raise the Fuhrer's spirits but any excitement over these achievements is overshadowed by Japan's polite, but stubborn refusal to conduct the war along the lines Hitler wishes.

At Hitler's direction, von Ribbentrop has been continually pressing the Japanese, through their German Ambassador, Oshima, to shift their major attack to India. Hitler has even gone so far as to invite Oshima to *'Wolfsschanze'* to make a personal appeal. On this occasion the Fuhrer advises Oshima that his forces are about to unleash an offensive against the Caucasus to secure the oil production there and once that had been accomplished, the road to Persia will be open.

If the Japanese now turn their attention to invading India, the Germans and Japanese would then been in position to catch the bulk of the British Far East forces between them in a massive pincer movement and destroy them.

Unbeknownst to Hitler, The Emperor of Japan had summoned Prime Minister Tojo to the palace and in view of the Japanese successes to date, has advised him: *'not to miss any opportunity to terminate the war.'*

Tojo had subsequently called in the German Ambassador, General Eugen Ott, and suggested that their two nations secretly approach the Allies with a view to solidifying their captured territories by negotiating a peace agreement. Tojo goes so far as to agree, as the personal representative of the Emperor, to fly to meet with Hitler in Berlin for discussions if the Fuhrer could see his way clear to send a long-range bomber to pick him up.

When informed of this offer Hitler is stunned. He had not expected any such suggestion and wanted no part of it. His response to the idea was polite, but not at all encouraging. Tojo was informed that Hitler could not possibly consider such a plan and that he would not risk having Tojo crash while being transported in a German aircraft.

By June the Fuhrer had given up on gaining direct Japanese aid in his planning.

He then turned his mind back to the defeat of Russia and his upcoming plan to drive into the Caucasus.

This attack, codenamed *'Blau'* had been delayed for weeks due to heavy spring rains and could not be launched by Marshal von Bock until the twenty-eighth of the month.

Initially, seventeen German and Six Hungarian Divisions were to drive toward Kursk and two days later, the eighteen Divisions of the formidable Sixth Army would strike out just to the south.

* * * * *

- Inner Circle -

- Speer -

Speer began to shift his attention away from the reorganization of arms and munitions, which was now doing well and began to concentrate his efforts on the organization of the manufacture of tanks and aircraft.

* * * * *

- Heydrich -

Heydrich's time in the SS had been a mixture of rapid promotions, reserve commissions in the regular armed forces and front-line combat service.

During the eleven years he served with the SS, Heydrich rose from the ranks, serving in every rank from private to full general.

He was also a major in the Luftwaffe, having flown nearly one hundred combat missions until July of nineteen forty-one when his plane was hit by Russian anti-aircraft fire. He had been able to make an emergency landing behind enemy lines after this incident, where he was able to avoid Russian troops and was eventually able to meet up with an advanced German patrol. Hitler was so concerned about this incident that he personally ordered Heydrich to return to Berlin to resume his SS duties.

Heydrich was the recipient of several Nazi party and military awards, including the *'German Order'*, *'Blood Order'*, *'Golden Party Badge'*, *'Luftwaffe's Pilot's Badge'*, the *'bronze'* and *'silver'* *'combat mission bars'*, and the *'Iron Cross'*, *'First'* and *'Second'* Classes.

Upon Heydrich's assassination, Hitler gave instructions for an elaborate State Funeral.

After the funeral held in Prague on the seventh of June, Heydrich's flower-draped coffin, resting in a castle courtyard, was passed by thousands of apparently grieving Czech and was then paraded on a gun carriage and moved with great pomp and ceremony along roadways lined by thousands of SS men holding torches, to the railway station. Here it was placed on a train for transport to Berlin.

A second, more elaborate State Funeral ceremony was then held in the new Reich Chancellery in Berlin on June ninth. Himmler gave the eulogy and Hitler attended to place all Heydrich's decorations on his funeral pillow. After the ceremony, the coffin was again paraded on a gun carriage, this time horse-drawn, through the streets to Berlin's Invalidenfriedhof military cemetery.

The grave was later given a simple wooden marker, while

the planning for the construction of a monumental tomb, ordered personally by Hitler, was arranged.

These wildly elaborate and extensive funeral arrangements for Heydrich were primarily orchestrated by the Nazis for propaganda reasons. It is of interest to note what the prime instigators of these public exhibitions, Hitler and Himmler, really thought of the loss of Heydrich, the investigation into his death, and the reprisals that followed over time.

Hitler privately believed Heydrich was the author of his own misfortune: *'Since it is opportunity which makes not only the thief but also the assassin, such heroic gestures as driving in an open, unarmoured vehicle, of walking about the streets unguarded are just damned stupidity, which serves the Fatherland not one whit. That a man as irreplaceable as Heydrich should expose himself to unnecessary danger, I can only condemn as stupid and idiotic.'*

Himmler, while surveying Heydrich's death mask after the Berlin funeral, was heard to remark: *'Yes, as the Fuhrer said at the funeral, he was indeed a man with an iron heart. And at the height of his power fate purposefully took him away.'*

Not the words of a man who was particularly upset by the recent turn of events.

It was despite these personal musings that the investigation into the assassination went forth with vicious determination.

As time went on the investigation, ordered by Hitler and executed by the SS, endeavoured to expand to include those who could even be remotely connected with the plan to remove Heydrich. Intelligence had already linked the villages of Lidice and Lezaky to the plot. The Gestapo indicated that Lidice was likely the assailants' suspected hiding place since several Czech army officers, exiled in England at the time, were known to have come from there and a resistance radio transmitter had been located in Lezaky.

As earlier agreed, after the funeral, Hitler met with

Himmler to discuss what form the final reprisals for the assassination would take.

On June ninth the Germans literally wiped out Lidice. One hundred and ninety-nine men were executed, ninety-five children taken prisoner, eighty-one of whom were later dispatched at Chelmno extermination camp and eight of whom, having been selected as holding Aryan characteristics were subsequently placed with German families for adoption. The one hundred and ninety-five women living in the town were promptly deported to Ravensbruck concentration camp.

In Lezaky all the adults, men and women were executed.

Both towns were then burned and the ruins of Lidice were then dynamited and flattened to the ground.

* * * * *

- Sonderkommando -

The *'Sonderkommando'* (Special Unit - work units of the death camps), which were composed almost entirely of Jews, were selected periodically from the deportees arriving at the concentration camps to be used as forced labour to carry out the disposal of the gas chamber victims.

The Sonderkommando members had the hands on responsibility for the removal of bodies. As such they were pivotal to the operation of the camps. They were granted much less squalid living conditions than other inmates and slept in their own barracks. They were also allowed to keep and use various goods such as food, medicines and cigarettes brought in by those deportees destined for the gas chambers and they were not subject to arbitrary, random killing by guards.

These men tended to live longer than other inmates. However because they were aware of what was taking place within the heart of the camps, they were considered to be *'Geheimnistager'* (bearers of secrets) and therefore had to be kept in isolation from the other camp inmates, with the exception of those who were about to enter the gas chambers.

Because they knew the truth of the operations, the Germans ensured they didn't live long enough to tell the tale. Roughly every four months they would be replaced by new arrivals.

The first responsibility of the newly chosen Sonderkommando would then be to dispose of their predecessors' corpses.

* * * * *

- Extermination Camps -

- Chelmno -

In a report dated June fifth nineteen forty-two addressed to the Obersturmbannfuhrer Rauff at the RSHA, camp inspector Becker, referencing the successful use of mobile gas chambers (trucks converted with hermetically sealed cargo areas) in the camp, wrote that using just three vans on the Eastern Front and operating without any breakdowns, they were able to process ninety-seven thousand soviet captives between December nineteen forty-one and June of forty-two.

Three such vehicles were now in operation at Chelmno.

Previous to this time the camp Sonderkommando, in addition to sorting victims' clothing and cleaning the vans after use, had been removing the bodies from the gas vans and burying them in mass graves.

Beginning in the summer of nineteen forty-two they stopped the burials which were time consuming and began burning the bodies in crematoria or on pyres in the forest camp.

* * * * *

-Auschwitz -

After the successful testing of Zyklon B gas, it had been adopted for use at Auschwitz. Two farmhouses had then undergone conversion to gas chambers. In January of forty-one the first had come on line and provisional gas chamber number two came on stream in June of forty-two.

* * * * *

- Concentration and Internment Camps -

- The Netherlands -

The Dutch civilian administration continued to function under German supervision after the Nazi occupation.

The Nazi commissioner, Arthur Seyss-Inquart had insisted on strict compliance with anti-Jewish measures and in January of forty-one, all Jews were ordered to report for registration. In excess of one hundred and forty thousand did as ordered.

In early forty-two more than three thousand Jews were sent to forced-labour camps in the Netherlands. Deportation from the Netherlands began in forty-two.

All Dutch Jews were ordered to move to ghettos in Amsterdam, while those who were stateless and who had entered the Netherlands during the nineteen thirties, were sent to the Westerbork transit camp. Jews from the provinces were then concentrated in the Vaght camp.

In late June of forty-two the occupying forces announced that the Jews were to be deported to labour camps in Germany. The majority of the Dutch police and railway workers cooperated in these deportations.

The trains the deportees boarded however, were not headed for Germany, but travelled directly to Auschwitz-Birkenau or Sobibor in occupied Poland.

* * * * *

- Low Countries -

- Belgium -

In the summer of forty-two the Germans converted the Dossin military barracks in Mechelen into a transit camp in preparation for the deportation of the Jews from Belgium. The location was chosen because it was situated about midway between the major Jewish population centres which were situated in Antwerp and Brussels and had good rail connections to the east.

Dossin consisted of a single three-story building surrounded by barbed wire in the populated area of the town, near the Dijle River and was well serviced by rail yards.

* * * * *

- Ghettos -

- Warsaw -

The deportations of Jews from nearby towns east of Warsaw, from Germany and other occupied areas, as well as that of several hundred gypsies, which had begun in April, was now almost completed.

The Warsaw Ghetto now held in excess of four hundred thousand people. As the numbers had risen, conditions had worsened.

In nineteen forty-one, well before this massive deportation order, over forty-three thousand of the inhabitants of this ghetto, close to one in ten, had died.

* * * * * *

- Unmanned Aircraft -

A final proposal for the development of the unmanned aircraft project was submitted to the Technical Office of the RLM on June fifth of nineteen forty-two. As Fieseler was to be the chief contractor, the project was renamed Fl 103.

On June nineteenth, Generalfeldmarschall Erhard Milch gave Fl 103 production high priority, and future development was undertaken at the Luftwaffe's *'Erprobungsstelle'* coastal test center at Karlshagen, part of the Peenemunde-West facility.

* * * * *

- The Family -

- Eric -

Mid-voyage, Eric was pleased to have relatively good weather so far in the trip back to Brazil.

His craft, as large as it was, seemed to be bursting at the seams from the number of passengers he had crammed aboard in order to empty the safe houses in Bordeaux before they could be discovered.

Under the current cramped conditions aboard the U-boat, the ability to travel on the surface in the evenings was no longer an opportunity to enjoyable a break for all aboard and a chance for exercise and fresh air. It had become an absolute necessity.

Luckily the weather had been cooperating wonderfully.

* * * * *

- The Countess -

Erika had returned aboard the family's private rail cars to the castle at Friedrichshafen and settled back into day to day life on Lake Constance with Ursula and her son-in-law, sharing with them her wonder of her new grandchild.

She was also continually inquiring of her daughter as to when another addition might be expected to join the family.

---

* * * * *

- Konrad -

After deplaning in Berlin, Konrad had exchanged goodbyes with Wilhelm and the Count at the airport and made his way separately into the city as he changed planes to continue on to *'Wolfsschanze'*.

He was anxious to sit down with his old mentor, Dr. Baron von Kliest to discuss the current ongoing research with him, but was planning on staying for only two days, as he did not want to be away from Gabriella and his new son any longer than necessary.

* * * * *

- The Count -

Two days before their scheduled meeting with Hitler, which had been set down for the second of June, Karl von Stauffer had sat Wilhelm down and carefully explained to him what he hoped to accomplish when seeing the Fuhrer.

Over drinks after dinner, the Count had carefully laid out the scenario for his son.

"By the meeting you must not only be conversant on the topic of this new flying bomb, which has caught the personal interest of the Fuhrer, Wilhelm. You must appear to Hitler as an expert on the availability of all of the new, so called, *'Super Weapons'* currently on the horizon, and leave him with no doubt as to the wonder of their potential and perhaps even more importantly, the key role you play in it their development."

Wilhelm frowned and set his cigar down in the ashtray on the table beside him.

"I understand what you are asking of me father, but I am not sure I understand why you want me there. You have others who are much more up on this unmanned flying machine specifically, as well as all the other proposals currently being worked on than I am…wouldn't it be better to take a number of them, instead of dragging me along."

The Count sucked in a deep breath, held it for a moment and then released it before speaking.

"I can't overstate the importance of this meeting for you Wilhelm. We have been presented with an opportunity to speak directly with Hitler at a time when few others can say the same.

The Fuhrer, by his message to me - the first for months I might add, has expressed a great deal of interest in these new weapons. Times are not going well for him as you well know. He obviously sees these types of projects leading to the manufacture of the super weapons of the future, weapons that can and will shatter our enemies."

Karl paused as he raised his glass and drank, then ensuring that he had Wilhelm's full attention he continued.

"What is important to us at this point in time is that you are removed from under Himmler's direct control. If even a portion of what we are hearing about what the SS is doing in the occupied territories is true, anyone associated with the SS-Reichsfuhrer, let alone one of his personal aides is going to be in a great deal of trouble after this war ends. Hitler's interest in this particular unmanned aircraft has given us an opportunity to accomplish exactly that. By the time we leave the meeting with the Fuhrer, I want him to be so impressed with your knowledge and commitment to these projects that he is convinced that without you at the helm they will not proceed.

I want him to decree that you be immediately removed from Himmler's staff and transferred to my staff with the instructions that you are to work solely on the project developments of Super Weapons. If he does that, Himmler will not even consider questioning such a move, and you will be able to distance yourself from his direct overview."

Wilhelm let out a deep sigh.

"Right. I'm beginning to understand why you wanted me fully briefed on this thing before we meet with him. Do you think it will work?"

The Count shrugged.

"I certainly hope so. I'll do my part by making the suggestion of such a transfer at the right time, but you'll be the one who will first have to convince him that it is something that is necessary for the successful continuation of this type of project to the production stage."

He added.

"And Wilhelm - we won't get a second chance at this, so don't let me down. You'll not only have to give Hitler confidence in this particular concept, you'll also have to sell him on the fact that without you, these type of weapons won't come to fruition. This may be the most important thing you do. It could well be something that decides whether you are alive or dead when Germany finally loses this doomed war."

CHAPTER TWELVE

- June -

- Air Operations -

There are two one thousand plane raids made against Germany by British Bomber Command, one against Essen and the other against Bremen. Additional targets struck are Dieppe, St. Nazaire and Le Havre in occupied France; as well as in Germany at Osnabruck and Emden.

Five hundred sorties are flown for a loss of two hundred and forty aircraft. Six thousand, nine hundred and fifty tons of bombs are dropped.

In the Mediterranean theatre, RAF bombers hit many targets in Italy and fly missions against Axis land forces in both Egypt and Libya.

On June twelfth US Liberator bombers hit oil installations at Ploesti.

* * * * *

- Maritime Warfare -

In the Atlantic a dozen U-boats are now operating in the Caribbean and a few are patrolling in the waters off Brazil. The British now have aircraft patrolling the Bay of Biscay, which have been fitted with the newly developed *'Leigh'* lights and some of the convoy escorts are now being refuelled at sea, which solves some routing problems and extends the range of the escorts.

The total Allied loss is one hundred and seventy-three ships amounting to a total tonnage of eight hundred and thirty-four thousand, two hundred. Axis submarines sink one hundred and forty-four of these, for a total of seven hundred thousand, two hundred tons.

* * * * *

- June First -

- Allies -

The first reports of *'gassings'* of Jews who have been deported to the east reaches the West.

* * * * *

- North Africa -

Rommel launches his attack on the 150th Brigade of the British 50th Infantry Division which he has now managed to encircle. He comes at them from the east against a position that has been specifically designed to defend against the west and they are quickly captured.

* * * * *

- Midway -

Twenty-five US submarines are now in position in the waters around Midway and the aircraft carrier USS *'Saratoga'*, repaired of the torpedo damage caused in January, sails from San Diego.

* * * * *

- June Second -

- Eastern Front -

The Germans renew the bombardment of Sevastopol. They have now been equipped with thirteen hundred artillery pieces, including two 24 inch *'Karl'* mortars and a massive thirty-two inch *'Dora'* railway gun and are being supported by aircraft of Fliegerkorps VII.

* * * * *

- North Africa -

Rommel dispatches his 90th Light Infantry and the Trieste Division south to take Bir Hacheim in order to free up his flank. The Free French units in place defend ferociously and although the Desert Fox supports his units with the 15th Panzer and heavy artillery he is unable defeat them.

* * * * *

- Midway -

The US carrier groups from Pearl Harbour join up northeast of Midway. The combined strength of the three carriers now in position amounts to two hundred and fifty aircraft and is comparable in numbers to that carried by the main Japanese force.

* * * * *

- Aleutians -

Aircraft from Kakuta's Japanese light carriers attack Dutch Harbour, but the Americans, who have been forewarned of the diversionary plan and recognize it for what it is, hold fast in their positions near Midway.

* * * * *

- June Third -

- Midway -

Air reconnaissance from the island locates the Japanese Invasion Group accompanied by their heavy support. A group of land based Flying Fortresses takes to the air against them. They have little success.

* * * * *

- London -

The British coal industry is nationalized.

* * * * *

- Malta -

HMS *'Eagle'* delivers another twenty-seven Spitfires.

* * * * *

- June Fourth -

- Midway -

The Battle of Midway opens with Admiral Nagumo's attack on the air defences of the island. He achieves a fair amount of damage. Both sides lose many aircraft, but by the end of the exchange the primary target of the Japanese, the island's airbase, is still functional.

In anticipation of large-scale American fleet support being sent from Pearl Harbour as a result of their move against Midway, after what the Japanese believe to be a surprise attack against the island, fourteen Japanese submarines are laying in wait between the island and Hawaii. They are intent upon delivering a shattering blow to the major American ships as they steam furiously to the defence of Midway.

The opposing fleet battle of the carriers begins and by the time the dust has settled the Japanese have received a disastrous defeat. Their carriers *'Akagi'*, *'Kaga'*, *'Soryu'* and *'Hiryu'* have all been sunk or scuttled. The only carrier lost by the Americans is the USS *'Yorktown'*.

It was a battle that the Japanese could not afford to lose. The balance of sea power has now permanently changed in the Pacific.

* * * * *

- Czechoslovakia -

Reinhard Heydrich succumbs to his injuries in Prague.

* * * * *

- June Fifth -

- North Africa -

At Gazala, British forces of the Eighth Army under the command of General Ritchie launch a major count-offensive against the Desert Fox's dug in forces in the Cauldron.

The elaborate anti-tank defensive positions of the Germans ordered by Rommel, coupled with the recovery of their critical logistics, decide the battle. By early afternoon on the day of the battle Rommel is clearly in control of the situation and promptly attacks the British position at *'Knightsbridge'* with the Ariete and 21st Panzer division. He subsequently overruns several of the British tactical headquarter positions disrupting the command and control of the British troops.

By day's end a goodly amount of the British armour has been destroyed and the tank numbers on both sides are now close to equal. However, the quality of the remaining German equipment is far superior to those machines left operational to the British.

* * * * *

- Washington -

The US declares war against Romania, Hungary and Bulgaria.

* * * * *

- June Seventh -

- Aleutians -

The Japanese successfully land a small occupational forces on Kiska and Attu.

* * * * *

- Eastern Front -

The Germans begin a major attack on Sevastopol, which is being supplied by a large Russian Black Sea Fleet. The defenders consist of seven infantry divisions and three marine brigades, which are all well under strength. The German attacking force has a strength of nine well equipped divisions, two of which are Rumanian.

* * * * *

- June Eighth -

- Australia -

A surfaced Japanese submarine fires several shells into a residential area in Sydney resulting in little damage.

* * * * *

- June Ninth -

- Czechoslovakia -

The SS obliterate the town of Lidice as part of the reprisal for Heydrich's assassination.

* * * * *

- North Africa -

Rommel renews his attack on the Free French positions at Bir Hacheim. Once again the defenders hold, but their situation is becoming perilous.

* * * * *

- Mediterranean -

An additional thirty two spitfires reach Malta.

* * * * *

- June Tenth -

- North Africa -

Rommel forces the Free French out of the fortress at Bir Hakeim.

* * * * *

- Pacific -

The carrier USS *'Wasp'* and the battleship USS *'North Carolina'* accompanied by their escorts, clear the Panama Canal and steam to join the Pacific Fleet.

* * * * *

- June Eleventh -

- Malta -

Two relief supply convoys set out for Malta. One, codenamed *'Harpoon'* sails from Gibraltar while the other *'Vigorous'*, leaves the harbour at Alexandria. They carry much needed food, fuel and ammunition.

* * * * *

- June Twelfth -

- North Africa -

Breaking out of the defensive positions at the Cauldron, Rommel begins to attack the British on the ridges between Knightsbridge and El Adem. At Knightsbridge, British counter-attacks are poorly coordinated. The British lose one hundred tanks and are left with only seventy that are operational, less than half the number Rommel has. In addition, as the Desert Fox's forces have taken the territory upon which the battle was fought. They are therefore able to recover and repair many of their damaged German tanks while the British correspondingly lose all equipment left immobile on the battlefield. The frustrated British can only watch from afar as Rommel scoops up anything worth salvaging.

* * * * *

- June Thirteenth -

-North Africa -

Rommel has a field day against British armour. He goes fully onto the offensive, destroying large amounts of British mechanized equipment at the Battle of Gazala. By the end of the day he threatens to encircle both the British 50th and 1st South African Divisions. He is now only fifteen miles from the Tobruk perimeter.

* * * * *

- June Fourteenth -

- North Africa -

At the Gaza line the British position has become unsustainable.

General Auchinleck authorized General Ritchie to withdraw from forward positions. In order to accomplish this breakout, the British 50th Division must first break through to the southwest, through an area occupied by the Italian X Corps and then turn east to rejoin the 8th Army. The RAF forces available in the area are largely outnumbered but make a valiant fight to cover the retreating forces.

The 1st South African is able to retreat along the coastal road but is very much aware of the danger of being cut off by Rommel's rampaging forces.

An ever watchful Churchill sends a telegram to Auchinleck which opens with: *'To what position does Ritchie want to withdraw the Gazala troops? Presume there is no question in any case of giving up Tobruk.'*

* * * * *

- Malta -

The relief convoys headed for the island are not faring well. *'Vigorous'* has been under air attack since shortly after leaving port and now sights a large Italian naval squadron steaming at speed toward it, and *'Harpoon'* now comes under attack.

* * * * *

- June Fifteenth -

- North Africa -

Auchinleck replies to Churchill with a telegram which reads in part *'...I have no intention of giving up Tobruk'*.

Part of Rommel's advance 15th Panzer force takes control of the main road east of Tobruk but they arrive just short of a chance to cut off the frantically retreating South African Division.

By evening the main body of Rommel's 21st Panzer has reached Sidi Rezegh.

* * * * *

- June Sixteenth -

- Malta -

Both relief convoys steaming for Malta have suffered serious losses and the Island is under heavy air attack.

'Harpoon' straggles into the harbour with only two of its original six transports having survived, one of which has lost part of its cargo as a result of having struck a mine. The tanker *'Kentucky'* has been sunk, meaning that there will be no significant amount of aviation fuel afforded by the convoy, something that is badly needed in view of dwindling RAF stocks on Malta.

Due to this very disappointing showing, the ravaged *'Vigorous'* convoy is ordered to turn tail and return to Alexandria.

* * * * *

- North Africa -

El Adem is evacuated by British forces as they face the reality of the hopelessness of forming any type of effective line of defense west of Tobruk.

* * * * *

- London -

Churchill, who is preparing to travel to the US, forwards a letter to His Royal Majesty, George the VI, in which he advises the King to appoint Anthony Eden to the post of Prime Minister. should he not survive the trip to America and back.

* * * * *

- June Seventeenth -

- North Africa -

The British attack Rommel near Sidi Rezegh, and in the ensuing battle the 4th Armoured Brigade loses one third of its tanks. Tobruk is now surrounded by the forces under the command of the Desert Fox.

* * * * *

- June Eighteenth -

- Washington -

Churchill arrives for high level talks with President Roosevelt and his advisers.

There is deep discussion with regard to the Russian pressure for the opening of a second front in Europe against Germany. A rough plan has been in the works for this to go ahead in forty-two, but it is agreed that this is simply not going to be possible under the current circumstances. Draft plans for some sort of joint activity in France or North Africa are suggested by Churchill, but no firm commitment is made in this regard.

A second topic of discussion revolves around discussion of future atomic research. It is agreed that Britain and the US should share their knowledge in this regard and that all future work on this file should be done in the US. Despite this fact, cooperation between the two counties on this project will continue to be less than smooth, especially now that development in America is quickly outstripping the progress being made in Britain.

The US *'Manhattan Project'*, a scientific approach to the construction of nuclear weapons, is launched.

* * * * *

- North Africa -

Tobruk is now surrounded by the *'Africa Korps'*.

Rommel is not deterred by the fact that his troops are nearing exhaustion. He issues orders for an attack on Tobruk to be commenced on June twentieth. He intends to unleash the 15th and 21st Panzer and Ariete in the southeast sector with the aim of driving a spearhead all the way through to the harbour. Kesselring sends in every bomber available to him in the Mediterranean to support the proposed attack.

* * * * *

- June Twentieth -

- North Africa -

Rommel's' offensive begins with a massive dive-bomber attack early in the morning. His ground forces then thrust determinately toward their goal and by the afternoon have ripped through the main defensive positions. They successfully reach the harbour by evening.

* * * * *

- Eastern Front -

After horrific fighting the Germans cut through the defenders to reach the harbour at Sevastopol.

* * * * *

- June Twenty-First -

- North Africa -

Rommel retakes Tobruk, capturing thirty-five thousand troops. Mountains of stores are captured, three million rations and five hundred thousand gallons of gasoline are a welcome sight to the Desert Fox, whose men are now very low on supplies of their own. The British are retreating rapidly and the road to Egypt is now open to the Germans.

Rommel sees this windfall as an opportunity to drive on to Egypt in pursuit of his bedraggled enemy. Going around Kesselring, who he knows is against this plan, Rommel makes the proposal directly to Hitler and Mussolini. A very thrilled Hitler not only approves of such a move but instantly promotes Rommel to the rank of Field Marshal.

* * * * *

- Washington -

Churchill receives the news from North Africa while in a meeting with Roosevelt and is visibly shaken by the information that Tobruk has fallen. Roosevelt, noting the Prime Minister's depressed state offers him immediate assistance. Three hundred Sherman tanks and one hundred self-propelled guns are quickly dispatched by the US to be used as reinforcements for the British Eighth Army.

* * * * *

- June Twenty-Second -

- Vichy France -

Vichy puppet Prime Minister, Laval, makes a radio broadcast to his people in which he belabours the desirability of a German victory and urges all Frenchmen to work hard in German industry.

* * * * *

- June Twenty-Third -

- North Africa -

Rommel's advance units cross the border into Egypt while the British Eighth Army withdraws to Mersa Matruh in disarray.

* * * * *

- June Twenty-Fifth -

- London -

US General Dwight D. Eisenhower arrives in London ready to assume the post of Commander of American Land forces in Europe.

* * * * *

- Eastern Front -

The Russians retreat from Kupyansk on the Oskol River east of Kharkov.

* * * * *

- North Africa -

Auchinleck removes General Ritchie from command of the British Eighth Army and takes direct control himself.

* * * * *

- June Twenty-Sixth -

- North Africa -

The Africa Korps now has only sixty operational tanks and the Italian Littorio Division about forty, giving Rommel a total of one hundred. The British forces facing him have two hundred tanks and have several fresh formations in position around Mersa Matruh. The new Field Marshal appears impervious to this imbalance in armour and he continues to advance with success.

* * * * *

- Germany -

Another RAF one thousand plane raid is launched. The target this time is Bremen.

* * * * *

- Eastern Front -

German forces drive toward Rostov-on-Don.

* * * * *

- June Twenty-Seventh -

- Germany -

RAF Bomber Command launches a heavy and highly destructive incendiary attack against Hamburg.

* * * * *

- June Twenty-Eighth -

- North Africa -

Rommel takes Mersa Matruh, which is situated approximately one hundred and forty miles from Alexandria. In so doing he captures yet another large quantity of British stores and equipment.

* * * * *

- Easter Front -

'Code Blue', the main German summer offensive, commences with the plan to capture Stalingrad and the Russian oil fields in the Caucasus. Bock's Army Group South drives east from Kursk toward Voronezh.

* * * * *

- Artic -

The British Home Fleet leaves Scapa Flow to provide distant escort cover for convoy PQ-17 which is composed of thirty-seven ships. The escort consists of two battleships, HMS *'Duke of York'* and USS *'Washington'* and the carrier HMS *'Victorious'*, with cruisers and destroyers in support.

* * * * *

- June Thirtieth -

- Artic -

The close-cover convoy protection for PQ-17 leaves Iceland with four cruisers, two of which are American, and three destroyers. The Germans sight the ships but do not engage.

* * * * *

- Eastern Front -

The Russian High command orders the evacuation of Sevastopol. The Black Sea Fleet, now much depleted, races to assist but can offer only very limited help.

* * * * *

- Washington -

II Corps is deployed to the European Theatre of war.

- Part Two -

CHAPTER THIRTEEN

- July -

- Hitler -

The German summer offensive, codenamed *'Blau'*, which had finally commenced on June twenty-eighth, was progressing well.

The Russians had ineffectively thrown in their tanks against the onslaught in a piecemeal fashion and within forty-eight hours the two German pincers had met and encircled a massive number of prisoners. The German advance units were now only a short distance from the Don and the strategic city of Voronezh.

Von Bock hesitated at this point, unsure of extending his supply lines and it isn't until July sixth that he takes the city. Hitler is disgusted with this hesitancy to take advantage of the initial overwhelming success of the attack. He relieves von Bock of his command.

As a shocked and disheartened von Bock heads west into forced retirement, Hitler, in order to get closer to the front, moves his headquarters deep into the Ukraine from 'Wolfsschanze' to a new compound, which he has once again coined after his self-chosen nickname of 'Wolf'.

This new advanced headquarters, christened 'Fuhrerhauptquartier Werwolf'' had been constructed in a pine forest approximately seven and a half miles north of Vinnitsa.

'Fuhrerhauptquartier Werwolf'' was built between December of nineteen forty-one and June of forty-two under a 'Top Secret' security designation. The site had been selected because of the Nazis proposed trans-European highway to the Crimean Peninsula, which would have intersected, when constructed, with this new Compound. It was close to the Wehrmacht regional headquarters at Vinnytsia and the Luftwaffe airbase located in Kalinovka, which was about fifteen miles away.

Hitler's personal accommodation at the compound was a modest log cabin built around a private courtyard which held his own concrete bunker. The remainder of the complex consisted of approximately twenty wooden cottages and barracks and three 'B' class bunkers surrounded by a ring of barbed wire and ground defensive positions which were connected by underground tunnels.

Two observations platforms were set up in the tall oak trees surrounding the pine forest. The entire area was encircled by defensive bunkers, anti-aircraft guns and tanks, as well as anti-tank ditches and minefields.

Encompassed within the compound was a tea house, barber shop, bathhouse, sauna, cinema and an outdoor swimming pool. The pool had been built solely for Hitler's use. Within the facility was a large vegetable garden which had been set up by the German horticultural company Zeidenspiner. This area was dedicated to supplying Hitler with a secure source of food. Two Artesian wells supplied the site with water and it had its own power generating facilities.

The bunkers were constructed of steel-reinforced concrete and had been built by 'Organization Todt' using some local Ukrainian workers by way of forced labour and Russian prisoners of war. Once construction had been completed, those who had been forced to do the work were executed to ensure the location and specifics of the compound remained secret.

While Hitler was in residence here, the complex was served by a daily three-hour long flight connection from Berlin to the airfield at nearby Kalinovka. Additionally a regular train connection from Berlin/Charlottenburg ran to the onsite *'Eichenbein'* station at *'Fuhrerhauptquartier Werwolf'*. It took thirty-four hours to travel from Berlin to the new complex by rail.

Hitler first took up residence here on July sixteenth of nineteen forty-two.

The weather was very hot, the bunkers humid and the conditions seemed to take a toll on the Fuhrer's disposition. The conditions within *'Fuhrerhauptquartier Werwolf'* led to Hitler catching severe influenza and he began running a temperature that reached into the high nineties.

He was both sick and depressed and arguments and episodes of explosive fury became regular occurrences.

Having convinced himself that the Russians were beaten, Hitler decided that he had sufficient troops to tackle not only his specified goal of taking the Caucasus but also to move simultaneously against Stalingrad. Halder, the Chief of the General Staff, somehow found the strength to openly disagree with the Fuhrer on this change of plan and was adamant in his view that such an operation was doomed to failure. He urged that the forces at hand must be solely concentrated on the original aim of occupying the Caucasus.

The back and forth arguments on the matter intensified and at one point Hitler told his personal adjutant; *'If I listen to Halder much longer, I'll become a pacifist!'*

At the daily conference held on July thirtieth the debate came to a head when Jodl solemnly stated that the fate of the Caucasus would be decided at Stalingrad, and that the Fourth Panzer Army, which had earlier been diverted, must be returned immediately.

Hitler exploded, but eventually agreed to this assessment.

In all probability if this tank army had never been shifted to the south in the first place, Stalingrad would have by now been in German hands.

This was not the only time that Hitler had suffered from critical overconfidence in his military strength. The first incident had been his determination to divide his forces to strike at Leningrad and the Ukraine simultaneously, despite the advice of his generals and in so doing, reducing the troops available for the attack on Moscow. If he had not done this, but instead stuck to his original plan, he would have in all likelihood taken Moscow.

Now, again against the advice of his generals, he was insisting on attempting to accomplish too much too quickly, by dividing his forces and stretching them too thinly, with the intention of taking both Stalingrad and the Caucasus simultaneously. Additionally, at a critical time in his fight on the Russian Front, the Fuhrer was siphoning off very significant resources, both in men and equipment for reassignment in order to deal with his obsessive plans to carry out the final solution to the Jewish question.

* * * * *

- Deportations -

On July fourteenth the Germans begin the deportation of Dutch Jews to Auschwitz.

On July sixteenth the seventy-four thousand Jews in Paris are rounded up and sent to Drancy Interment Camp.

On July nineteenth Himmler orders *'Operation Reinhard'*; the mass deportation of the Jews in Poland to extermination camps.

On July twenty-second deportations from the Warsaw Ghetto to Treblinka begin. Deportation of the Belgian Jews to Auschwitz also commences.

On July twenty-third, Treblinka officially opens.

* * * * *

- Concentration Camps -

- Auschwitz -

On July seventh, Himmler grants permission for sterilization experiments.

On July seventeenth, Himmler arrives for a two day visit to Auschwitz-Birkenau. He is here to inspect ongoing construction and expansion which includes four large new gas chambers and crematoria. He takes the time to observe the extermination process from start to finish, watching as two trainloads of Jews arriving from Holland are processed.

Pleased with his inspection, he promotes the Camp Commandant, Rudolf Hoess.

By early nineteen forty-two, the death rate at Dachau had outstripped the capacity of the old crematorium originally built by Topf & Sohne. Plans were then drawn up in April for a more efficient four-furnace crematory which, from its early planning, was to contain five gas chambers. On July twenty-third the order was issued from the SS headquarters in Berlin to commence construction of the crematorium at the envisioned cost of one hundred and fifty thousand Reichsmarks.

* * * * *

- Extermination Camps -

- Treblinka -

Treblinka was the last of the secret extermination camps to be constructed specifically for *'Aktion Reinhard'* (Operation Reinhard). It was completed and came into operation on July twenty-third nineteen forty-two.

The two parallel camps of Treblinka were located fifty miles northeast of the Polish capital of Warsaw near the

Malkinia/Sokolow Podlaski railway junction. This junction, connected to major cities in central Poland and near the Treblinka town railroad station, was a spur leading to earlier gravel pits which had been located in the area. Due to the pre-war work done at the gravel pits, heavy machinery was present to assist in the building of the camps. This location was well-connected by rail, centered between some of the largest Jewish ghettos, those of Warsaw which held approximately five hundred thousand and that of Bialystok holding sixty thousand and it was isolated from any large residential areas.

Treblinka I had originally been constructed as a forced-labour camp intended for Poles and Jews in nineteen forty-one. New barracks and barbed wire fencing nearly seven feet high were erected in the fall of forty-one. The workforce used to build it were garnered by way of arresting those nearby for a variety of charges and then sentencing them to hard labor. This was carried out by the local Gestapo office located in Sokolow. Initially all were sentenced to six months but inevitably these were extended indefinitely. Twenty thousand such prisoners were used in its construction for forced labour in the large quarries, while it was in operation. Few of those who were held in Treblinka lived to tell the tale. Working twelve to fourteen hour shifts in the quarries, these prisoners would eventually also supply the firewood necessary to feed the open area crematoria that were to later be built at Treblinka II.

In July of nineteen forty-two, Jews and non-Jews were separated within the camp. The majority of the men in the camp worked in the quarries which were spread over forty-two acres and supplied road construction material for the German military and therein played a large part in the strategic road-building programme necessary for the attack on the Russians. Women prisoners worked in the sorting barracks where they repaired and cleaned military clothing that was delivered regularly by freight trains. Treblinka II was designed to be divided into three parts, denoted as Camp 1, Camp 2 and Camp 3. Camp 1 was the administrative compound where the guards lived. Camp 2 was the receiving area where the incoming transports of prisoners were offloaded and Camp 3 was where the gas chambers were located. It was built by two groups of German Jews who had been expelled from Berlin and imprisoned in the Warsaw Ghetto. SS-Hauptsturmfuhrer, Richard Thomalla, who headed the construction team had selected these men because they could speak German. Construction had begun on April tenth of nineteen forty-two, after Belzec and Sobibor had already come on stream.

The camp was constructed on approximately thirty-five acres of land and was surrounded by a double row of over eight foot barbed wire fencing. As was the case in other death camps, the fencing was interwoven with pine branches to obstruct the viewing of the camp's operations from outsiders. Additional prisoners from the surrounding settlements were brought in to construct a new railway ramp within Camp 2 to allow for the receiving of prisoners. This was finished by June of forty-two.

The first section of the camp to be completed was Camp 1, the administrative and residential compound. The main gate for access by road traffic was erected on the north side of the camp. The barracks were constructed of materials brought in from Warsaw. The kitchen, bakery and dining rooms used by the German administrators were equipped with high-end items that had been expropriated from arrested Jews. There was a laundry, tailor and shoe repair service available to them as well. Separate quarters near to, but fenced off from the SS-barracks, were the barracks for the female serving, cleaning and kitchen workers.

The next section to be constructed was Camp 2. This was where the railway unloading ramp extended from the Treblinka line into the camp. Here the forced laborers were ordered to construct a platform surrounded by the barbed-wire fence and erect a new building that was camouflaged to look like a normal railway station, complete with a wooden clock and fake railroad terminal signage. Behind a second fence, just over three hundred feet from the track itself, two long barracks were built. These were to be used by the arriving deportees, separated by sex, for undressing and were each provided with a *'cashiers booth'*, which supposedly collected money and jewellery from those arriving, for *'safekeeping'*. The hair of the women and children was also shorn off in a separate building.

All of the buildings in this camp, including the barber barracks, contained piles of clothing and the other belongings of the arriving prisoners. To the right of the barracks there was a fake infirmary showing a large red cross. This building was surrounded by a barbed-wire fence and was where the sick, old, infirm or *'difficult'* prisoners were immediately brought directly from the arriving trains and promptly taken to the rear of the building. Here, a deep open pit had been dug. Deportees arriving at this building were then led out a back door to the edge of the pit, shot one by one and pushed in.

Camp 3 was the last part of the construction phase. It was completely screened off from the railroad tracks by a large earth embankment. The gas chambers were constructed at its center. The remaining three sides were fenced off from the other parts of the camp.

Leading away from the undressing barracks was a fenced off path that wound through the forested area and directly into the gas chambers. In the initial stages of operation at the camp, the bodies were to be taken out the other side of the chambers and dumped directly into huge burial ditches which were one hundred and sixty feet long, eighty-two feet wide and thirty-three feet deep.

* * * * *

- Ghettos -

- Warsaw -

Wholesale deportations to Treblinka began.

The Germans ordered the Jewish council, headed by Adam Czerniakow, to select and organize the groups to be marched to the *'Umschlagplatz'* (deportation point'), which was connected to the Warsaw/Malkinia rail line.

In this instance, although he did not call for open resistance toward the Germans, Czerniakow refused to do as ordered when asked to sign the deportation order. Instead, he committed suicide by swallowing a cyanide capsule on the twenty-third of July.

The SS moved in and took direct charge of deportations. Rather than wasting time making up lists of those would be transported, they would simply surround a whole building and send the Jewish police in to force all the occupants out until the required number for that specific transport was achieved, then march them straight to the *'Umschlagplatz'*.

* * * * *

- Transit Camps -

- Occupied France -

In nineteen thirty-nine more than two hundred thousand Jews resided in Paris. The majority of these were eastern Europeans who had recently immigrated to France. Approximately half of the Jewish population of Paris left the city after the Germans invaded in May of nineteen-forty.

After the French armistice with Germany in June of nineteen-forty, Paris became the seat of both the German military government and the Gestapo. The persecution of the Jews in Paris began almost immediately after occupation. In October of nineteen-forty seven synagogues were bombed in central Paris.

Between nineteen forty and forty-one the Germans arrested about ten thousand Jews in the city and a like number fled to the unoccupied zone in the south. The start of systematic mass deportations of foreign and stateless Jews began in nineteen forty-two. Jews holding French citizenship or who held valid German work permits were exempted at this time. The French police actively assisted in the roundups for these deportations. The majority of these individuals were sent to the Drancy Transit Camp, the remainder were interned at Pithiviers and Beaune-la-Rolande before onward transport to camps in occupied Poland. In mid-July of nineteen forty-two nearly thirteen thousand Jews were rounded up and interned in the Velodrome d'Hiver, a sports arena in south-central Paris, which became a makeshift assembly centre for onward shipment to Drancy.

From Drancy the Jews were transported to Auschwitz.

In nineteen forty-two, thirty thousand Jews were deported from Paris. Thousands had gone into hiding or left the city.

* * * * *

- Netherlands -

The Westerbork Transit Camp was located in the Dutch province of Drenthe, near the towns of Westerbork and Assen. This camp had originally been established by the Dutch government in October of nineteen thirty-nine to intern Jewish refugees who had entered the Netherlands illegally. Germany had occupied the Netherlands in May of nineteen forty. In early forty-two the Germans decided to enlarge the camp and convert it into a transit camp for Jews. The systematic roundup of Jews from the Netherlands and their shipment to Westerbork began in July of nineteen forty-two.

The residency of Jews at Westerbork was routinely short-term. Sixty thousand went from the camp to Auschwitz, thirty-four thousand to Sobibor, five thousand to the Theresienstadt ghetto and four thousand to the Bergen-Belsen concentration camp.

* * * * *

Mechelen Transit Camp -

Mechelen was located in Belgium.

In late July of forty-two the Germans ordered all Jews to report there, ostensibly to be sent onward to work camps in Germany. In reality they were to be deported directly to Auschwitz. Few Jews reported willingly. The Germans then began to arrest Jews and Gypsies throughout Belgium and intern them in Mechelen.

* * * * *

- Eric -

The third in the series of four super U-boats had been completed in March of this year and, as he had with the second, Eric had personally selected the officers and crew for that craft. It had completed its sea trials only weeks before he'd arrived in Bordeaux and with the pressure of having to empty the safe-houses of their human cargo in anticipation of the cut off of visas for Jewish specialists, the U-boat had immediately sailed for Brazil with its first cargo.

Eric was now in overall command of all three of these specialized craft.

It was with some trepidation that Eric neared the coast of Brazil.

This was due to the fact that, as the super subs had to be kept off the official radar of the Kriegsmarine, each maintained radio silence when at sea and he was therefore unable to keep tabs on their individual progress when they were not in port. The second U-boat was supposedly on her way back to Bordeaux and if all had gone as planned, he expected to find the third moored and unloading in the underground chamber below the mining operation in Brazil when he arrived.

Hopefully nothing untoward had interfered with their scheduled trips, but until he reached Brazil, he had no way of knowing for sure.

This concern was somewhat counter-balanced by his eagerness to see Heidi again.

* * * * *

- Friedrichshafen -

The family's private rail cars had been pushed into their barns under the castle by the little yard engine. The powerful little machine was now a permanent fixture at the castle as it was used almost daily to shunt the arriving and departing freight cars from occupied France up and down the spur from the rail line at the bottom of the mountain. The Countess Erika was pleased to be back with her daughter and son-in-law in the peaceful surrounds overlooking the town. Upon their arrival earlier in the month, the Count and Wilhelm had spent only two days at the castle before continuing on to Berlin by train.

Karl had made the decision to leave the private railcars in Friedrichshafen rather than use them for the trip to the German capital, due to the increased bombing raids into the heart of Germany and the expanding risk of having them damaged or destroyed if moved from the protection provided by the mass of the castle.

Erika, already delighted with her visit to her first grandchild had, upon her return, immediately thrown herself into preparations for the next arrival, interviewing additional staff to be taken on for the care of Ursula's baby if and when it came, and overseeing the complete renovation of the nursery.

Ursula was of course inundated with her mother's regular enquires as to progress in that regard and she and Friedrich were encouraged to spend a good deal of their free time working toward the event.

Satisfied at being told that it was important and secret work required for the war effort, and involved as she was in the planning for her next grandchild, Erika displayed little interest in what her daughter and son-in-law were doing deep below the castle.

Ursula was very content. She was kept busy during the day cataloguing and arranging for the safe storage of the stream of booty arriving from occupied France and looked forward each evening to the intimate attention of her husband as they laboured to satisfy Erika's wish for an additional grandchild.

For the three of them the war seemed far off and of little concern.

* * * * *

- Oslo -

Konrad was now dividing his working hours between the development and expansion of the Lebensborn project in Norway and his newly shared research into genetics with his early mentor, Doctor, the Baron von Kliest.

Gabrielle was surprisingly content with her new role as mother and homemaker, and was striving to become the center of the expanding social circle of senior members of the occupying German forces in Norway.

Konrad was deeply in love with her and although happiest when working, tended to suffer without complaint, as he was drawn in to play his part as host or escort at a continuing round of events organized by his young, beautiful, and energetically outgoing wife.

* * * * *

- Berlin -

The meeting with Hitler had taken much longer than the Count had anticipated.

The Fuhrer had initially been solely concerned with garnering information on both the development and possible deployment of the unmanned aircraft. Bormann, expecting the discussion to be brief, had slotted in only one hour for the meeting.

Wilhelm had learned his topics well and the Fuhrer had listened quietly for the first fifteen minutes before asking a few specific questions. As Wilhelm provided in depth answers,

Hitler became increasingly hyper and more animated as he began to envision the power and effectiveness of such a weapon. After Wilhelm had finished answering his questions, an obviously very pleased Fuhrer spent forty-five minutes expounding on how effective the proposed machines would be in bringing England to her knees without the risk of losing of a single drop of German blood.

It was then that Karl took the floor and began to advise Hitler on a long list of other *'super weapons'* that were either on the drawing boards or in the initial stages of development.

Wilhelm waited until his father had finished speaking and then moved forward to stand at the Fuhrer's desk. He removed some design schematics from his large leather folder and spread them on the desk in front of Hitler.

"Another example, Mein Fuhrer. The proposed Me-262, our first jet-powered aircraft. We hope to have it test flown this month. It is far faster and better armed than anything the enemy has ever dreamed of. Built in sufficient numbers, it will sweep the skies clean of Allied aircraft and give the Fatherland absolute air superiority wherever it's deployed."

The Fuhrer stood and began to scan the sheets in front of him. He took some time with each page of the complex plans and finally rolled them up and handed them back to Wilhelm before rubbing his hands with obvious glee and moving out from behind his desk.

Hitler, eyes sparkling with delight, then began to pace furiously, waving his arms about as he asked for additional information on each project. It was Wilhelm who then answered the majority of these questions.

A knock came at the door and Hitler, who was in mid question, spun around abruptly as it opened and Bormann stuck his head inside. Before the man could speak the Fuhrer shouted at him.

"Not now...the entire future of Germany may well rest on what takes place here today!"

Bormann promptly snapped his head back through the opening and pulled the door closed.

Hitler continued where he had left off and the exchange between the Fuhrer and Wilhelm went on for another hour before a vibrant Hitler finally nodded and settled back down into the big chair behind his elevated desk.

His eyes locked with the Count's as he spoke.

"You do not know how wonderful this has been for me. I am surrounded by defeatist, outdated Military commanders and forced to take personal control of the military, leaving me overburdened with the problems of state and I have no time available to me to allow myself the luxury of keeping abreast of these wonderful developments.

This meeting strongly affirms my original foresight in selecting you for the position you currently hold, Count von Stauffer. Today you and your son have lifted a tremendous weight from my shoulders and have clearly demonstrated how important your work is to the fulfilment of my dreams for the Fatherland. Unlike many others, you do your duty and ask nothing of Germany. You work diligently without complaint, overseeing and keeping me abreast of the wonderful discoveries that only we, the German people, can ever hope to achieve. "

He smiled across at them as he shifted his gaze toward Wilhelm.

"The apple did not fall far from the tree Count...young Wilhelm here follows in your footsteps. He is a remarkable young man. Germany owes you both a great debt and you should be proud of him."

It was now or never.

Karl nodded solemnly and then made his pitch.

* * * * *

By the time Count and his son walked out of Hitler's office forty minutes later and crossed the now well populated waiting area, SS-Obergruppenfuhrer, Count Karl von Stauffer had been transferred from the SS to the Wehrmacht and promoted to the rank of *'Generalfeldmarschall'*.

Wilhelm von Stauffer had also been transferred from the SS to the Wehrmacht and raised two grades in rank to that of Major, deftly removing him from the oversight of his former SS master. Hitler further ordered that he be removed from all other responsibilities and appointed as an aide to his father. He was instructed to head a new department which was to be solely responsible for the future oversight, design and development of super weapons. He was to be responsible to no one in the Reich, other than his father, and the Count would report only to the Fuhrer himself.

In a nutshell, Wilhelm's activities were to be top secret and he was responsible to, and would only report directly to, Germany's newest Generalfeldmarschall, Count Karl von Stauffer.

A memo to Bormann by the Fuhrer directing that any future request for a meeting with him originated by the Generalfeldmarschall was to be treated as a priority and scheduled within twenty-four hours of receipt of such request. An order reflecting these changes, under Hitler's signature and addressed to the SS-Reichsfuhrer, Heinrich Himmler, among several others, was in the process of being typed as Wilhelm and his father left the building.

CHAPTER FOURTEEN

- July -

- British Air Operations -

Bomber Command sends raids against Danzig, Hamburg, Bremen and the Industrialized Ruhr. Daylight attacks are made against occupied France and from July fourth onward the USAAF joins in on these sorties.

* * * * *

- Maritime Warfare -

The presence of additional Allied convoy protection available on the US east coast is expanded south from Florida and is already having a very positive effect in the prevention of merchant shipping losses.

A distinctive line mid Atlantic is drawn which will serve to denote the division of responsibility for both eastern and western authorities. CHOP (Change of Operational Control), clearly provides boundaries for the convoy escort vessels, removing previous ambiguity.

HF/DF (High Frequency Direction Finding) sets are now being fitted aboard escort vessels which removes the need for these ships to rely on shore-based directional finding services, which can often be hit or miss.

The Germans lose eleven U-boats while Axis submarines sink ninety-six ships amounting to one hundred and seventy-six thousand, one hundred tons. The total Allied losses reaches one hundred and twenty-eight ships for a total of six hundred and eighteen thousand, one hundred tons. The increased convoy presence along the US coast causes the Germans to remove some U-boats from that area to shift them deeper into the Atlantic. U-boats become quite active off Sierra Leone.

* * * * *

- July First -

- North Africa -

Rommel begins his first assault on the British defenses at El Alamein.

* * * * *

- Artic -

German intelligence advises of the convoy PQ-17, which is bound for Russia and early on this date, U-225 and U-408 sight the convoy. Eight additional U-boats are immediately dispatched to the location.

* * * * *

- July Second -

- London -

Concern over Churchill's ability to run both the country and the war leads to motion of censure in the House of Commons but this is resoundingly defeated when the vote is taken.

* * * * *

- Artic -

Convoys QP-13 and PQ-17 pass each other at sea causing the Germans to confuse the specific locations of both fleets.

Air and U-boat attacks are attempted against the out-bound QP-17 but these are unsuccessful.

The *'Tirpitz'* and the heavy cruiser *'Hipper'* accompanied by six destroyers leave their base at Trondheim.

- July Third -

- North Africa -

The Italian Ariete Division is all but wiped out by the New Zealand 2nd Division and their supporting artillery.

* * * * *

- Artic -

The German battle cruiser *'Lutzow'* and the pocket battleship *'Admiral Scheer'* sail from Narvik with their destroyer escort and proceed to join the battleship *'Tirpitz'* at Altafiord. Shortly after leaving port, *'Lutzow'* and three of the destroyers run aground.

* * * * *

- Guadalcanal -

The last of the resistance faced by the invading Japanese is destroyed and they are now the occupying force.

* * * * *

- July Fourth -

- Eastern Front -

The German siege of Sevastopol ends in success. Russian casualties are massive. The Germans also take ninety

---

thousand prisoners at the overall cost of twenty-four thousand casualties to their own forces.

* * * * *

- Artic -

The Germans achieve their first successes against PQ-17. The British First Sea Lord, certain that the major German warships will soon be brought to bear and only too aware of the superior firepower of the German capital ships, fears a confrontation. In addition, he is conscious of the fact that the Luftwaffe has the range to comfortably reach the scene. He orders that the convoy scatter and that all close-cover warships accompanying the convoy, return to port.

* * * * *

- Eastern Front -

Hoth`s Fourth Panzer Group reaches the Don River near Voronezh and on his left flank Weich`s Second army is also making gains against the Russian defenders.

* * * * *

- July Fifth -

- Artic -

The Germans sink thirteen vessels from PQ-17. The German capital ships are withdrawn when it becomes obvious that the Luftwaffe and the U-boats have the situation well in hand.

QP-13, now into the relative safety of the Denmark Strait sails into an area of Allied mines and loses four ships.

* * * * *

- July Seventh -

- Eastern Front -

Voronezh is taken by the Germans. Units of Army Group South begin to drive along the Donets Corridor.

* * * * *

- Artic -

The Germans sink another eight ships from PQ-17. Convoy stragglers will continue to crawl into various Russian ports over the next several days. Twenty-four ships are lost in total. When they go down, at the cost of five lost German planes, three thousand, three hundred and fifty vehicles, four hundred and thirty tanks and two hundred and ten aircraft plus ninety-six thousand tons of additional equipment, go down with them.

By all accounts, it is an Allied disaster of enormous proportions.

* * * * *

- July Ninth -

- Eastern Front -

In preparation for the offensive against the Caucasus the command system in the south for German forces is reorganized. Army Group South is divided into two. The first Group, (A), under the command of General List is composed of First Panzer Army, Seventeenth Army and Eleventh Army. Group (B), commanded by General Bock is formed using Fourth Panzer Army, Second Army and Sixth Army.

Group A is to advance from south of the Donets and capture Rostov then cross the Don and overrun the oilfields before regrouping on a line from Batumi on the Black Sea to Baku on the Caspian. 'B' is ordered to advance north of the Don and establish a protective front for 'A'.

* * * * *

- July Tenth -

- North Africa -

As part of Auchinleck's plan to force Rommel to burn up his short fuel supply, he orders the recently arrived Ninth Australian Division to attack the weak positions of the Italian Sabratha Division near Tell el Eisa, forcing Rommel to send them reinforcements. Over the next few days he continues to push Rommel to waste fuel by hitting the various Italian positions and repeatedly causing the Desert Fox to rush in armour to bail them out.

* * * * *

- July Eleventh -

- North Africa -

Short of fuel and ammunition, Rommel now faces a stalemate as his forces reach El Alamein.

* * * * *

- July Twelfth -

- Eastern Front -

The Russian High Command appoints Marshal

Timo shenko to a newly constituted Stalingrad Front. German forces have reached Lisichansk and Kanteminovka.

* * * * *

- July Thirteenth -

- Eastern Front -

Hitler suddenly decides to add Stalingrad to his list of must-haves for the summer campaign. He orders Army Group 'B' to break off from its covering role and sends it against Stalingrad.

* * * * *

- July Fourteenth -

- North Africa -

Units of the 1st British Armoured Division move against the south of Ruweisat Ridge. Losses are great on both sides but little ground is gained.

* * * * *

- Malta -

Supplies are brought in by submarine and HMS *'Eagle'* delivers an additional thirty-one Spitfires to the island.

* * * * *

- July Sixteenth -

- Vichy France -

The puppet government under Laval orders the French police to arrest thirteen thousand, one and fifty-two Jews and hold them at the Winter Velodrome for deportation.

* * * * *

- July Seventeenth -

- Eastern Front -

Hitler now decides that Army Group 'A', with the loss of support from 'B', will not have enough punch to fight its way across the Don. He promptly strips 'B' of the Fourth Panzer Group, which he then sends in support of 'A'. The weakened 'B' has now lost it armoured spearhead.

It immediately begins to lose a good deal of its momentum.

* * * * *

- North Africa -

The British advance around Miteirya Ridge forces a desperate but successful German counter-attack. Field Marshal Rommel's supply problems have reached a desperate state and he suggests a retreat to *'Generalfeldmarschall'* Kesselring.

* * * * *

- July Eighteenth -

- Bavaria -

The first test flight of the jet-powered Me-262 prototype is made at Leipheim near Gunzburg.

* * * * *

- July Nineteenth -

- Atlantic -

Grand Admiral Karl Donitz realizes that the situation off the eastern shores with regard to convoy protection has now changed radically. He orders the withdrawal of the last two U-boats patrolling in the area and sends them to other assignments.

* * * * *

- Eastern Front -

Despite Hitler's interference and adjustment in respective strengths both Army Groups 'A' and 'B' are progressing well. Voroshilovgrad and Kamensk are taken and the troops have reached the Don as far east as Tsimlyansky.

* * * * *

- July Twentieth -

- New Guinea -

The Japanese troops landing in the Buna-Gona area begin to move across the Owen Stanley mountain range as they thrust toward Port Moresby in the south-eastern part of the island. The beleaguered small band of Australian defenders begins to fight a rearguard action along the Kokoda Track as they retreat.

* * * * *

- July Twenty-First -

- North Africa -

A frustrated Rommel sends reports to the OKW providing details as to his specific shortages of men, equipment and supplies. The British read the coded messages thanks to the code-breaking abilities of *'Ultra'* and immediately decide that the time is ripe for an attack against the *'Desert fox's'* forces.

Eighth army has three hundred tanks, while Rommel has given his strength as fifty each for both the Germans and the Italians under his command. Unfortunately despite the much weakened Africa Korps situation, the British supporting armour and artillery is, once again, poorly deployed for support. By this point, the best troops available to the British Eight Army, the Australians and the New Zealanders, are becoming extremely disillusioned by this repeated failure by its supporting firepower.

* * * * *

- July Twenty-Second -

- Warsaw Ghetto -

Treblinka is opened in Poland and the systematic deportation of the Jews from the Ghetto begins.

* * * * *

- North Africa -

British forces attacking south of Ruweisat are taking heavy losses which include the destruction of the 23rd Armoured Brigade; however, Rommel is suffering losses he can no longer afford and both sides now prepare to hold their ground and regroup.

The British supply lines are now relatively secure and close by in the Nile Delta. Rommel is facing a much more difficult situation in securing his own supply relief. Malta is also now in a much stronger position to harass the Axis convoys through the use of both air and sea units.

* * * * *

- New Guinea -

The Retreating Australians have now been chased all the way down the Kokoda Trail to Kokoda itself and having arrived, they now take up a defensive line.

* * * * *

- London -

The American deposition of planners in London is advised that Roosevelt agrees with the British that *'Operation Sledgehammer'* (the Second Front scheduled for nineteen forty-two in Europe) is not possible. He instructs his negotiators to agree to *'another place'* for US troops to fight instead. The planning for *'Operation Gymnast'* in North Africa is dusted off, renamed *'Torch'* and discussed at length.

* * * * *

- July Twenty-Fourth -

- Eastern Front -

The Germans take Rostov-on-the-Don and the Russians are in a general retreat along the Don River.

* * * * *

- July Twenty-Sixth -

- North Africa -

A second attack against Rommel fails.

* * * * *

- July Twenty-Seventh -

- Eastern Front -

Army Group 'B' clears the Russians out of the Don elbow and begins an attack on the important position at Kalach.

* * * * *

- July Twenty-Ninth -

- New Guinea -

After three days of heavy fighting the Japanese take the city of Kokoda, which is located halfway along the Owen Stanley pass to Port Moresby.

* * * * *

- Eastern Front -

Army Group 'A' south of the Don continues to make good progress and captures Proletarskaya. Hitler now recognizes that his earlier removal of the Fourth Panzer Army from Group 'B' has left it without its armoured thrust and this has led to an unimpressive performance. He now reverses his order and sends them back to Group 'B'.

Hitler's vacillation has been costly as the Fourth Panzer Amy has spent most of its time running back and forth and has spent little time actually fighting. It also now become clear to Hitler that the need to take Stalingrad is now of the utmost importance and he worries that he has left Group 'A' with a massive and very strategically-vital task and perhaps with less strength than will be called for to accomplish the task.

* * * * *

- July Thirtieth -

- East Indies -

The Japanese occupy several small islands between Timor and New Guinea with a view to strengthening their planned campaign against Port Moresby.

* * * * *

- Eastern Front -

The Germans advancing from Rostov take Bataisk on the Don.

* * * * *

- July Thirty-First -

- Solomon Islands -

US bombers attack targets on Tulagi and Guadalcanal.

CHAPTER FIFTEEN

-August -

- Hitler -

Rommel had won an unexpected victory in North Africa with the taking of Tobruk which was the cornerstone of the British defences and had then pushed all the way to El Alamein situated only sixty-five miles from Alexandria.

The overall situation appeared to the Fuhrer as favourable.

A massive cloud on the horizon had raised its ugly head however, when the news of the Japanese losses at Midway reached the Fuhrer. The fact that his ally had lost not only four of its carriers, but also the very cream of the crop of its naval aviators, hit Hitler hard.

The balance of power in the Pacific had shifted and this was not good news. Thereafter Hitler's spirits dipped and tension began to mount during the military conferences held at *'Fuhrerhauptquartier Werwolf''*.

During one meeting held on August twenty-fourth, Halder requested that a unit presently under heavy Russian attack be permitted to retire to a shorter line.

There was a deadly silence in the room for a few seconds and then Hitler turned to face Halder and, his outrage a palpable power, exploded, complaining that his Army Chief of Staff always came to him with the same proposal:

'*Withdraw!*'

The silence in the room after his shouted response was deafening and Hitler continued.

"I expect my commanders to be as tough as the fighting troops."

Halder had learned over time to accept this type of

comment from Hitler, but on this occasion, the tense atmosphere came to a head for him and he made a forceful response in which he expressed the opinion that thousands of brave Germans were falling in the field of battle simply because their commanders were not being allowed to make reasonable military decisions based on the circumstances occurring in their individual operations. The other officers in the room were astounded, not so much because they disagreed with Halder's view but because they were fully cognisant of how Hitler would likely respond. At this point in the war, one did not even consider the idea of disagreeing forcefully with the Fuhrer. It simply wasn't done.

Hitler, rendered speechless for a few moments, stared at Halder with cold, blazing eyes and then, regaining his composure with difficulty, his tone hoarse with affronted shock, he lowered his voice.

"Colonel General Halder, how dare you use language like that in front of me? Do you think you can teach me what the man at the front is thinking? What do you know about what goes on at the front? Where were you in the First World War? And you try to pretend to me that I don't understand what it's like at the front. I won't stand that! It is outrageous."

As one, the other officers in the room lowered their gaze and moved quickly out, closing the door behind them. It was mutually felt that Halder's days at *'Fuhrerhauptquartier Werwolf''* were numbered.

Toward the end of the month German forces entered the outskirts of Stalingrad. Russian communications had been disrupted and imminent victory seemed near. Hitler's dark mood did not reflect this auspicious development and he became paranoid, exclaiming that both his commanders in the field and those at headquarters were deceiving him.

He began to accept little advice and absolutely no criticism of his decisions. List, who had replaced Bock, was now a recurring target for the expression of Hitler's displeasure and after the last conference of the month, the Fuhrer began to openly and publically level insults at the man.

He too, was now being written off by those surrounding the Fuhrer and was no doubt facing replacement in the near future.

Hitler's megalomania was at a peak. He was incapable of making mistakes and any military failure was now laid directly at the feet of his commanders. He was convinced that he was surrounded by traitors.

This paranoid determination was reinforced for him when, in late August, a spy ring called the *'Die Rote Kapelle'* (The Red Orchestra) was exposed by the Gestapo. This group included prominent Germans who were spying for Moscow.

Hitler promptly became convinced there was a spy operating in his headquarters. How else could the enemy know of his secret plans and make the critical decisions necessary to thwart them?

* * * * *

- Inner Circle -

- Speer -

- Manpower shortages -

By nineteen forty-two German industry was short well over one million workers.

Albert had been in his new position for six months and was proving himself very capable. Production had increased this month over the month of February by twenty-seven percent for guns and twenty-five percent for tanks. The production of ammunition had almost doubled, an increase of ninety-five percent.

Hitler was pleased and now that Speer had successfully mobilized all the resources that had, for various reasons, been sitting idle before he took over, he began to look for other ways to capture them. Two weeks after taking up his new post, Speer had convinced Hitler that all non-military building projects, including those underway at Obersalzberg, Hitler's personal compound, should be suspended until the war had been won. He had then addressed a meeting of all the *'Gauleiters'* and *'Reichsleiters'* at which he had expressed his opinion on the matter and with the intent of bringing an end to the private plans of these men to expand and improve their personal situations in a feathering their own nests, used this agreement with Hitler to drive the point home.

"Consideration of future peacetime tasks must never be allowed to influence a decision. I have instructions from the Fuhrer to report to him in the future on any such hindrances to our armaments production, which from now on can no longer be tolerated."

In other words, winning the war required belt tightening in order to ensure materials were not wasted for non-military purposes and that they, those in charge, needed to present a good example by putting an end to all such endeavours.

Not surprisingly, after the meeting he was approached by many of those in attendance who were in full agreement with such a plan but who requested that their personal building projects should be exempted from the general rule. Those holding powerful positions within the new Reich intended for the most part to lead the good life, and that meant personal building projects. Speer found himself fighting an uphill battle.

Bormann was the worst of the group. He resented Speer's growing influence with Hitler and through devious means, managed to convince Hitler that the ongoing projects proceeding under his direction at the Obersalzberg compound need not be considered for such cuts and three weeks later Speer found himself having to re-convince the Fuhrer that it must be halted. Hitler gave him assurances that this would be done, but in fact the work went on.

And Bormann wasn't alone.

Hitler insisted that the derelict castle of Klessheim near Salzburg be rebuilt into a luxurious guesthouse. He also encouraged a Gauleiter to renovate a hotel and the Posen Castle and this went ahead, as did a personal private residence for the Gauleiter involved, which was located nearby. Robert Ley, the head of the German Labour Front fought for the continuation of the construction of a pigsty on his model farm, claiming that this was a war priority since it was important to food production.

Gauleiter Friz Sauckel determined that the construction of the *'Party Forum'* in Weimar must not be affected and building continued.

The fabrication of two personal trains, one for Ley and the other for Keitel, was also begun.

Himmler ordered the construction of a country lodge for his mistress near Berchtesgaden.

The Fuhrer, his paranoia and his belief that he was destined by God to fulfil his elaborate plans for a new Germany, became extremely conscious of his personal safety. He ordered new bunkers built before he would take up residence in any new headquarters and the thickness of these bunkers had to be increased on a regular basis to reflect the progressive rise in the size of allied bombs.

If the Fuhrer needed such protection, then surely other members of the upper echelon, who were flushed with their own self-importance, needed similar fortifications. Goering had extensive underground installations built not only at his massive hunting lodge conversion at Karinhall, but also at the isolated castle at Veldenstein near Nuremberg, which he rarely graced with a visit. The Reichsmarschall also ordered that the road between his personal residence at Karinhall and Berlin, forty miles away through primary forested county, was to be provided with concrete shelters at regular intervals. Needless to say, the *'Gauleiters'* and *'Reichsleiters'* took note and many promptly ordered the building of their own private bomb shelters.

An *'uphill battle'* was an understatement.

And then there was the problem of a growing manpower shortage being suffered by the armaments plants to deal with. Many of these industries were working only a single shift each day and sitting idle at night due to a lack of labourers.

Speer had intended to transfer his hard-won, freed up construction workers from the non-war related construction projects to armaments production. Not surprisingly he found that the petty bureaucratic nature of the Nazi political system would again raise its ugly head.

When Albert approached the head of the *'Business Department for Labour Assignment'* within the *'Four Year Plan'*, who fell under Goering's jurisdiction, the Ministerial Director, Dr. Mansfeld told him that, without the agreement of the Gauleiters, he lacked the authority to transfer the released construction workers from out of the districts where they were currently employed Albert knew from experience that these individuals would solidly close ranks against him if any of their privileges were threatened. Additionally Goering was highly unlikely to give him any cooperation at this point.

In order to solve this particular problem, Speer decided that he would have to find himself an ally from within the membership of the Gauleiters to join his own staff as well as avoid dealing with Goering by approaching Hitler for special powers before the matter reached the ears of the Reichsmarschall and thereby accomplish an end run around Goering by presenting him with a fait accompli.

The man Speer wanted from within the ranks of the Gauleiters was an old friend, Karl Hanke who had been appointed Gauleiter of lower Silesia in January of forty-one. Albert went directly to Hitler and explained the situation.

Hitler listened and offered his tentative support for the proposal. They agreed to discuss the matter again in the near future.

He had not anticipated Bormann's reaction however, and Bormann, who was head of the party hierarchy and therefore controlled the appointments of Gauleiters and who, was already displeased with the influence Speer had with Hitler had no intention of having Hanke, an outspoken supporter of Alfred's appointment, shifted to a powerful position under Speer.

Bormann took the move as an infringement into his personal realm and began to take steps to prevent such a transfer from taking place.

Unaware of Bormann's indignation, Speer met with Hitler two days later and again raised the idea with the Fuhrer. This time Hitler agreed with the main thrust of the plan but objected to Speer's choice of Hanke, saying:

"Hanke hasn't been a Gauleiter long enough and doesn't command the necessary respect. I've talked with Bormann. We'll take Sauckel."

In addition Hitler advised Albert that Sauckel would remain a direct subordinate to Bormann. Speer had just experienced a successful inner-circle end run, orchestrated against himself, and due to Hitler's tendency to avoid unnecessary confrontation with those who surrounded him, the situation was about to become even more convoluted.

Courtesy of Bormann, Goering had by now got wind of the proposal. He went to Hitler and complained that Speer's plan was an interference in his administration of the Four Year Plan.

Hitler mollified Goering and told him he would mull the matter over and get back to him.

Hitler once again demonstrated his indifference toward administrative concerns by deciding that he would appoint Bormann's man, Sauckel, to the position of *'Commissioner General'* and then place that position under the umbrella of Goering's Four Year Plan organization.

He summoned Speer and Sauckel to his headquarter and then gave them the document authorizing the appointment. He told the two men that there could no longer be any such thing as a labour shortage, stating:

"The area working directly for us embraces more than two hundred fifty million people. Let no one doubt that we will succeed in involving every one of these millions in the labour process."

Hitler left no doubt as to where the labourers needed for the armaments industries were going to come from. He ordered Sauckel to bring the needed workers in by any means whatsoever. Sauckel immediately gave his pledge to eliminate all labour shortages and to provide replacements for all German specialists who were drafted into the services.

* * * * *

- Deportations -

The Germans begin to transport the Croatian Jews to Auschwitz.

Beginning on August twenty-sixth, seven thousand Jews are arrested in Vichy France.

* * * * *

- The Count -

Few in Germany would welcome a summons by SS-Reichsfuhrer Heinrich Himmler, and Karl von Stauffer was no exception. But a summons had come and it had also included Wilhelm.

The evening before they were to fly out to *'Fuhrerhauptquartier Werwolf"* for *the* scheduled afternoon meeting with Himmler, he and his son settled in the library with brandy and cigars and discussed how they were going to handle the command performance. Karl had anticipated some form of reaction from Himmler over the outcome of his and Wilhelm's session with Hitler and he had already made some notes on how to manage it, with a view to minimizing the fallout.

They began to study these carefully and expanded on them where they recognized a need.

* * * * *

- Fuhrerhauptquartier Werwolf -

The last half hour of the flight from Berlin had been somewhat uncomfortable due to the stifling heat radiating from the August sun but flying conditions had been ideal and Karl and Wilhelm, sporting their new Wehrmacht uniforms, alighted buoyant and rested at the Luftwaffe base at Kalinovka.

The Count had initially been informed that an SS staff car would be sent to await their arrival at the airfield to transport him and Wilhelm the fifteen miles to the compound but he had politely declined the offer, choosing instead to arrange to have a Wehrmacht driver and vehicle detailed for that purpose.

This decision was the first card Karl intended to play in the upcoming meeting with Himmler. Despite his recent promotion, Himmler still outranked him and it was Karl's way of respectfully demonstrating to the SS-Reichsfuhrer that he no longer felt it necessary to accept SS support in his day to day operations.

The Count had no intention of taking action that might incite Himmler's displeasure unduly. His aim was that of maintaining a delicate balance between himself and the SS-Reichsfuhrer, but he felt he had to set the stage for the meeting on his terms, not Himmler's.

Himmler was a rising star within Hitler's inner circle by this point in the war. He had accomplished this mainly by stepping into the void over the problem of solving of the Jewish problem for Hitler and after doing so, he had steadily risen in power within the Reich.

The degree to which his position had heightened had been clearly demonstrated by the alliance that Bormann had recently formed between himself and the leader of the SS. Karl was certain that it was due to that alliance that Himmler had called the meeting and that the Reichsfuhrer had been fully apprised by Bormann of the specifics and results of his and Wilhelm's earlier meeting with Hitler.

The Count had been able to achieve his goal with the Hitler Meeting. The Fuhrer had willingly placed him in a position that determined a demonstrable independence from influence by anyone in the Reich but himself. This bubble of responsibility and authority in which Hitler had placed Karl insured that he was reasonably insulated from outside interference in his activities, even by a person of Himmler's importance but the Count was not a fool and he knew only too well that those under the direct protection of the Fuhrer one day, could well find themselves without it the next.

Karl, at his own manipulation, was now walking a tightrope and he had no intention of giving Himmler any reason to feel threatened by this new shift in the balance of power surrounding Hitler. It was his intention at this meeting to impress upon the SS-Reichsfuhrer that little if anything of importance had changed in their relationship and that the decision to reassign him and Wilhelm to the Wehrmacht had been something that the Fuhrer had decreed without personal consultation with him and was something that he, as a good soldier and German citizen had been obliged to accept without question.

He and Wilhelm settled themselves into the rear of the large 770 series open Mercedes Wehrmacht staff car and quietly discussed, yet again, their intended approach to Himmler as the powerful vehicle smoothly made its way to the secure Eastern Front command compound.

* * * * *

The meeting was to take place in Himmler's personal train which was sitting on a spur line at the compound railway station. Karl was not surprised to be informed by one of Himmler's aides upon their arrival that the Reichsfuhrer was in consultation with the Fuhrer and would unfortunately be delayed.

The Reichsfuhrer sent his apologies and asked would the Generalfeldmarschall please join him for luncheon as soon as he was free and in the interim make full use of the facilities available aboard while he waited.

As Karl had predicted, Himmler had now played his first

card of the hand. He and Wilhelm would be expected to cool their heels until well after the appointed time for the meeting. This was to demonstrate clearly to Karl just who was the more important, he or the Reichsfuhrer.

The Count had his own next card to play and he did so with a straight face.

"Please thank the Reichsfuhrer for his courteous offer and inform him that unfortunately we will be unable to take advantage of his kind suggestion, in that the Fuhrer has requested that I and my son, lunch with him..."

He pointedly looked at his watch and frowned.

"We had anticipated being through with our meeting with the SS- Reichsfuhrer by this point and unfortunately, we will be unable to wait here any longer, as the Fuhrer has scheduled the lunch for the top of the hour. Perhaps you would be good enough to explain our predicament to Herr Himmler and advise him that we will make ourselves available to him as soon as the Fuhrer is finished with us."

Without waiting for a response The Count turned on his heel and Wilhelm followed him out onto the platform and back into the waiting staff car for the short ride to Hitler's personal quarters.

* * * * *

It was early evening before Karl and Wilhelm, who had bought several super weapon files down with them to show Hitler, arrived back at Himmler's personal train.

They were immediately ushered into the Reichsfuhrer's office car where Himmler was sitting behind his desk in the process of appending his signature to several official documents using his customary green ink. Appearing engrossed for a few moments in clearing his desk he waved them to chairs across from him and they sat down. In due course Himmler set his pen down and handed the papers to an aide who had been standing patiently behind him and then as the aide filed out of the room the Reichsfuhrer lifted his gaze to them and smiled, although the smile never reached his cold penetrating eyes.

"Ah, Feldmarschall, welcome. I'm sorry for my inability to see you at the appointed time, but as you can see, the pressures of war never offer much respite. I wanted to personally congratulate both you and your son on you promotions and thank you for the wonderful service that you have been providing for the Fuhrer. He speaks very highly of your work. While I am sorry to lose you both from our SS-ranks and somewhat surprised at this change, based upon the obvious importance to the Fuhrer of your new positions, I can see why he might wish to take such action and of course I would never question his decision to do so."

Karl nodded and returned the smile.

"Yes Herr Reichsfuhrer, we too were taken by surprise by the Fuhrer's decree, but like you, we live to serve Adolf Hitler and I would never consider questioning any of his decisions."

There was a pregnant pause as the two men gazed across the desk at each other. Karl made no move to break the silence, nor did his contemplation waver.

I've accomplished what I wanted. Himmler is unsure of how to handle the situation. I'm certain there was much more this man had intended to say at this meeting, but he has brushed that aside due to the way I've handled it. Himmler is angry. That is obvious. But, he is also impressed by my performance and it's now up to me to smooth things over and leave the meeting, with the delicate balance between us that had been in place before the shift in responsibilities and authority had occurred, still intact.

I don't want this man as my enemy. I just want to keep a low profile with him and keep him at arm's length for my own and my family's protection.

Himmler who had obviously been reassessing the situation dropped his eyes, cleared his throat and spoke, carefully choosing his words.

"Yes, yes, well we all do our duty and accept whatever arduous tasks the Fuhrer sees fit to impose upon us. That goes without saying. I simply wanted to personally congratulate both of you."

Karl dutifully nodded his appreciation for the thought.

Sure you did you devious bastard. That's why you summoned us all the way out here. Just to congratulate us.

"Suffice to say Herr Reichsfuhrer that I see no reason why this new situation should in any way affect the previous good working relationship we've experienced and I assure you that I will continue to see to it that you are promptly apprised of any new developments in our research that I feel you will find of interest. You may be certain that both Wilhelm and I know full well how you have supported us in these trying times and look forward in the future to maintaining our strong bonds with the SS and its leader."

This time the smile did make it to Himmler's eyes, if only briefly.

"My thoughts exactly Herr Generalfeldmarschall. As usual, you move directly to the crux of the matter. We understand each other then. I thank you for taking time from your busy schedule to see me and again offer my congratulations on your promotions."

It had gone well and the Count was not about to jeopardize the situation by further conversation. He stood and Wilhelm followed suit as they clicked their heels together and saluted. As he turned to leave he let out s sigh of relief.

Yes Herr Reichsfuhrer, and I will keep a weather eye on any knives that may be approaching my back, as will you, I am sure!

CHAPTER SIXTEEN

- August -

- Allied Air Operations -

RAF Bomber Command sends raids against Frankfurt, Mainz and Duisberg and a Pathfinder Force is created to locate and mark targets for future bomber raids.

US bombers begin independent raids on occupied France as well as joining the RAF against communications targets in France.

* * * * *

- Maritime Warfare -

A total of one hundred and twenty-three Allied ships are sunk for a total of six hundred and sixty-one thousand, one hundred tons. Submarines take one hundred and eight of these for a total tonnage of five hundred and forty-four thousand, four hundred tons.

U-boat operations are centered on the main North Atlantic convoy routes and off the coast of Brazil, with a few working in the areas of the Caribbean and the Gulf of Mexico.

The US launches the carrier *'Independence'* and the battleship *'Iowa'*.

* * * * *

- August First -

- Easter Front -

Army Group 'A' continues its advance, capturing the town of Salsk and pushing on to the Kuban River near Kropotkin. Group 'B' hammers at the Russian forces in the bend of the Don near Kalach and Kletskaya.

* * * * *

- August Third -

- North Africa -

A disgruntled Churchill, accompanied by General Brooke, arrives in Cairo to assess the activities of the Eighth Army. The British Prime Minister is dissatisfied by the performance to date and is looking to replace the commanders.

* * * * *

- Malta -

U-boats supported by the Luftwaffe decimate a convoy en route to the island.

* * * * *

- Eastern Front -

Group 'B' continues to pound Kletskaya and the Fourth Panzer Army has crossed the Don at Kotelnikovo. First Panzer has split to mount two attacks from its position on the Kuban, the first east toward Stavropol and the other south toward Maykop.

* * * * *

- August Fifth -

- Washington -

The military planners from the US and Great Britain meet for joint planning for *'Operation Torch'*.

* * * * *

- Atlantic -

A U-boat wolf pack forms to attack convoy SC-94. Over a period of several days, eleven ships go down, however two U-boats are sunk and four suffer damage.

- August Sixth -

- North Africa -

Churchill selects General Alexander to command in the Middle East and General Gott is placed in tactical control of Eighth Army.

* * * * *

- Eastern Front -

Army Group 'B' hammers the Russian defences in the Don elbow and the Seventeenth Army from Group 'A' takes Tikhoretsk.

* * * * *

- August Seventh -

- Operation Watchtower -

The Guadalcanal Campaign is launched by US forces as they invade Gavutu, Guadalcanal, Tulagi and Tanambogo in the Solomon Islands.

* * * * *

- North Africa -

General Gott is killed on his flight back to Cairo and Churchill selects General Montgomery as his replacement.

* * * * *

- Aleutians -

A US naval task force bombards the Japanese-held island of Kiska.

* * * * *

- August Eighth -

- Solomon Islands -

The US make additional landings. Those troops on Guadalcanal meet little initial opposition, while the other landings are meeting heavy resistance.

During a naval confrontation near Guadalcanal, the US loses three cruisers and the Australians, one.

* * * * *

- Allied Command -

Roosevelt and Churchill agree that *'Operation 'Torch'*, the second front against the Germans, which is to go ahead in North Africa, is to be commanded by US General Dwight Eisenhower.

* * * * *

- Eastern Front -

Group 'A' consolidates its gains near the Kuban River and then continues its drive south. 'B' captures Surovniko.

* * * * *

- August Ninth -

- India -

There are several riots pushing for independence and Mahatma Gandhi is arrested.

* * * * *

- Solomon Islands -

The Japanese naval operations on the eighth have forced an interruption in the unloading of US transports off Lunga Point, leaving the Marines short of heavy equipment and without half their supplies.

* * * * *

- Eastern Front -

The First Panzer Army takes Maykop and the Seventeenth, Krasnodar. They find that the defenders have destroyed the oil refineries at Maykop prior to fleeing.

* * * * *

- August Tenth -

- North Africa -

Rommel begins attacks in the vicinity of El Alamein.

* * * * *

- Solomon Islands -

The Japanese heavy cruiser *'Kako'* is sunk by a US sub while steaming from the earlier naval encounter at Guadalcanal to her home base at Rabaul.

* * * * *

- August Eleventh -

- Mediterranean -

While on convoy duty, the carrier HMS *'Eagle'* is sunk by U-73.

* * * * *

- New Guinea -

The Australian defenders are forced out of Deniki on the Kokoda Trail and retrench five miles away near the summit of the Trail.

* * * * *

- Vichy France -

Puppet Prime Minister Laval give a public speech in which he states: *'The hour of liberation from France is the hour when Germany wins the war.'*

* * * * *

- Eastern Front -

German forces take Kalach on the west bank of the Don River.

* * * * *

- August Twelfth -

- Moscow -

Churchill informs an unhappy Stalin that there will be no Allied second front launched in Europe in nineteen forty-two.

* * * * *

- New Hebrides Islands -

Strong US reinforcements are landed on Espirtu Santu to build a base for the support of the Guadalcanal campaign.

* * * * *

- New Guinea -

The Japanese begin landing a strong contingent of troops at Buna.

* * * * *

- Mediterranean -

The relief convoy for *'Operation Pedestal'* is attacked continually. One merchant ship is sunk in the morning and in the evening, as the escorts withdraw, the carrier HMS

'Indomitable' is damaged and a destroyer sunk. Then a cruiser and two freighters are sunk and another two cruisers, a transport and the US tanker *'Ohio'* are damaged.

* * * * *

- August Thirteenth -

- North Africa -

Montgomery assumes command of the Eighth Amy and Alexander replaces Auchinleck.

* * * * *

- Mediterranean -

The doomed convoy for *'Operation Pedestal'* takes more hits. In the morning the cruiser HMS *'Manchester'* is sunk along with five more freighters. Later in the day two more freighters are sunk. Only four of the merchantmen straggle into the harbor at Malta and the damaged tanker *'Ohio'*, under tow, later makes it in at Valetta.

* * * * *

- August Seventeenth -

- Eastern Front -

German forces take Pyatigorsk and Yessentuki in the Caucasus.

* * * * *

- August Eighteenth -

Patrick Laughy

- Pacific -

Japanese reinforcements land at Taivu, Guadalcanal. Australian troops land at Port Moresby. US aircraft destroy the Japanese air power at Wewak, New Guinea.

* * * * *

- August Nineteenth -

- Western Europe -

'Operation Jubilee' the ill-conceived, ill-planned and ill-fated British raid made at Dieppe France, is launched. The raid consists of over six thousand infantrymen, predominantly Canadian and is supported by a Canadian armoured regiment.

Justified, after the fact, with having the aim of proving that it was possible to land and gather intelligence as well as to destroy some coastal defences, port structures and strategic buildings, it was in reality a sop to Stalin, to prove that the British were seriously committed to the idea of opening a Western Front as well as a propaganda exercise to boost morale in the United Kingdom.

None of the supposed aims claimed were met. The landings took place at five in the morning and by ten-thirty on the evening of the same day, commanders were forced to call a retreat. The action was a slaughter and unmitigated disaster. Of the six thousand, and eighty-six men put ashore, sixty percent were either killed, wounded or captured.

* * * * *

- August Twentieth -

- Guadalcanal -

The new air base at Henderson Field receives its first

aircraft, a group of thirty-one fighters.

* * * * *

- August Twenty-First -

- Guadalcanal -

US forces receive much needed supplies and the Japanese move against Henderson Field without success. In an exchange at the Tenaru River, a Japanese *'banzai'* charge results in massive casualties for the Imperial Army.

* * * * *

- August Twenty-Second -

- Declaration of War -

Primarily in response to the recent sinking of Brazilian ships, Brazil declares war against the Axis countries.

* * * * *

- August Twenty-Third -

- Stalingrad -

The Germans launch a massive air raid against the city.

* * * * *

- August Twenty-Fourth -

- Solomon Islands -

The naval battle of the Eastern Solomons begins and

results in the loss of the light carrier, *'Ryujo'* for the Japanese and a badly damaged US carrier, the USS *'Enterprise'*.

* * * * *

- Berlin -

Hitler appoints Otto Georg Thierack as the Reich Minister of Justice with a mandate to set aside any or all German written law.

* * * * *

- New Guinea -

Japanese assault troops from Buna land on Goodenough Island in preparation from a move into Milne Bay.

* * * * *

- August Twenty-Fifth -

- Solomons -

Japanese transports headed for Guadalcanal are attacked by the US aircraft now on the island and two are damaged and an escorting destroyer is sunk. They decide to abandon daylight transports and revert to supplying their forces through the use of destroyers at night.

* * * * *

- Eastern Front -

There is heavy fighting along the Terek River near Mozdok in the Caucuses.

* * * * *

- August Twenty-Sixth -

- New Guinea -

The battle for Milne Bay begins with Japanese forces landing and launching a full-scale assault against the Australian base near the eastern tip of New Guinea.

* * * * *

- August Twenty-Seventh -

- Eastern Front -

Marshal Georgii Zhukov is appointed to the command of the Stalingrad defence. The Luftwaffe is delivering heavy air strikes on the city daily. The Russian perimeter around Stalingrad is gradually drawing in. In the south the Germans have crossed the River Terek and captured Prochladrii.

* * * * *

- Solomons -

The US aircraft carrier *'Saratoga'* is attacked and damaged by the Japanese submarine I-26. That leaves USS *'Wasp'* as the only American carrier still operational in the Pacific.

* * * * *

- August Twenty-Eighth -

- Guadalcanal -

Japanese reinforcements are brought in at night by destroyers.

* * * * *

- August Thirtieth -

- North Africa -

The battle of Alam Halfa in Egypt, a few miles south of El Alamein, begins as Rommel moves to drive the British out of Egypt.

* * * * *

- Luxembourg -

Luxembourg is formally annexed into the German Reich.

* * * * *

- Guadalcanal -

Henderson Field receives eighteen more fighters and twelve dive bombers.

* * * * *

- August Thirty-first -

- New Guinea -

The Japanese decide to evacuate their troops from Milne Bay in order to concentrate on the attack against Guadalcanal. They lose one thousand men before the operation is completed making the first Japanese setback on land since the start of the war.

* * * * *

- Guadalcanal -

An additional twelve hundred Japanese troops are landed.

* * * * *

- Eastern Front -

Defeating stiff Russia resistance, the Germans reach a point sixteen miles from Stalingrad.

* * * * *

- Luxembourg -

A general strike against conscription begins.

CHAPTER SEVENTEEN

- September -

- Hitler -

Hitler, convinced that all his moves appear to be anticipated by the enemy, is becoming seriously paranoid. There had to be a spy at work.

On September seventh the Fuhrer sends Jodl, who was one of the few staff officers who remained within his good books, to the Caucasus to find out why List wasn't making better progress in the mountain passes leading out to the Black Sea.

After an extended meeting with List, who was the commander of the Mountain Corps, Jodl determined that with the forces available to him the current situation facing the German commander was unwinnable. He flew back to *'Fuhrerhauptquartier Werwolf''* and reported directly back to Hitler, informing him of his assessment of the situation and that in his estimation, this was despite the fact that List had been adhering strictly to his instructions as ordered.

Hitler lurched to his feet and shouted:

"That's a lie!"

He went on to berate Jodl, accusing him of having colluded with List, and telling him that his job had been to transmit orders to List only, not evaluate or assess the situation.

Jodl was completely blindsided by the outburst. His reply was blunt.

"If you wanted a mere messenger, why didn't you send a young lieutenant?"

Infuriated by the response and further convinced that he was a victim of lies, a glaring Hitler stalked out of the room and stomped off to his personal bunker.

All future briefing conferences, from that point onward, took place in Hitler's personal quarters and the atmosphere at these meetings was beyond chilled, with Hitler pointedly refusing to shake hands with any staff officer and secretaries recording every word of the discussions and each order Hitler issued. Hitler was determined that there would never be another occasion when his orders were *'misunderstood'* or *'disputed'*. For months the Fuhrer refused to have his much enjoyed meals surrounded by his inner circle and staff. He ate alone in his private rooms, his only companion, a recent gift from Bormann, his dog Blondi.

German military staff officers had been summarily chastised. Not one of them felt secure in his position.

On the ninth of September Hitler summarily removed List and took personal command of Army Group 'A'. Rumours began to circulate that Halder, Jodl and Keitel would soon follow.

At military conferences Hitler still held fast to his confidence for success on the Eastern Front. At one of these, attended by General von Weichs of Army Group 'B' and General Friedrich Paulus, the field commander tasked with taking Stalingrad, at which both men warned the Fuhrer that the long and lightly held Don front on the northern flank was of concern due to its lack of depth, Hitler made light of the situation. He simply assured them that the Russians were rapidly running out of steam and that any resistance left at Stalingrad was a, *'purely local affair'*. They need not fear the strength of the Don flank as the Russians were now incapable of mounting any major counteroffensive. He advised them that the trick now was to; *'concentrate every available man and capture as quickly as possible the whole of Stalingrad and the banks of the Volga.'*

In order to ensure this took place he proposed to reinforce Paulus' Sixth Army with an additional three divisions.

In fact, in so doing, he had reached a relatively solid evaluation of the situation. The Russian defenders were in disarray and massive desertions were taking place, not only of infantrymen but many officers up to and including the rank of General. The Luftwaffe was already mining the Volga at the rear of the city of Stalingrad and German advanced units were ranging throughout the center of the city and had seized the main railroad station and reached as far as the waterfront.

This situation was fluid however. Russian reinforcements were being ferried across the river in great numbers and by the fifteenth of the month, resistance his begun to firm up. On that date the railroad station changed hands several times and Paulus was forced to narrow his attack.

Hitler's mood began to worsen with this news and when Warlimont, Jodl's deputy, returned to these military conferences in Hitler's quarters after a two week absence he found the change in the Fuhrer striking, convinced that: *The man's confidence has gone with realization that the Russians cannot be beaten.'*

Gerhard Engle, Hitler's adjutant noted in his diary; *'He trusts none of the generals...he would promote a major to a general and make him chief of staff, if he only knew such a man. Nothing seems to suit him and he curses himself for having gone to war with such poor generals.'*

On September twenty-fourth Hitler decides to remove General Franz Halder, his Chief of the General Staff (OKH), who has displeased him above all others with his continual prophesies of doom, but whose military competence he values highly. On that date he summoned Halder and once the man is seated across from him says.

'You and I have been suffering from nerves. Half of my exhaustion is due to you. It is not worth while going on. We need National Socialist ardor now, not professional ability. I cannot expect this of an officer of the old schools such as you.'

Halder was deeply hurt and disappointed. His eyes glistened with the threat of welling tears as he listened to his leader. Hitler took this as weakness which, as far as he was concerned, demonstrated further grounds for dismissal.

Halder rose and without a word in his own defence, simply said: *'I am leaving'* and walked out of the office.

Hitler replaced Halder with Kurt Zeitzler, promoting him two full ranks to that of Major General. Up to this point Zeitzler had been almost exclusively a staff officer, not a commander. He was regarded as energetic, efficient and noted for his ability in managing the movement of large mobile formations.

In Zeitzler's first meeting with Hitler, surrounded by approximately twenty other senior officers, Zeitzler did not toady. He stood silent as Hitler complained at some length that the General Staff tended to doubts and fears and functioned in an atmosphere of defeatism. When the Fuhrer had finished with this tirade, Zeitzler said.

"Mein Fuhrer, if you have any further objections to the General Staff, please tell them to me under four eyes but not in the presence of so many other officers. Otherwise you must seek a new chief of the General Staff."

He then saluted Hitler and marched out of the room.

You could have heard a pin drop in the room as the remaining officers, pointedly staring down at their boots, awaited the inevitable explosion from Hitler, but it never came. Zeitzler had impressed Hitler. The Fuhrer instead grinned and finally said.

"Eh, he will be back, ja?"

Those leaving the room had hope that there might now be a new spirit of defiance at military conferences with this new man at the helm, but that idea was quickly dispelled. In his first address to the members of the OKH, Zeitzler quickly clarified his position.

"I require the following from every staff officer: he must believe in the Fuhrer and in his method of command; he must on every occasion radiate this confidence to his subordinate and those around him. I have no use for anybody on the General Staff who cannot meet these requirements."

From Hitler's perspective, he had picked the right man.

On September thirtieth of nineteen forty-two, Hitler returned to the Berlin Sportpalast to deliver a speech at the opening of the Winter War Relief program. Hitler was not at his best on this occasion. For him, it was a short and not particularly inspired speech, delivered without the usual animation and sparkle. However it does give us a chance to experience what his hand-picked audience experienced on that evening, as to his confidence and determination.

This is an English translation of that speech:

'My German countrymen and countrywomen! It is now a year since I was last able to speak to you and to the German people from this place. In retrospect, it is in many ways to be regretted, first because I myself very much regret not being able to stand oftener before the nation, and second because I am naturally afraid that my speeches thereby are becoming worse rather than better, for in this regard practice is necessary. My time is unfortunately much more limited than the time of my worthy adversaries. Naturally he who can travel around the world for weeks at a time, with a broad sombrero on his head, wearing a white silk shirt here, and some other outfit there, can naturally occupy himself much more with speeches

All this time I have really had to be busy managing and doing rather than speaking. Besides, I cannot of course speak every week or every month. For what am I to say? What has to be said will be said by our soldiers. Moreover, the subjects on which I might speak are naturally more difficult than the subjects of the discourses of my adversaries, who are accustomed to send their numerous chats over the world from the fireside or other places. The subject matter of my possible speeches is more difficult, for I do not deem it proper to occupy myself now with the shaping of things for the future. I consider it more appropriate for us to occupy ourselves with that which the immediate present demands of us.

Naturally it is very simple to concoct an Atlantic Charter. This nonsense will of course be valid for only a few, very few years. It will simply be cast aside by hard facts. For other reasons also it is somewhat easier for our opponents to talk, for now they have suddenly discovered our party program after many years of vain effort. And we now see with astonishment that they promise the world for the future just about what we have already given our German people and for which we, in the final analysis, were involved in a war by the others it is very witty, when, for example, a President says: "We wish in the future that everyone should have the right not to suffer from want," or something similar. To this one can only say: It probably would have been much more simple, if this President, instead of plunging into a war, had used the whole working strength of his country to build up useful production and to care for his own people, so that want and misery might not reign and 13,000,000 people might not be unemployed in a region which has only 10 people per square kilometer to support. These men could have accomplished all these things.

When they now appear and suddenly represent themselves to the world as saviors, and declare, "In the future we will see to it that there shall be no want, as in the past; that there will be no more unemployment, that every man will own a home"-these owners of world empire should have been able to do that in their own countries long ago-before we did it ourselves. They suddenly discover nothing but the basic principles of the National Socialist program

Now when I hear that a man says-I believe it was Mr. Eden, but one really doesn't know what nonentity is speaking over there-when he now says, "This is the difference between the Germans and us: the Germans have a faith and we also have a faith; but the Germans believe in something in which they don't believe, while we believe in something in which we really believe-." To that I can only say: If they truly believe in what they profess to believe, they should have been able to acknowledge this belief sooner. Why have they declared war on us? For their aims are certainly not very *different from our own. We have not only believed in something, but have also acted upon what we believed in! And now we believe that we have to strike the enemy until final victory is won. That is what we believe-Naturally, we cannot reach common ground with these people over the concept of "belief."*

He who believes, for example, that Namsos was a victory, or who believes that Andalsnes was a victory, or who believes that even Dunkirk was quite the greatest victory in the history of the world, or who believes (it is all the same to me) that any expedition that lasts 9 hours is an astonishing and encouraging sign of a victorious nation-with such a one we, with our modest successes, cannot of course be compared. For what are our accomplishments as compared with these? If we push forward a thousand kilometers that is really nothing-an absolute failure!

If we, for example, in the last two months-it is really only for two months that war can be carried on sensibly in that country-have pushed to the Don, down the Don, finally reached the Volga, attacked Stalingrad-and we shall take it, too, you can depend on that-that is nothing at all. If we push on to the Caucasus, then that also is nothing. If we occupy the Ukraine, if we get the Donetz coal into our possession, all that is nothing. If we are getting 65 or 70 percent of Russian iron, that is nothing at all, absolutely nothing. If we actually open up to the German people, and thereby to Europe, the largest grain area of the world, nothing. If we secure for ourselves the sources of oil there, that is also nothing. All that is nothing.

But when Canadian vanguards with a small English tail as appendage come to Dieppe and manage to hang on there-one may say painfully-for nine hours-to be destroyed in the end-that is an encouraging, an astonishing sign of the inexhaustible, victorious power which is the British Empire's own! In contrast to that, what is our air force, what is the performance of our infantry, what is the performance of our tank arm, what by comparison is the accomplishment of our engineers, our railway construction troops and so forth, of our whole gigantic traffic system which has opened

up and re-built half a continent in a few-one may even say months? That is nothing!

U-boats, also nothing, of course. Even back in 1939 they were nothing. At that time Churchill came out and said: "I am able to give you the good news that the U-boat danger may be regarded as disposed of once and for all. We have destroyed more U-boats than the Germans had altogether. Or-one moment-that was not, no, that was not Churchill; that was Duff Cooper. But as I said, each one of these is a bigger swashbuckler than the other, and you are constantly getting them mixed up.

The fact that we have thrown them out of the Balkans, that we conquered Greece, that we occupied Crete, that they have been chased back in North Africa, all that, too, is nothing. But if, let us say, a few men land anywhere at all to take us unawares at a lone advance post-then those are deeds, those are accomplishments. Anyone who thinks that way will never understand our beliefs. But if the English really believe in what they pretend to believe-seriously-then one can only be sorry for their intelligence.

In any event, in contrast with these deeds, of course, they also have claims on the future. They say: "The second front will come!" When we moved eastward, they said: "The second front is already under way! Attention! About face!" We, however, have not stood at attention, and have not about-faced, but have calmly marched forward. In that connection I shall not say, though, that we have done nothing to prepare for a second front. When Mr. Churchill says: "We wish now to leave it to the Germans to ponder in their anxiety where and when we shall open it." I can say to Mr. Churchill merely: "So far you have never caused me any anxiety."

But he is right in saying that we must ponder. If I had an opponent of stature, of military stature, then I could calculate pretty closely where he would attack. But when one faces military idiots, one cannot know, one cannot know where they will attack. It may be the craziest sort of undertaking, and that is the one unpleasant thing-the fact that in the case of these mentally sick or perpetually drunk persons one never knows what they are really up to.

For this reason we must naturally be prepared everywhere, and I can give Mr. Churchill assurance-whether or not he chose with cleverness and military shrewdness the first spot at which he wished to start the second front; opinions in England are already divided on this, and that will be evident on all sides from now on-that it does not matter where he is looking for the next spot. He can call it good luck anywhere if he can remain on land for nine hours.

In my eyes, the year nineteen forty-two already has behind it the most fateful trial of our people. That was the winter of forty-one to forty-two. I may be permitted to say that in that winter the German people, and in particular it's Wehrmacht, were weighed in the balance by Providence. Nothing worse can or will happen. That we conquered that winter, that "General Winter," that at last the German fronts stood, and that this spring that is, early this summer, we were able to proceed again, that, I believe, is the proof that Providence was content with the German people.

It was a very difficult and a very hard test and trial, you all know that. And in spite of that, we not only got over that most difficult time, but we managed very calmly to organize the attacking divisions, the motorized and tank formations anew, which were designed to initiate the resumed offensive. This offensive is now taking its course not in the manner which our enemies may have imagined. Is it not necessary, however, that we should proceed according to their formula, *because up to now these formulas have certainly not been very successful.*

I believe that if we look back we can be satisfied with the three years that we have left behind. It was always a very sober goal that was set up. Often very daring, where it had to be daring. Deliberate, where it could be deliberate. Cautious where we had time. Careful where we believed we had to be very careful-but we were also very bold where boldness alone could save us.

For this year we had laid out a very simple program. First: Under all circumstances to hold what had to be held. That is, to let the others advance where we ourselves did not intend to go forward, as long as they want to advance. To hold unflinchingly and wait to see who will be the first to weaken.

Second: To attack relentlessly where the attack is necessary. The goal here is very clear: destruction of the right arm of those international plotters of capitalism, plutocracy, and Bolshevism. It is against the greatest danger which ever hovered over our German people in modern times that we have defended ourselves for over a year now and against which we must proceed.

And here we set ourselves some goals, and I may mention them quite briefly, just in the form of catchwords, to make you aware, and to make every German aware, of what was accomplished in these few months. The first goal was the safeguarding of our dominating position on the Black Sea by the final mopping-up of the Crimean Peninsula. Two battles, the battle for Kerch and the battle for Sevastopol, served this purpose. If in these three years our opponents, I dare say, had achieved only one single such success, we would not be able to speak with them at all, because they would not be on the earth, but floating in the clouds. Blown up by nothing but imagination.

After we brought that into order, it appeared necessary

to us that a bubble which existed at Volkhov be removed. It was pinched off and the enemy destroyed or taken prisoner. Then came the next task, preparation for the break-through to the Don. Meanwhile, the enemy at this time selected a great operational objective, namely, of breaking through from Kharkov to the bank of the Dnieper, in order in this way to bring about the collapse of our entire southern front.

You will probably still recall with what enthusiasm our opponents followed these operations. They ended in three battles with the complete annihilation of more than 75 divisions of our Russian foe. After that followed our attack in our own great offensive. The goal was: First, to take from the enemy his last big wheat regions. Second, to take from him the last remaining coal which can be made into coke. Third, to move up to his sources of oil, to take them, or at least to isolate them.

Fifth (he does not mention a "fourth") the attack was to be carried on to cut off his very last and greatest communication artery, namely the Volga. And here the goal set was the region between the bend of the Don and the Volga, and the locale set was that of Stalingrad, not because this locality bears the name of Stalin-that is altogether a matter of indifference to us-but exclusively because this is a strategically important point. And since in general we realized that with the elimination for Russia of the Dnieper, Don, and Volga as communication lines about the same thing results for Russia or even worse that would result for Germany if we should lose the Rhine, the Elbe, the Oder, or the Danube. For, on this gigantic river alone, the Volga, in six months about thirty million tons of goods are shipped. This corresponds to a whole year's shipments on the Rhine.

This is cut off and has been cut off now for some time. The occupation of Stalingrad, which will also be carried through, will deepen this gigantic victory and strengthen it, and you can be sure that no human being will drive us out of this place later on. Now, as far as the further objectives are concerned, you will again understand that I do not speak of them because they are objectives which are being pursued at the present time. Mr. Churchill is talking about that. But the moment will come when the German nation will have had these further objectives made fully clear to them.

But I must now tell you a seventh (there is no mention of any sixth-Ed. Note) thing: That we set as another task for ourselves-naturally, the organization of this gigantic territory which we have occupied. For we did not care to say that we have marched so and so many thousand kilometers, but in reality we aim to make this vast territory secure for the conduct of our war and, in a wider sense, not only for feeding our people and safeguarding our raw materials, but for the support of all Europe.

To this end, first of all, traffic had to be put in order. The English too have achieved things in this sphere. For example, they have built a railroad from Egypt to Tobruk, which now serves us in extraordinarily good stead even though they finished it in a fairly short time. What does it count for in comparison with the railroads which we must build? And, indeed we wish to build them not so that they should be useful to the Russians, but for ourselves.

There are tens and tens of thousands of kilometers of railroad lines which we now put in operation again, or have put in operation long since, thanks to the energy and efficiency and devotion of many tens of thousands of German soldiers, railroad engineering troops, men of the Todt Organization, other organizations and so forth, of the Reich Labor Service, for example.

This vast net of communications, which today is already operating again for the most part on German rail gauges, was completely destroyed. Not only hundreds, but thousands of bridges had to be built anew, blasted sections had to be removed, crossings had to be rebuilt. All that happened *within a few months and, making allowances for circumstances, will be completed within a few weeks.*

Now, my party comrades, you will understand one thing. There are people, on the side of our opponents, who say: "Why do you stop suddenly?" Because we are prudent, because-let us say-we do not first run to Benghazi or still farther, in order then to be obliged to run back again, but because we stop somewhere long enough to establish our lines of communication. Naturally people who do not have military schooling will not grasp this. For this reason they have not been successful. All those, however, who have even the slightest military schooling, will grant that the area which we conquered in a few months is absolutely unique in world history.

And I say this also because there may be also among us some smug old reactionary, who suddenly says: "Indeed, what is the trouble? They have been at a standstill for a week now." Yes, my dear old smug reactionary, you're on the wrong track. Why don't you go there yourself and try "regulating traffic?" The German people, I know, has in its entirety unlimited confidence in its military leadership and the achievements of its soldiers. It knows very well that there will be no pause without reason.

We are not only bringing our communications into order, but we must build roads, for the blessed land of the proletarians and the peasants unfortunately has no roads, or only fragments of roads. So these must be built. The first really tremendous roads there are being built by our organizations. In many regions roads must be laid out through swamps, regions in which it was formerly believed that communication was altogether impossible. If somebody now remarks: "Well, the Russian manages to get through,"well, he is a kind of swamp man anyway. That we have to admit. He is not a European. For us it is simply somewhat harder to move forward in this morass than it is for this nation born in the morass.

Secondly, behind it we are organizing our agriculture also. Proof: the territory is to be opened up after all, and that isn't so simple either, for it isn't a question of what is sown and what is reaped but it is a question of practical value coming into evidence here. That means that these products are brought to the railway over endless stretches; that they can be loaded; that we can readjust part of this whole agriculture; that thousands of tractors which are damaged or eliminated be replaced or repaired, or that some other substitute be found for them.

And I can only tell you, that what has been accomplished here is really tremendous. While the front is fighting up ahead, some soldiers are fighting a few kilometers behind the front with the sickle and the scythe. They are already tilling the fields again, and behind them are our Labor Service Girls and their agricultural organizations. And when some blockhead-I can't call it anything else-take Duff Cooper or Eden or some such fellow, if you like-says: "That was a big mistake for the Germans to have gone into the Ukraine, to say nothing of the Kuban region," then he will see whether we made a mistake in going into these wheat regions.

The first, if only modest results of this action we were able to impart to the German people already to our good fortune-I may well be permitted to say. But you may be convinced that we are only at the beginning. The whole past year was one of battle. A horrible winter. And now we are fighting again. But even during this coming year this region will be organized entirely differently and the English can depend on that. We now understand how to arrange this. And finally farther behind that follows the organization of general economy, for this whole economy must be gradually brought into operation. Thousands of businesses and factories, canning factories and so on, mills and so on, all this *must be brought back into operation. It has all been destroyed.*

And behind all this is mining. This also must be exploited. In order to do this one must have electric current, and I can tell you if you could see how we are working there and what we are creating there and how we know precisely, on such a day this work will be done, and on such a day this electric power will be added; how we produce on this predetermined date so and so many thousands of tons of coal per day, and on another predetermined date so many thousands of tons. We no longer need to transport coal from Germany to the east, but on the contrary, we are going to build up our own industrial states there. Then you would understand that even at a time when apparently nothing is being done, nevertheless tremendous things are being achieved.

And then there is the liberation of the populace from the oppression of a Bolshevik power which spiritually, even today, holds millions of people there in a state of despair, and one may well say, of fear, of which one can hardly have any idea in Germany and other countries. It is the fear of the Commissar. It is the fear of the G. P. U., the fear of the whole regime, which still fills millions of people. All that will gradually be eliminated and is being eliminated, and there are many regions where the whole population is already working with us by the millions, and there are other regions in which it is already fighting in our ranks and on our side.

The result of this whole gigantic activity, which I have only been able to point out to you with a few sentences, are tremendous. While in the north of Europe, in the west, and on all other fronts we are on the defensive, we are here fulfilling one of the greatest prerequisites for the organization of Europe for war and for this war.

Of course you know that our enemies are constantly accomplishing miracles,-uh-of course there is not a tank that they build which isn't the best tank in the world, of course there is not a plane which isn't the best in the world. When they build a cannon, one measly cannon, then it is the cannon par excellence, the most amazing cannon in the world. They make a new machine gun or a new automatic pistol. It's a marvel, this pistol. They say this new pistol is absolutely the biggest invention in the world.

Then if you take a look at this junk you can only say that we wouldn't even put it in the hand of a German soldier. In everything they are far superior to us. Of course they are ahead of us in their incomparable generals. They are ahead of us in the bravery of their individual soldiers. Of course, any Englishman can handle three Germans just like that. Only unfortunately he can't find them, can he? They are superior to us in their equipment. What is a German tank worth against an English one, to say nothing of an American one, and so on? What is a German plane worth against one of theirs? But at any rate, the great heroes of this war, they will someday be written down in history on our side. And in this, history will only be honoring justice and truth.

And then on our side there is the further development of our alliances, the cooperation with our allies, first and foremost with our oldest ally, with Italy. Not only on one front do we fight jointly, but on a whole series of fronts. And that is good, for it shows that all the hopes of these enemies who believe they can dissolve this alliance are idiocy, are madness. We know very well what would happen to our two countries, indeed, we learn from the goals set by these enemies, from the crazy and idiotic goals they set up, what the fate would be of the German and the Italian peoples, but we know, beyond that, what the fate of Europe would be, if that other world could ever win a victory.

If they say today "Yes, of course, we would then take over the protection of Europe against Bolshevism," then I can only say in reply: "England had better see to it that she knows how to protect herself against Bolshevism." We do not need her protection! We got rid of Bolshevism within, we shall also get rid of it outside. That we have proved. But if, in a country, archbishops hold sacred Masses and have on one side of their altar cloth the Bolshevik symbol, then I see a black fate for that country. We know better what that leads to. The English will find that out yet. Perhaps fate will punish them just as it once punished the old Germany for thinking it could deal with these people. Germany and Italy, just like Spain and a whole number of other European nations, such as Rumania and so on, have taken care of the problem. Whether the other world will also take care of it is still to be revealed by this war.

But that this other world will not take care of us, of that you may be assured. If we take together all of our allies and those who are fighting on our side, Rumanians and Hungarians, Croats and Slovaks, and above all the Finns in the north, and then the Spaniards and so forth; when we take them all together, then we can really say that this is already a European crusade today. And then there are the Germanic volunteers of our Armed Elite Guard and the Legions of individual European states. It is really Europe which has gathered together here, just as it did in olden times against the assaults of the Huns or the Mongols. And now also, since I spoke to you last, Japan has likewise entered this war. Of course it too has only suffered defeats, and of course, the Japanese generals are absolutely no good as against these incomparable heroes, these famous generals of England, to say nothing of America.

MacArthur! What kind of general is that! What is a little Japanese against him! Only these Japanese took Hong Kong, and they made themselves masters of Singapore, and they took possession of the Philippines, and they are installed in New Guinea, and they will take complete possession of New Guinea, and they occupied Java and Sumatra.

But of course all this is nothing against the endless victories which England and America have won there. Battles, naval battles, such as the world has never seen before. Only Roosevelt will of course not say a word about the losses, in no case will he express himself normally, and never say what he thinks. We certainly know these heroes too well. It is today really a worldwide alliance, not only of the have-nots, but of all the peoples who are fighting for honor and decency, and who are determined to get rid of this vilest coalition that the world has ever seen.

In speaking of that I must come to something else. I have already mentioned that as early as 1939 neither Churchill nor Duff Cooper had completely destroyed the German U-boats. There were no more U-boats. And then from time to time reports kept coming again and again: "But now they are finally eliminated." Since then their success, supported by the heroic efforts of our air force formations, has grown greater from month to month.

Now our adversaries explain: "We have enormous defense resources. We have new methods. The British and American genius has invented entirely new machines, with which we will tame this danger." I can tell you one thing: The German genius does not rest either. We also are working. Our U-boats have exceeded all previous accomplishments by far, and I can assure the gentlemen that this will not change. We are remaining uninterruptedly up to date, of that you can rest assured. Also uninterrupted is not only continued construction but especially new construction of weapons. Up to the present we have appeared every year with a new weapon, which has been superior to the enemy's. It will continue to be so in the future.

Therefore we can also, if we examine the collective result, confirm that the last months of this year have also been successful and that those in the future will surely also be successful. Now of course besides the second front, they

have another method. The man who invented bombing warfare against the innocent civilian population declares that soon this bombing warfare will be ex-
panded very strongly against Germany.

I would like to express one thing here: In May, 1940, Mr. Churchill sent the first bombers against the German civilian population. I warned him at that time and for almost four months but of course in vain. Then we struck and indeed so thoroughly did we strike, that he suddenly began to cry and declared, it was barbarism and it was terrible. England would take revenge for it. The man who has all of this on his conscience! If I take no note of the war-monger general of this war, Roosevelt-the one to blame for all of this-he (Churchill) was the one who then dared to represent himself as innocent.

Again today they are conducting this warfare and I would like to express one thing here: The hour will come this time also in which we will answer. May both of the chiefs of this war and their Jewish backers not begin to squirm and whine if the end for England is more horrible than the beginning? On the first of September, 1939, we made two pronouncement in the Reichstag session of that date: First, that now that the, have forced this war upon us no amount of military force and no length of time will ever be able to conquer us; and second, the if Jewry is starting an international world war to eliminate the Aryan nations of Europe, then it won't be the Aryan nation which will be wiped out but Jewry.

They have drawn nation after nation into this war. The men who pull the strings of this demented man in the White House have managed actually to draw one nation after the other into this war. But to just the same degree a wave of anti-Semitism has swept over nation after nation. And it will move on farther. State after state that enters this war will one day become anti-Semitic.

In Germany too, the Jews once laughed at my prophecies. I don't know whether they are still laughing, or whether they have already lost the inclination to laugh, but I can assure you that everywhere they will stop laughing. With these prophecies I shall prove to be right.

The *historic successes of these last months have been so stupendous that it is really necessary to think of those to whom we owe these successes. For we read in the newspapers of great victories, of great battles of encirclement; but often for weeks we also read nothing at all except that "the operations are progress in," or "the operations are progressing favorably," or "such and such fronts are quiet" or "on other fronts attacks have been repulsed." My comrades, you have no idea what is concealed under the simple words of the communiqué of the Highest Leadership of the Armed Forces. The communiqué must remain terse. In it we must try to find an equilibrium in order to view the actual deeds with regard to their importance in relation to the whole.*

That does not mean merely that the fighting, where it is wholly unimportant measured by the events of the war, is easier for the individual German soldier than where it is a matter of very great decisions. It is always the man and his life that has to be taken into consideration. Often there are hundreds of thousands of brave soldiers of all service branches-the infantry, the army, engineers, artillery, squadrons of the Armed Elite Guard, squadrons of the air force or, at sea, our warships, on the surface and under water-all of them, at such a moment, often for days at a time, must risk their lives, and you then read nothing more than "Defensive fighting," or "Attacks of the enemy repulsed," or "Enemy who broke through destroyed," or "A break-through accomplished," "Advance in such-and-such a region," "Crossing of such-and-such a stream," "Capture of such-and-such a city. "You do not realize what is hidden beneath these words in the way of human heroism, and also of human pain, and suffering, and we may say, often anxiety too, naturally, deathly anxiety on the part of all those who, especially for the first time, are placed before the trial of God in this highest court.

All that reads simply, and is nevertheless infinitely hard. It similar to the situation in the World War when many soldiers returned home and were asked; "How is it really?" And then finally they had to realize it cannot be explained to someone who has not experienced it. One cannot tell him. He who has not lived through it himself doesn't know what it is; he does not understand it, one cannot tell him about it, and it is for this reason that many remain silent altogether and say nothing, because they have the feeling: "You just can't describe how it really is." And this is especially true when one has a barbaric, bestial opponent, as the one in the east, an opponent of whom one knows that he knows no pardon, an opponent who recruits not among men but actually among beasts. There is infinite suffering, infinite devotion, infinite heroism -infinite energy behind all these dry statements. When you read that so and so has received the Knight's Cross that is a very brief description which is published in the local, probably in . . . press. But what this description embraces in detailed achievement, the great mass of our people will not be able to conceive.

It is impossible for the individual to know exactly what it means when a pilot shoots down thirty, forty or firtyplanes, when he shoots down eighty, when he shoots down one hundred; those are not one hundred battles, because in them oftentimes he risks his life a thousand times; or when he finally shoots down one hundred and fifty, or one hundred and eighty, or t planes that is more than were ever shot down in the last war.

Or when U-boat commanders attack again and again, when commanders of the same U-boat carry out their assignments again and again, mine-sweeping units perform their assignments, it is always an uninterrupted service which one can only mention-I might say-in one sentence,-a service of many weeks and months of continuous devotion of their lives against a sentence which is then printed in a newspaper.

If we keep this in mind, then we must realize that with all that the homeland is doing, it cannot thank its soldiers anywhere nearly enough. And that doesn't apply only to our soldiers; it applies to all the soldiers of the other nations allied with us who are fighting on our side.

And here there is something else to be mentioned, namely that the German Army does not carry on it's fighting, say, like the English. We don't always send others to the places that are especially dangerous, but we regard it as our duty, as a matter of course, yes, and as an honor for us, to bear this burden of blood ourselves in full, honest measure. We have no Canadians and Australians to pull the chestnuts out of the fire for us, for we are fighting beside our allies as loyal, absolutely honorable associates.

But we consider all this also necessary, for out of this battle, perhaps the most difficult in our history, there will come in the end that which always hovered before us National Socialists who came out of the first World War, namely, this great Reich of a community of the people bound close together in sorrow and joy. For this war does really bring to birth one great bright aspect-namely, the great comradeship. What our party always strove for in peace, to form a community of the people out of the experience of the First World War - that is now secured.

All the German racial stocks carry their share. Otherwise the founding of the Greater German Reich would have been only an act of constitutional law. As it is, it is an eternal document signed with the blood of all . . . a document which no one can destroy now, against which all *the talk and babble of our enemies will be completely ineffectual, but above all a document which gives this State not only its form of authority, but its inner substance. You will also note, if you read the Knight's Cross citations, the simple man, the corporal or the non-commissioned officer, along with the sergeant-major, with the lieutenant and with the general, and, if you see the promotions of our young officers, the National Socialist community of the people here begins to make its appearance to its full extent. There are no longer any birth certificates.*

There is no former station in life, there is no conception of capital, there is no origin; there is also no more of our so-called education of former times. There is only one standard of value that is the standard of the upright, courageous, faithful man; the capable man, the determined and daring man who is fit to be the leader of his people. In reality an old world has been torn down. From this war arises, established by blood, the community of the people, the hope of the old National Socialists after the last war, who were able to transmit our creed to the nation.

And that perhaps is the greatest blessing for our people in the future, that we will come out of this war improved in our community and absolved in our community and absolved of so many prejudices, that after this war it really will be proved how right the party program of our movement was and how correct, moreover, our entire National Socialist approach was, because one thing is certain: No bourgeois state will survive this war. In this case everyone sooner or later will have to declare where he stands.

Only the one who is able to weld his people to a unit, not only politically but also socially will come out of this war as the victor. That we National Socialists laid this foundation, we owe - I personally owe, to the experience of the First World War. But, because the Greater German Reich has to fight this second war through, to that it will, one-day, be able to attribute a reinforcementand a deepening of this program.

That is why I am convinced today that they, the last remnant of a past from which they have learned nothing, who are hoping somewhere, by idle talk, or in one way or another, to experience some day, perhaps, a new dawn of their class world, will come to grief and suffer shipwreck. World history will push them aside, as if they were not there at all. It is ridiculous even to fight against this fate. And besides, as a soldier returning from the Great War, I once expounded this world philosophy to the German people and created the foundation of the Party.

Do you believe that some German would be able to offer the soldier returning victoriously from this war another Germany than the National Socialist Germany in the sense of a real fulfillment of our ideas of a true community of the people? That is impossible. And in the future that will surely be, perhaps, the most blessed benefit of this war. Special expansion is not the decisive thing, but the decisive thing will be the filling of this space with a closely-knit, strong people, which must recognize this to be the most essential principle.

Among this people not only does every soldier carry the marshal's staff in his knapsack, and indeed not only in theory, but truly, but also among this people every single fellow citizen finds the road open, which his genius, industry, bravery, effort or preparedness in general might open to him.

I would like at this moment to refer to the homeland front. It also has to endure hardships. The German worker is working hard. Last spring, when the question arose of bringing out new defense weapons, I had the experience of noting how in numerous factories workers not only worked ten and eleven hours a day, but even renounced their Sundays for weeks and weeks and weeks, with the one thought only-to give the front weapons.

I must point out, that in general the German worker

accomplishes tremendous things and that he is true to the present state, to its leadership, and above all to his soldiers, to his comrades and labor colleagues. I must, however, point out that just so does the country population fulfill its duty- that millions of German women have aligned themselves into this labor process, that the peasant women today accomplishes the work of two men. And finally I must point out that even our professions which require mental activity have sacrificed themselves fully, that here also millions upon millions sacrifice everything, in spirit and in thought, inventing and working in order to arm the nation and in order never again to give the front the example it gave in 1918.

Therefore, if I can say to the homeland today that it can be perfectly at ease, whether in the east or the west, in the north or the south, because the German front of our soldiers stands immovable, then I can say to the front, in exactly the same way: German soldier, you may rest assured; behind you stands your homeland, which will never leave you in the lurch. And that is no empty phrase. The good ones among our people from all strata of life are being welded together more and more into an indissoluble community, and this community will again reveal itself particularly, in the great relief work that we have to carry out this winter.

I have already pointed out often, that it would easily have been possible for us to take another road, but we did not do so because of the simple realization that it is better to acquaint the individual compatriot himself with the tasks which fall to the country and thus affect this individual, but above all to remind the more fortunate persons of the suffering of the less fortunate ones, to show them by continuous propaganda all that must still be done in order really to be able to speak here of a community of the people in the true sense of the word. It is not here a question of lip-service, but to this end every individual must devote all his *means, willingly to serve this community, and no one has any right to exclude himself from this work, especially at a time when millions of others have to defend the community with their blood.*

I address this appeal to the entire German people in the name of its soldiers particularly and of all others who sacrifice themselves in the armament factories or on the land or anywhere else. But in this hour I want to assure you of one thing: namely, that we shall mercilessly destroy every saboteur of this community. Just a few weeks ago an English newspaper, in a lucid hour, wrote very correctly for once that one should not laugh at the German Winter Aid Collections. It said that it is true that if in England one person enriches himself at the expense of the others he gets at most a few weeks or months in prison and then lives better than any soldier at the front can live, but that anyone who commits a sin against the community in Germany is practically on the way to the grave. This newspaper is right.

At a time when the best of our nation must serve at the front and must serve there with their very lives, there is no place for criminals or good-for-nothings who destroy the nation. Whoever profits on the things designated for our soldiers, can count on being ruthlessly eliminated. Whoever profits on that which so many of the poor amongst our people have sacrificed for our soldiers shall not expect to find any grace.

Every German must know that everything he gives to his soldiers or to the suffering homeland really reaches those who deserve it or who were meant to have it. And above all no habitual criminal shall have the illusion that a new crime will save him beyond this war. We will take care that not only the decent fellow will die at the front but that under no circumstances the criminal or indecent fellow at home will live through this period.

I do not wish that a German woman, who perhaps has to go home from her place of work at night, constantly has to watch out anxiously that no harm will be done to her by some good-for-nothing or criminal. We shall eliminate these single cases. We have eliminated them and the German people owe it to this fact, that there is so little trouble now. I believe that I am acting in the spirit of the preservation of our community, but above all the spirit of the front. The soldiers demand the right that while they are risking their lives out there, their families, their wives and their other relatives be protected at home. At this moment I also have to assure the front of something else, of the boundless bravery with which this German homeland on its part too accepts and endures the war even where it strikes them and strikes them with dire severity.

I know a city, a Frisian city. I wished to evacuate it a long time ago, because it was attacked time and again. I wished to take the children away, and the women, in order to bring them to safety. It was out of the question. Again and again they went back to their city and they could not be taken away, although this city has suffered so severely.

Here, too, countless deeds of heroism were accomplished, not only by men but also by women. And not only by women but by boys who have hardly reached the fifteenth, sixteenth or seventeenth year. They set to work with their whole beings, in the knowledge that they are one single community in this war, consecrated to one another, and know very well that either all must survive victoriously together or be destined for extermination together. If a soldier did not know that, you could not expect him to risk his life under these dismal circumstances. Conversely, the homeland, too, must know it, so that it will measure its own contribution accordingly.

And, therefore, I expect that the new Winter Relief will be an especially strong document of this indissoluble community spirit so that the nation will thereby give the whole world a testimonial, something besides a stupid lying, plebiscite; a testimonial of their sacrifice, in which they declare: We stand behind our soldiers, as our soldiers stand before us. And we both stand together before our people and before our Reich and under no circumstances will we ever capitulate.

Let our adversaries conduct this war as long as they are able to do so. What we can do in order to beat them, we certainly will do. That they ever will beat us is impossible and out of the question." Nationalist Socialist Germany and the states which are allied with her will come out of this war with a glorious victory as young nations, as real peoples' states.'

* * * * *

- Inner Circle -

- Himmler -

Himmler and Bormann added a third member to their power group within the inner circle of Nazi hierarchy. The new man was Erich Koch.

Koch had been appointed as Chief of Civil Administration of Bezirk Bialystok and had also been appointed *'Reichskommissar'* in the *'Reichskommissariat Ukraine'* on the First of September, giving him command of the Gestapo and uniformed police. His first act as *'Reichskommissar'* had been to close all local schools, declaring that:

"Ukraine children need no schools. What they'll have to learn will be taught them by their German masters".

He was a brutal man and was heard to remark:

"If I meet a Ukrainian worthy of being seated at my able, I must have him shot."

Himmler felt that he was just the man to round out their little clique.

* * * * *

- Speer -

Albert was very much aware of Himmler's rising star and the support the man gleaned from his close association with both Bormann and Koch. He also knew that Goering strongly disliked him, if not in public, at least in fact and that the only other member of the inner circle who was still in Hitler's good graces, was the Propaganda Minister, Joseph Goebbels.

He and Goebbels had initially fallen out over Speer's stand on the Propaganda Minister's earlier extramarital fling with the Czech actress Lida Baarova. By this time in the war, however, Speer's importance had risen dramatically within the inner circle and Goebbels, who was finding himself being routinely sidelined by the Himmler, Bormann and Koch trio, found it advantageous to forgive Speer for what he saw as his previous transgressions.

When, in the summer of nineteen forty-two, Speer sensed a certain defrosting of their earlier relationship, he asked him to put his propaganda apparatus to work to speed the production of armaments. Goebbels, very eager for an ally by this point, quickly acquiesced, and soon newsreels, magazines and newspapers were required to publish articles on the subject.

With Goebbels's new support, Speer's popularity and influence increased markedly, making his job much easier.

* * * * *

- Wernher von Braun -

Wernher Magnus Maximilian Freiherr von Braun, while in his twenties and thirties was the central figure in Nazi Germany's rocket development program. Von Braun had graduated from the *'Technische Hochschule Berlin'* in nineteen thirty-two with a degree in aeronautical engineering. He had an early interest in rocketry and felt that he needed to learn more about physics, chemistry and astronomy to reach his goal, which was the exploration of space. He entered the *'Friedrich-Wilhelms-Universitat'* for post-graduate studies and graduated with a *'Dr. Phil.'* degree in physics in nineteen thirty-four. He took further studies at *'ETH Zurich'*.

He was tapped by the German army for part of their team working on research into rocket development in thirty-four and this group, which was working at *'Kummersdorf '*, successfully launched two rockets that rose to a height of two miles by the end of that year.

Von Braun applied for membership in the Nazi party on November twelfth of nineteen thirty-seven. In nineteen forty, at Himmler's request, von Braun, still working for the army, became a member of the SS.

He was highly interested in the American physicist, Robert H Goddard's, research in the field and using plans from various journals incorporated his ideas into the building of the *'Aggregat'* (A) series of rockets.

* * * * *

- Peenemunde -

On April second, nineteen thirty-six the Reich Air Ministry paid seven hundred and fifty Reichsmarks to the town of Wolgast for the purchase of the whole Northern peninsula of the Baltic island of Usedom.

The *'Heeresversuchsanstalt Peenemunde'* (Peenemunde Army Research Center) (HVP) was founded in nineteen thirty-seven as one of five military proving grounds under the *'Heeres Waffenamt'* (German Army Weapons Office).

The property was to be shared by the Luftwaffe and the Army.

The Luftwaffe immediately began working on their

research facility on the site and the Army, acting on orders from the Commander in Chief of the German Army, Walther von Brauchitsch, quickly began construction of their own separate facility designed for rocket research. By the middle of nineteen thirty-eight the army research personnel from Kummersdorf had packed up and headed to their new location at Peenemunde.

The Army moved its research team, including von Braun, into *'Peenemunde Ost'* which consisted of *'Werk Ost'* and *'Werk Sud'*, while the Luftwaffe settled into *'Peenemunde West'* or *'Erprobungsstelle der Luftwaffe'*, which was their new flight test site.

Von Brauchitsch then ordered construction of an *'A-4'* production site at Peenemunde and in January nineteen thirty-nine, Walter Dornberger, who as an artillery Captain had earlier arranged for Von Braun to receive a research grant from the Ordnance Department and who was now the military commander at Peenemunde, appointed von Braun as technical director and created a subsection of the unit specifically for planning the Production Plant for the 'A' project, which was to be headed by G. Schubert, a senior Army civil servant.

* * * * *

- The A4 Project -

During nineteen thirty-six, von Braun's rocketry team working at Kummersdorf investigated the installation of liquid-fueled rockets in aircraft. Ernst Heinkel, the German aircraft designer and manufacturer whose company was named *'Heinkel Flugzeugwerk'*, was enthusiastic about the project and supported their efforts, supplying one He 72 and two He 112's for their experiments.

In June of thirty-seven, one of the 112's was flown with its piston engine shut down during a successful flight, which utilized von Braun's rocket powered engine alone. This demonstration proved that an aircraft could be flown satisfactorily with a back-thrust system affixed to the rear. Von Braun's engines were using a mix of alcohol and liquid oxygen.

During the same period experiments being conducted by German engineer, Helmuth Walter, a pioneer researcher into rocket engines and gas turbines, was conducting experiments on hydrogen peroxide based rocket engines and moving towards lighter and simpler engines that definitely seemed more compatible for use in aircraft. His firm, located in Kiel, was given a commission by the RLM to build a rocket engine for the He 112.

Von Braun's engines used direct combustion and created fire, while Walter engines had hydrogen peroxide and calcium permanganate as a catalyst and used hot vapours produced from a chemical reaction. Both engines created thrust and provided high speed. Test flights using the Walter rocket fitted to a He 112 proved it to be the better of the two engines, as it was more reliable, simpler to operate and less dangerous to both the aircraft and the test pilot.

* * * * *

- Mechelen Transit Camp -

In August of forty-two the Germans started to empty this camp of Belgian Jews and Gypsies who had been previously interned. Two transports, containing approximately one thousand Jews, now left each week for Auschwitz-Birkenau.

* * * * *

- Concentration Camps -

On September the ninth, in order to prevent contamination of ground water, the practice of burying bodies at Auschwitz was stopped. Open pit burning commenced and all the previously buried bodies, numbering approximately one hundred and seven thousand, were dug up and burned as well.

On September twenty-sixth, the SS begin to cash in on the growing mounds of possessions and valuables confiscated at Auschwitz and Majdanek. Seized German currency was sent to the Reichs Bank. Foreign currency, gold, jewels and other valuable were sent to the SS Headquarters of the Economic Administration. Watches, clocks and pens were distributed to the troops at the front. Clothing was cleaned and distributed to German families.

* * * * *

- Ghettos -

- Warsaw -

Toward the end of September of forty-two the mass deportations ended, leaving only about fifty-five thousand prisoners remaining in this ghetto. The SS now established a special section, called *'The Werterfassung',* which was used to collect and sort the belongings of the victims slated for shipment to Germany. Following these mass deportations, the ghetto was reduced in size and divided into three separate sections.

* * * * *

- Lodz -

After occupation, the Germans had created a ghetto in Lodz, a Polish city located approximately seventy-five miles southwest of Warsaw. Before the war this city had contained the second largest Jewish population in the country.

The establishment of this facility took place in February of nineteen-forty. One hundred and fifty thousand Jews were forced into this ghetto. An additional forty-five thousand individuals were added in forty-one and forty-two. Beginning in May of nineteen-forty, the Germans started to establish factories within this ghetto and by August of forty-two nearly four hundred of these had been set up.

Their primary product was textiles, especially uniforms for the German army. Conditions within the camp were horrendous and deportation from Lodz had begun in January of forty-two. The Jewish administrators strongly supported the factories, hoping that what they produced in the factories for the German war effort would save them from having to fill far higher German deportation orders.

Major deportations from this ghetto ceased in September of forty-two.

* * * * *

- Eric -

Eric waited impatiently for the conning tower hatch to be opened and then shielded himself with his cap from the falling water droplets as he followed a deckhand out of the sub. Upon reaching the deck and after giving his eyes a few seconds to adjust to the bright lighting, he turned his gaze to the four U-boat pens and was pleased to see that the newest U-boat which had left from Bordeaux just before him, was riding easily at her moorings in slot number three.

His primary concern as to its safety satisfied, he turned his attention to the completion of his docking maneuvers as other members of the crew moved into their positions in preparation.

This was accomplished in short order and he then turned the ship over to his second in command , shook his cap free of moisture, placed it on his head and moved directly to the gangplank. As soon as it had been secured in place he moved downward to the cement dock area and walked directly across to the control bunker. The door opened as he approached and his distant cousin Hans burst out and engulfed him in a firm bear hug. They were both laughing as they parted and looked each other up and down. Hans spoke first.

"It's good to see you again my friend."

He stepped to one side of the doorway and waved Eric inside as he continued.

"The Captain of the other U-boat advised us you would be arriving shortly and that your cargo would be primarily human. We've arrange quarters for everyone I think, and I've just notified Grandfather of you arrival, so we can expect to see a surface welcoming committee arriving shortly to guide them to their new accommodations. I came ahead to speak to you about your father's last letter which arrived with the last crew. He had anticipated that Brazil might be at war on the Allied side by the time you arrived and suggested that all those uniformed members here, change from uniform to civilian clothing. We've done that and I assumed that you would wish that your crew should follow that example during your stay with us, at least any of them who will be rising above to the surface, so I have brought clothing for that purpose."

Eric smiled and nodded.

"Good. Yes, Father and I discussed this awhile back and we agreed that as soon as Brazil declared war we would be obliged to have a low profile here. We should not have anyone in uniform wandering about above the *'Operation Fatherland'* levels.

The other U-boat left on schedule for Bordeaux?"

Hans nodded and grinned.

"Yes everything seems to be going smoothly as far as I know. As usual, we can expect a coded telegram notifying us of its arrival in port, which I expect will be any day now."

* * * * *

- Friedrichshafen -

Based on several days of mild morning sickness as well a general sense of biological change within, Ursula was of the opinion that she was pregnant. She had gone so far as to share this belief with Friedrich, but had said nothing to her mother as yet.

Despite the mildly upset stomachs in the mornings, she felt extremely well overall. She was tremendously busy with her work, as there appeared to be no end to the number of rail cars arriving not only from France, but now also from other occupied territories. Her days cataloguing and storing artworks had also been expanded more and more by the added need to arrange for the securing of a much expanded amount of other valuables, jewels, gold, silver, rare books and manuscripts.

She was as yet still not absolutely positive that she was indeed pregnant and due to her expanding workload, found little time to dwell on the situation. She also knew that if she was to share the information with her mother, Erika would promptly side with Friedrich, who was already suggesting that she cut back on her work and rest more.

One was bad enough! She didn't need both of them hassling her. She felt just fine, better than she ever had and she was quite capable of doing her job at this point. Perhaps, if she was right and it was true, well then she might consider cutting back, but certainly not for several months.

* * * * *

- Oslo -

Konrad had just returned from a second trip to Berlin to consult with Baron von Kliest about their advancing joint research on genetics.

He'd arrived back in time to accompany Gabriella to a dinner party witch was being held for visiting Nazi officials and it wasn't until they'd returned home to the mansion late in the evening that he had a chance to bring her up to date on his trip.

They were enjoying a cognac and preparing for bed when he spoke.

"Von Kliest is urging me to join him on a permanent basis. We are reaching some extraordinary conclusions and he feels we should be working full time together on the research. I have pretty well set up all the Lebensborn clinics here that are necessary and personally would look forward to the move as I think he is right, but I told him that I would have to discuss it with you before I made the commitment. I spoke with your father about it while I was there and he thinks it might not be a bad idea. He told me that the research project has now been given a high priority by the Fuhrer and that Himmler is backing it strongly. They are considering moving the research out of Berlin....the bombing is getting quite heavy and your father believes that it could be arranged for the new facility to be constructed at Friedrichshafen where it would be well out of the danger zone."

Gabriella, who was seated at her dressing table removing her stockings and had no particular interest in returning to Berlin had begun to frown when he started speaking.

She had left her past in Berlin and was not anxious to find herself in the position of having to face up to it if she returned. However, at this last bit of information the frown had slipped away and she seemed to brighten.

"Almost all of the family would be together if we were to move back to the castle. Eric will be at sea of course and father probably wouldn`t be able to leave Berlin other than for short visits, but the others are already there."

As he responded, Konrad lowered his voice slightly.

"You must not repeat what I now tell you, do you understand?"

Gabriella looked at him quizzically and nodded.

"All right."

Konrad continued.

"I'm no good at politics and don't really have much of a grasp on how the war is going for us, but your Father is of the opinion that Germany will lose the war. In fact he went so far as to say that it is only a matter of attrition at this point and Germany cannot win an extended war of attrition. His prediction is that the war will be over as early as nineteen forty-four.

He believes that at this juncture, Himmler would agree to and even encourage my joining the Baron in this line of research and thinks we should take advantage of this opportunity to return to Germany. Your father is concerned about the family being too far apart when the end approaches and would prefer that we are all together when that time comes as, he has definite plans for our future after the war."

Gabriella nodded her understanding and her mind seemed to drift a little before she spoke.

"Mother would certainly welcome that and we would definitely all be comfortable at the castle. We would have every amenity there and although I have enjoyed our time here, I must say that I wouldn't find a chance to leave an occupied land where we are at best tolerated to return to a land filled with friendlier faces unwelcome."

She nodded absently as she stood and turned to face him.

"I think perhaps you should take up the position Konrad."

CHAPTER EIGHTEEN

- September -

- Allied Air Operations -

- Western Europe -

Dropping more than six thousand tons of bombs, British raids are made against Wilhelmshaven, Bremen and Duisburg. The US targets are in France and the Low Countries, where the fledgling American forces drop two hundred tons.

* * * * *

- Maritime Warfare -

- Atlantic -

The patrol areas for the U-boats remain unchanged. Attacks against targets off Trinidad are the easiest pickings. North Atlantic convoys are reorganized to sail from New York to the United Kingdom rather than from the Canadian ports of Sydney and Halifax, making it easier to form coastal convoys in conjunction with the main convoys. Support groups are organized to provide backup for the naval escorts. These ideally include an escorted carrier and are sent in to bolster firepower to any hard-pressed convoy. Additionally, Leigh Light aircraft come into service with RAF coastal command.

Total Allied shipping losses are one hundred and fourteen ships for Five hundred and sixty-seven thousand, three hundred tons. Subs sink ninety-eight of these for four hundred and eighty-five thousand, four hundred tons.

* * * * *

- Mediterranean -

Combined British air and naval forces sink a full one-third of the supply ships being sent to the German and Italian forces. Rommel is still suffering from supply shortages and he is infuriated when he learns that many of the supplies and vehicles that are successfully landed are sent to inactive Italian units in Libya. By this point in the war, only about one-third of Italy's prewar fleet of merchant ships remains in operation. The remainder have been either sunk or captured.

* * * * *

- September First -

- Guadalcanal -

'Seabees', the men of the Navy's Construction Battalion, begin to arrive.

* * * * *

- Eastern Front -

- Stalingrad -

German units have now reached the suburbs and fierce battles are raging. The Russian Sixty-Second Army is in real danger of being cut off.

* * * * *

Eastern Front -

Troops, both German and Rumanian contingents from the

German Eleventh Army, cross from Kerch and land on the Taman Peninsula.

* * * * *

- North Africa -

Rommel's forces make weak attacks. One of his Panzer Divisions is out of fuel and the Fifteenth makes little progress while delivering the British Eighth Armoured Brigade a powerful lesson in the use of anti-tank guns.

* * * * *

- September Second -

- North Africa -

Rommel makes the decision to pull back to regroup. Montgomery decides to hold his positions and doesn't give chase.

* * * * *

- Eastern Front -

The German Eleventh and Seventeenth Armies push ahead and approach Novorossiysk. First Panzer grinds slowly toward Grozny.

* * * * *

- New Guinea -

The Japanese begin to reinforce Buna, sending one thousand troops from Rabaul.

* * * * *

- September Third -

- Stalingrad -

The Russians pull out all the stops, actively conscripting men and boys into the army to assist in the defence of the city.

* * * * *

- North Africa -

The New Zealand Division holding defensive position around Alam Nayil is ordered to move against the retreating German lines, but despite ferocious fighting, they achieve little.

* * * * *

- September Fourth -

- Stalingrad -

As their troops reach the Volga south of the city, the Germans send over one thousand planes against the city.

* * * * *

- US -

The *'Manhattan Engineering District'* is formally created. Research and development of the atomic bomb has begun.

* * * * *

- Vichy France -

The puppet government sets up the *'Service du travail obligatoire'* (Compulsory Work Service) or STO. This is a forced enlistment and deportation of hundreds of thousands of French workers to Nazi Germany, where they will work as forced labour for the German manpower-starved war effort. In return the German government agrees to release one French prisoner of war for every three workers that are provided to the Reich.

* * * * *

- September Fifth -

- New Guinea -

Australian and American troops rout the Japanese forces at Milne Bay, Papua. This is the first outright defeat for the Japanese land forces in the Pacific war.

* * * * *

- September Sixth -

- Eastern Front -

The Germans take the Black Sea port of Novorossiysk.

* * * * *

- North Africa -

After retreating from Alam Halfa, Rommel returns to his original defensive positions. Intelligence tells him of the massive reinforcements Montgomery is receiving for the Eighth Army. He is very much aware that if this imbalance in support continues, he will not be able to defeat the British. He digs in, preparing vast and elaborate fixed defences consisting of dug-in field guns, barbed wire, minefields and booby traps.

* * * * *

- September Seventh -

- Guadalcanal -

Six hundred Marine Raiders carry out a commando raid against the Japanese base at Taivu, seriously disrupting their plans for an attack against the main American position.

* * * * *

- September Eighth -

- Vichy France -

The government dismisses General de St. Vincent, the Military Governor of Lyons, for refusing to help arrest Jews residing in his area.

* * * * *

- New Guinea -

The Japanese compel the Australian forces in the Owen Stanley Range to retreat from their position near Efogi.

* * * * *

- September Ninth -

- US -

Japanese planes drop incendiaries in Oregon forests for the second time. The small fire that was the result of an earlier attempt is not repeated on this occasion.

* * * * *

- Eastern Front -

Hitler removes General List from the command of Army Group *'A'* and assumes personal command.

* * * * *

- Madagascar -

The British make landings at Majunga, with the intention of occupying the entire Island.

* * * * *

- September Twelfth -

- Cape of Good Hope -

U-156 sinks the liner *'Laconia'* just south of the Equator. She is transporting servicemen's wives and children and Italian prisoners of war. The U-boat commander, Captain Leutnant Hartenstein surfaces and gives aid and then sends a radio message to the Allied forces in plain language. As a result of his broadcast, the U-boat is attacked by an American plane.

German Admiral Doenitz orders that no further similar rescue attempts are to be made by U-boats. He then arranges for Vichy ships from Dakar to be sent to finish the rescue work.

* * * * *

- Eastern Front -

The Russian perimeter around Stalingrad has shrunk to a length of about thirty miles. The tough and uncompromising Russian General, Vasily Chuikov, is appointed to the command of the Sixty-Second Army to deal with the rising danger of collapse.

* * * * *

- Guadalcanal -

The carrier USS *'Wasp'* flies in aircraft to bolster the American forces which are under heavy Japanese attacks around *'Bloody Ridge'.*

* * * * *

- September Thirteenth -

- Stalingrad -

German forces surround the city and a state of siege commences.

* * * * *

- North Africa -

Units of the British Long Range Desert Group attack airfields at Benghazi and Barce. Amphibious landings attempted at Tobruk are unsuccessful and result in heavy casualties.

* * * * *

- September Fourteenth -

- Artic -

Over the next few days the convoy PQ-18 reaches Russia with much better results than its predecessor. It has been provided with a significantly larger escort force, including a carrier. While thirteen merchant ships are sunk, the majority of the merchantmen make it through and the costs to the Germans for the sinkings are considerable. They lose two U-boats and twenty aircraft.

* * * * *

- Guadalcanal -

The Japanese attempts to take Henderson Field grind to a halt. To date they have taken twelve hundreds casualties and been unable to accomplish their task.

* * * * *

- New Guinea -

The Australian defenders on the Kokoda Trail are pushed back to Imita Ridge, leaving the Japanese only thirty miles from Port Moresby.

* * * * *

- September Fifteenth -

- Solomons -

With three torpedo hits, the Japanese sub I-19 sinks the carrier USS *'Wasp'* off Guadalcanal. A destroyer is also sunk

* * * * *

- Aleutians -

The Americans begin a series of bombing runs on the Japanese occupied island of Kiska.

* * * * *

- September Fifteenth -

- Port Moresby -

US troops arrive to reinforce the battered Australian defenders.

* * * * *

- September Sixteenth -

- Eastern Front -

There is extremely heavy fighting around the Mamayev Kurgan Hill at Stalingrad. This strategic location changes hands several times over the next few days.

* * * * *

- New Guinea -

Local air superiority and support from American troops means that the combined Allied force can regroup and begin planning for an offensive against the Japanese invaders.

* * * * *

- September Seventeenth -

- US -

All atomic research in the States is placed under the military control of General Groves. Groves, concerned about security and the eventual American control of the research material, makes him less than willing to share his results with the British.

* * * * *

- September Eighteenth -

- New Guinea -

After evaluating their supply situation, Japanese General, Horii, begins to pull some of his troops back to the area around Buna and Gona.

* * * * *

- Guadalcanal -

With the arrival of six transports bringing supplies and the 7th Marine Regiment as reinforcements, the Americans have reached a strength of about twenty-three thousand men and are now well supplied.

* * * * *

- Madagascar -

The British land troops on the east coast at Tamatave.

* * * * *

- Stalingrad -

The Russians expand the transport of troops across the Volga at night. The battle of the *'grain silo'* begins and the Germans are forced to retreat.

* * * * *

- September Nineteenth -

- Libya -

The German defenders repulse the Allied attack launched against Jalo.

* * * * *

- September Twentieth -

- Eastern Front -

The town of Terek in the Caucasus is taken by the Germans.

* * * * *

- Greece -

The offices of the pro-Nazi *'National-Socialist Patriotic Organization'* are blown up by the Greek *'PanHellenic Union of Fighting Youths'* in order to thwart German attempts to raise a Greek volunteer legion for deployment to the Eastern Front.

* * * * *

- September Twenty-First -

- Sweden -

Pro-Nazi candidates for the national election fair extremely poorly.

* * * * *

- September Twenty-third -

- North Africa -

Rommel flies to Berlin for medical treatment.

* * * * *

- New Guinea -

Additional American reinforcements land at Port Moresby and the Australian Commander in Chief, General Blamey, now takes personal command with orders from MacArthur to go over to the offensive.

* * * * *

- Madagascar -

The Capital, Tananarive, is taken by the British.

* * * * *

- Guadalcanal -

The *'Third Battle of Matanikau River'* begins with a Japanese naval bombardment and reinforcements are landed. The invaders come close to destroying Henderson Field but are unable to take it and their land forces are decisively driven back.

* * * * *

- September Twenty-Fourth -

- Eastern Front -

Hitler removes General Halder as Chief of Staff at OKH and replaces him with General Zeitzler.

* * * * *

- Guadalcanal -

Overnight two Japanese destroyers on resupply missions are damage as the US Navy gains experience and strength in the area.

* * * * *

- September Twenty-Seventh -

- New Guinea -

Japanese forces begin to retreat down the Kokoda Trail in the face of strong Australian attacks.

* * * * *

- September Twenty-Eighth -

- Stalingrad -

A small number of Russian forces manage to cross the Volga near Rzhev in the central section of the front.

* * * * *

- September Twenty-Ninth -

- Madagascar -

The British land forces at Tulearon on the southwest coast of the island.

CHAPTER NINETEEN

- October -

- Hitler -

A commando raid made by the fledgling *'Small Scale Raiding Force'* (SSRF), against the German occupied Channel Island of Sark, ends with the small British force successfully taking five German soldiers prisoner.

After having tied their hands and while they were escorting their prisoners back to the beach in preparation to leave the island, their charges begin to struggle and shout for help. In order to prevent their discovery and capture by other German troops, the British quickly execute all but one of their prisoners.

When Hitler hears of this incident he is appalled and furious. Subsequently on the eighteenth of October nineteen forty-two he issued his infamous *'Commando Order'*.

It read as follows:

TheFuhrer	**SECRET**
No. 003830/42g.Kdos.OWK/Wst	**F.H.Qu 18.10.1942**
12 copies	**Copy No.12.**

For a long time now our opponents have been employing in their conduct of the war, methods which contravene the International Convention of Geneva. The members of the so-called Commandos behave in a particularly brutal and underhand manner; and it has been established that these units recruit criminals not only from their own country but even former convicts set free in enemy territories. From captured orders it emerges that they are instructed not only to tie up

prisoners, but also to kill out-of-hand unarmed captives who they think might prove and encumbrance to them, or hinder them in successfully carrying out their aims. Orders have indeed been found in which the killing of prisoners has positively been demanded
of them.

In this connection it has already been notified in an Appendix to Army Orders of 7.10.1942, that in future, Germany will adopt the same methods against these Sabotage units of the British and their Allies. i.e., that whenever they appear, they shall be ruthlessly destroyed by the German troops.

I order therefore:-

From now on all men operating against German troops in so-called Commando raids in Europe or in Africa, are to be annihilated to the last man. This is to be carried out whether they be soldiers in uniform, or saboteurs, with or without arms; and whether fighting or seeking to escape; and it is equally immaterial whether they come into action form Ships and Aircraft, or whether they land by parachute. Even if these individuals on discovery make obvious their intention of giving themselves up as prisoners, no pardon is on any account to be given. On this matter a report is to be made on each case to Headquarters for the information of Higher Command.

Should individual members of these Commandos, such as agents, saboteurs etc., fall into the hands of the Armed Forces through any means - as, for example through the Police in one of the Occupied Territories - they are to be instantly handed over to the S.D. To hold them in military custody - for example in P.O.W. Camps, etc., even if only as a temporary measure, is strictly forbidden.

This order does not apply to the treatment of those enemy soldiers who are taken prisoner or give themselves up in open battle, in the course of normal operations, large scale attacks; or in major assault landings or airborne operations. Neither does it apply to those who fall into our hands after a sea fight, nor to those enemy soldiers who, after air battle, seek to save their lives by parachute.

I will hold all Commanders and Officers responsible under Military Law for any omission to carry out this order, whether by failure in their duty to instruct their units accordingly, or if they themselves act contrary to it.

(Signed) A Hitler

* * * **

- Inner Circle -

This order was forwarded by the OKW on the following day with a cover letter reading:

HEADQUARTERS OF THE ARMY SECRET
No. 551781/42G.K.
Chefs W.F.St/Qu. F.H. Qu.   19/10/42
22 Copies   Copy No.21.

The enclosed Order from the Fuhrer is forwarded in connection with destruction of enemy Terror and Sabotage-troops.
This order is intended for Commanders only and is in no circumstances to tall into Enemy hands.
Further distribution by receiving Headquarters is to be most strictly limited.
The Headquarters mentioned in the Distribution list are responsible that all parts of the Order, or extracts

taken from it, which are issued are again withdrawn and, together with this copy, destroyed.

Chief of Staff of the Army
(Signed) JODL

* * * * *

- Alfred Rosenberg -

As head of the *'Reich Ministry for the Occupied Eastern Territories',* Rosenberg had presented Hitler with his original plan for the organization of the conquered Eastern territories. In it he had suggested the establishment of new administrative districts to replace the previously Russian-controlled territories. These were to be governed by new *'Reichskommissariats'* and were to be specifically named *'Ostland '*(Baltic countries and Belarus) and *'Ukraine'* (Ukraine and nearest territories). Rosenberg believed that these steps would encourage certain non-Russian nationalism and promote German interests for the benefit of future Aryan generations in accord with the geopolitical, *'Lebensraum im Osten'* plans. This would then provide a buffer against Russian expansion in preparation for the total eradication of Communism and Bolshevism by decisive pre-emptive military action.

Based on these plans, once the Wehrmacht had invaded Russian-controlled territory, they would immediately implement the first of the proposed *'Reichskommissariats'* of Ostland and Ukraine.

This had been done, *'Ostland'* being assigned to Hinrich Lohse on July seventeenth, nineteen forty-one and *'Ukraine'* assigned to Erich Koch on September first of that year respectively.

Unfortunately the new organization of these administrative territories almost immediately led to conflict between Rosenberg and the SS over the treatment of the Slavs under German occupation.

Rosenberg was Nazi Germany's chief racial theorist and he considered Slavs, though lesser than Germans, to be Aryan and was not pleased with the treatment being meted out to non-Jewish occupied peoples. His initial plans, which Hitler had accepted at the time they were drawn up, had proposed the creation of buffer satellite states made up of Greater-Finland, Baltica, Ukraine, and the Caucasus.

Rosenberg, unlike the others in the Nazi hierarchy, advocated a policy designed to encourage anti-communist opinion. He issued a series of posters announcing the end of the Russian collective farms and annulled all Russian legislation on farming, restoring family farms for those willing to collaborate with the occupiers. He was of the firm belief that a good portion of the Slavs could become supporters of a new German regime if it offered the removal of the harsh Russian systems that Stalin had initiated.

But, although Rosenberg could be considered as a fringe member of the inner circle, he was still in awe of and afraid of Hitler. He simply would not assert himself when in the Fuhrer's presence and Himmler, who was quite definitely one of the stars of the inner circle and who had now aligned himself with both Bormann and Koch, had a very different view of how the Slavs should be treated. To him they were either redundant or only good for slave labour.

Needless to say, Himmler's view was that the 'New Order' was essentially a war of conquest and extermination and as a result he saw to it that Rosenberg's German propaganda efforts designed to win over Russian option were at best patchy and inconsistent.

Himmler and his two staunch supporters saw to it that Rosenberg's influence with Hitler was continually undermined. In an attempt to reduce the onslaught, Rosenberg agreed to fire his current appointee to the leadership of the 'Political Department' and his liaison for the Ukrainian, Caucasian, Russian and other émigré groups, Georg Leibbrandt. Leibbrandt held similar beliefs to Rosenberg and was his staunchest supporter. He was continually pressuring

Rosenberg to by-pass Bormann and go directly to Hitler in order to have the draconian practices of Himmler and his crew, with regard to the administration of the newly occupied territories, stopped.

Unfortunately for Rosenberg, Leibbrandt's subordinates stepped into the void and continued submitting new suggestions to Rosenberg complaining of the handling of the Slavs and urging him to speak directly to Hitler about it. One of these was a thirteen page memorandum from Otto Brautigam, who had spent seven years in Russia. The Germans he said, had been greeted as liberators but the occupied peoples had soon discovered that the slogan *'Liberation from Bolshevism'*, was merely a blind for enslavement. Instead of gaining allies against Stalinism, the Germans were creating bitter enemies. The document went on to say:

'Our Policy has forced both Bolsheviks and Russian nationalists into a common front against us. The Russian fights today with exceptional bravery and self-sacrifice for nothing more or less than recognition of his human dignity. The Russian people must be told something concrete about their future.'

At the sight of this document Rosenberg trembled in fear. Not a very brave man at the best of times, under the present circumstances it is likely that this memorandum never went any further than his own office.

* * * * *

- The A-4 Project -

The first successful flight by a prototype of von Braun's long-range ballistic missile took place at Peenemunde on October third of nineteen forty-two. The weapon was still in the early developmental and testing phases however.

* * * * *

- Ratlines -

Planning for a system of escape routes for Nazis and other fascists who foresaw a need to flee Europe should the Axis powers lose the conflict, later referred to as *'Ratlines'*, began as early as nineteen forty-two. These escape routes led mainly to havens in South America, particularly Argentina, Brazil, Uruguay, Chile and Bolivia. Lesser destinations included the US, Canada and the Middle East.

There were two primary routes. The first went from Germany to Spain and then onward to Argentina. The second from Germany to Rome, Rome to Genoa and then to South America. Initially these routes developed independently but over time they functioned under one umbrella.

The origins of these first lines of escape grew out of ongoing negotiations taking part between the Vatican and Argentina, both before and during the war. As part of these negotiations, Pope Pius XII who believed that the Axis powers would win the war, proposed open borders for would-be immigrants from Europe. The Vatican succeeded in getting the Argentinians to agree that after the war, European Catholics, who felt themselves in mortal danger, could immigrate to their country.

The Argentine Foreign Minister cabled his Ambassador to the Vatican suggesting that the two neutral states, Argentina and the Vatican, might mediate the eventual peace.

On October sixth of nineteen fourth-two, Ambassador Llobet replied to the Foreign Minister that he had met with a representative of Pius XII, Monsignor Luigi Maglione, who: *'suggested to me that the pontiff would be interested in knowing the willingness of the government of the Argentine Republic to apply its immigration laws generously, in order to encourage at the opportune moment European Catholic immigrants to seek the necessary land and capital in our country.'*

The intention of the Vatican to join Argentina in the mediation of a peace after the Axis powers had won the war was to allow Germany to gain a bridge to the western hemisphere. The peace as the two parties envisioned it was also to be sweetened for the mediators themselves in that it would allow Argentina to take control of the Falkland Islands and the Vatican to be named as the governor of the city of Jerusalem.

Subsequently, a German priest stationed in Rome, Father Anton Weber, who headed the Rome branch of the St. Raphael Society, an organization that gave assistance to Catholic immigrants, traveled to Portugal with the intention of continuing on to Argentina, to lay the groundwork for the future immigration of Catholics. These steps taken by the Catholic Church would later be exploited by the Nazis who wished to flee Germany and the occupied countries toward and after the end of the Second World War.

* * * * *

- Lebensraum -

SS involvement in the process of influence with regard to the occupied territories was growing with each rise of Himmler's star-status within the inner circle.

Under Rosenberg's original plan, two more administrative divisions in addition to *'Ostland'* and *'Ukraine'* were to be created in the occupied trattorias. These were to be *'Reichskommissariat Moskowien'*, which would include Metropolitan Moscow and large tracts of European Russia, followed by *'Reichskommissariat Kaukasus'* in the Caucuses.

Himmler intended to see to it that the SS ensured that *'The Final Solution'* to the Jewish question, as well as the enslavement of Slavic inhabitants as slave labourers for use on the estates granted to SS soldiers after the conquest of Russia, became a reality. This despite Rosenberg's position on the handling of the Slavs.

Himmler's perpetual striving to see to it that the SS wormed its way into all aspects of life in the new Reich and continued to enrich his own struggle to build a personal empire, recognized no boundaries.

The Reichsfuhrer's view of the future was that each of these new SS *'soldier peasants'* would be expected to father at least seven children and that all German women would have as many children as possible in order to populate the newly acquire Eastern territories. To facilitate this policy of extreme fertility, he ordered the *'Lebensborn Program'* expanded and the creation of a state decoration to be known as the *'Gold Honor Cross of the German Mother.* This new award was to be given to German women who bore at least eight children for the Third Reich. He and his ally, Martin Bormann, began to push for new marriage legislation to facilitate population growth. The envisioned new law would allow all decorated war heroes to marry an additional wife. Himmler's SS plans envisaged a German population of three hundred million by the year two thousand.

* * * * *

- Deportations -

On the fifth of October, Himmler ordered all Jews in concentration camps in Germany to be sent to Auschwitz and Majdanek.

On the twenty-fifth of the month, Himmler ordered the deportation of Jews from Norway to Auschwitz.

On the twenty-eighth the first transport from Theresienstadt concentration camp, located approximately forty miles north or Prague, arrived at Auschwitz.

* * * * *

- Ghettos -

- Minsk -

Between November of forty-one and October of forty-two, over twenty thousand prisoners from Germany and the Protectorate of Bohemia and Moravia were deported to Minsk. A good number of these had been given *'Special Handling'* upon their arrival in Maly Trostinets, a small village located about eight miles to the east. The remainder were housed in a separate ghetto in Minsk. Here they were segregated, German Jews from local Belarusian Jews. Little contact was permitted between the residents of the two ghettos.

Inmates here were used as forced labour on projects in factories constructed within the ghetto, as well as on projects outside in the Shiroka Street labour camp and the operas house, where Jewish private property was sorted and stored.

* * * * *

- Mizocz -

This Polish ghetto was located in the town of Mizocz. On October twelfth the seventeen hundred occupants were surrounded by Ukrainian auxiliaries and German police in preparation for its liquidation.

Once rounded up the internees were marched to a ravine where they were shot and buried.

* * * * *

- Concentration/ Transit - Camps -

- Janowska -

In September of forty-one, the Germans set up a factory in the suburbs of Lvov, on Janowska Street. It was one of the network of factories owned and operated by the SS which were called *'Deutsche Ausruestungswerke'* (DAW), and were staffed by forced labourers who worked mostly in carpentry and metalwork. The SS constructed a camp to house these workers next to the factory in October of that year.

In addition to use as a forced-labour camp, Janowska was also employed as a transit camp during the mass deportation of Polish Jews to the *'Special Handling'* centers during forty-two. Arriving inmates underwent a selection process there similar to that used at Auschwitz-Birkenau and Majdanek. Those classified as fit for work remained in the camp as forced labourers and those rejected as unfit were deported to Belzec or shot at the Piaski ravine which was located just north of the camp.

Over the summer and fall of forty-two, thousands of internees were deported from the Lvov ghetto to Janowska.

* * * * *

- Medical Experiments -

- Horst Schumann -

SS-Major, Dr. Horst Schumann was born in *'Halle an der Saale'* on May first, nineteen-six. He joined the Nazi party in nineteen thirty and the SA in nineteen thirty-two. He received his medical degree in nineteen thirty-three and commenced his medical career as an assistant doctor in the Surgical Clinic of the Halle University. In nineteen thirty-four he accepted employment in the Public Health Office in Halle. He was then recruited into the Air Force as a physician in thirty-nine.

In October of that year he met with Dr. Viktor Brank in Hitler's chancellery and as a result joined the *'Aktion T4'* Euthanasia program in early October of thirty-nine. Here he worked in Block 30 in the women's hospital.

In January of nineteen-forty, he became head of the Grafeneck Euthanasia Center in Wurttemberg and in the early summer of that year moved to the Sonnenstein Euthanasia Centre. He then became part of the commission of doctors named *'Aktion 14f13',* who accepted the responsibility for transferring weak and sick prisoners from Auschwitz,

Buchenwald, Dachau, Flossenburg, Gross-Rosen, Mauthausen, Neuengamme and Niederhangen concentration camps to the euthanasia killing centers.

On July twenty-eighth of forty-one, Schumann arrived at Auschwitz. On August eleventh of forty-two, Himmler, in a letter sent to SS-Oberfuhrer Brack, expressed an interest in sterilization experiments involving the use of x-rays. Schumann took an interest in this problem of finding the best way to sterilize Jews and others of inferior genetic makeup and in nineteen forty-two set up an X ray station at Auschwitz in the women's camp. Here men and women were forcibly sterilized by being positioned repeatedly for several minutes between two x-ray machines with the rays targeted at their sexual organs. Many of the personally-selected individuals died after great suffering or were gassed immediately because their radiation burns rendered them unfit for work. In confirmation of the results, men's testicles were removed and forwarded to Breslau for examination. Ovariectomies were performed on the females by the Polish prisoners, Dr. Maximillian Samuel and Dr. Wladyslav Dering.

* * * * *

- Eric -

With the exception of a welcoming extended-family dinner, Eric had found little free time since arriving back in Brazil.

Leaving the unloading of the U-boat to his crew, he spent the first several days assisting Hans in settling the latest U-boat load of passengers into newly completed housing.

Single men, who were in the majority, were to be provided with one bedroom apartments, while those who had managed to bring family members with them were given small houses.

In addition, he inspected the barracks that had been recently finished in the growing town that had sprung up to support the mineworkers. There were two of these completed and several more under construction. They would initially be used for his own U-boat crews while ashore and as time went on, for those unmarried immigrants, who would be expected towards, and after, the end of the war.

It also took him two days to tour the now-producing mine itself and more importantly, the vast underground *'Operation Fatherland'* research and development facilities now functioning below the mine.

During these busy days he found little free time and although Heidi was often accompanying him and Hans as they made their rounds of the massive and still growing facilities, he found no time to be alone with her.

She was seated beside him at meals and on numerous occasions and there had been physical contact between them, feet under the table, arms and shoulders brushing, surreptitious handholding and on one occasion a brief kiss while enjoying after dinner drinks on the large patio.

This wasn't, of course, unexpected. Both she and Eric continued to flirt and seek each other's company, just as they had on his earlier trips. But as much as Eric understood the need for their relationship to proceed within the bounds of locally acceptable behaviour, which he was painfully aware was considerably more strict in Brazil than it would have been in modern Germany, he very much wanted to make love to his beautiful fiancée and unless he was reading the signals emanating from her completely wrong, she was more than ready to comply.

He was also cognisant of the fact the other members of his expanded family in Brazil were very well aware of both their feelings on the matter and appeared to be enjoying the rising frustration registered by both participants.

It wasn't until four days before he was due to sail again for Bordeaux that the situation was to be remedied, however. For it was then, after he had taken care of his other duties and responsibilities, that Hans and his Grandfather, the Brazilian family patriarch, took him aside after dinner and the three of them retired to the old gentleman's library for port and cigars, that the topic was addressed openly.

The cigars had no more than been lit, when the elderly gentleman faced him squarely.

"I have noticed that you and my Heidi are itching to ah - how shall I put it - advance the level of your relationship."

Hans almost choked on his cigar as he struggled to withhold his mirth at the statement. His grandfather gave him a sharp look before continuing.

"You are a virile young man and she is ready for womanhood so that is to be expected. I also appreciate the fact that you, who are experience in this area I am sure, have held yourself in check and performed like a gentleman. However, under the circumstances, the war, and the necessity for you to be away for long periods, it has been recognized that certain allowances might be made. "

Hans, whose eyes had rolled up into his head, chuckled and raised his hand.

"Grandfather if I may, I think I could express this delicate matter more expeditiously, if you would allow me."

The old man shrugged and nodded his head before raising his glass to his lips and emptying it. Hans set his own glass down and shifted slightly to face Eric.

"My mother has discussed this with Heidi and my sister has made it plain that she is not prepared to accept the status quo. My mother sympathises with her and they have had an in-depth discussion resulting in the possibility that, providing Heidi does not find herself pregnant before the wedding, certain conjugal activity could take place between the two of you before you leave for your return trip to Bordeaux."

Eric didn't know what to say and only nodded. A satisfied Hans smiled and continued.

"Heidi has been thoroughly briefed by our mother on what that entails and the various ways of dealing with it. However, as it takes two to tango and well, to put it concisely, we would need your word that you will see to it that she will have no difficulty in getting into her wedding gown."

The benefits of such an arrangement being obvious to him, Eric had no hesitancy in agreeing to fulfill that particular request.

That evening and for the next three days, Heidi and Eric were allowed to slip away after dinner and nothing was said when they arrived somewhat dishevelled and in tandem, for breakfast the next morning although one couldn't help but note that Heidi's complexion had become radiant and that she could not keep her eyes off Eric who was likewise affected. Additionally the tension in the air that had earlier surrounded all concerned. had disappeared overnight.

* * * * *

- Ursula -

Confirmed!

Ursula's pregnancy was confirmed by her doctor and as her Mother was about to return to Oslo within a few days with the family's private railcars in order to pick up Gabriella's family for the return trip to the castle, she informed her mother of her condition immediately. A delighted Erika, threw herself enthusiastically into rushing the remodelling of the nursery and arranging for additional staff, with renewed determination.

* * * * *

- Gabriella -

Konrad had indeed received Himmler's active support for the move to join the Baron in his genetic research.

The job Konrad had been sent to fulfill in Norway had, by all accounts, gone well and it appeared to Himmler that the accomplishments from Konrad's endeavours could be reasonably expected to produce an end result in Norway that was predicted to rival Germany's own *'Lebensborn'* hopes for the expansion of the Aryan peoples.

He informed Konrad that while the *'Lebensborn'* program would improve the outlook in the short-term, he had very high expectations that the results of the genetic research would likely lead to a more successful achievement in the reaching of the long-term goal of doing everything possible to meet the expanding births that the ever-growing Reichs would require in the future.

* * * * *

- Wilhelm -

As a result of the successful launch of the *'A-4'*, Wilhelm, who was now heavily involved in the research and development of super weapons, had just returned from Peenemunde.

At the site he was provided with a showing of the film taken during the successful flight and upon request, been provided with a copy of that highly classified depiction.

Upon his return to Belin he'd run the film for his father and the Count had suggested they take advantage of their new-found ability to meet freely with the Fuhrer, to be the first to present him with the results of the test flight.

As the Countess intended to pick him and Wilhelm up on her return trip from Oslo with Gabriella and her family so that they could join them for the onward leg of the journey to the castle, he quickly requested a meeting with Hitler and found it rapidly granted.

He and Wilhelm immediately set out for *'Fuhrer-hauptquartier Werwolf'* the next day and upon arrival, spent almost three hours with Hitler, who was ecstatic with the successful launch depicted on the film and decreed that he would use it and the flying bombs to drive the British into submission.

He invited Wilhelm and the Count to join him for lunch.

The invitation to lunch was noted with displeasure by Hitler's regular entourage at the forward compound, who had been exiled from sharing meals with Hitler since his recent bout of paranoia and his resulting general mistrust for his military advisors.

CHAPTER TWENTY

- October -

- Allied Air Operations -

RAF Bomber Command targets Cologne, Essen and Flensburg.

British and US aircraft strike at France by both night and day and from British bases, RAF bombers hit targets in Italy with emphasis on Milan, Turing and Genoa.

In total the British drop four thousand, one hundred tons and the US, three hundred tons.

* * * * *

- Battle of the Atlantic -

Total Allied shipping losses amount to six hundred and thirty-seven thousand, eight hundred tons. Axis submarines account for ninety-four ships or six hundred and nineteen thousand tons. The most promising hunting grounds for U-boats are off the coast of Trinidad.

* * * * *

- October First -

- New Guinea -

Australian forces begin to move forward along the Kokoda Trail while a US contingent moves over the parallel Kapa Kapa Trail, with the intention of joining with the Australians to cut off the Japanese retreat at the Kumusi River.

Additionally there are planed landings along the north coast, between Milne Bay and Cape Nelson.

* * * * *

- October Second -

- Ireland -

The British cruiser HMS *'Curacao'*, escorting the liner, *'Queen Mary'* which has been converted to a troop-transport, collides with the massive ship and is sunk off the coast.

* * * * *

- South Pacific -

The US begins construction of a base on Funafuti Atoll in the Ellice Islands.

* * * * *

- October Fourth -

A British commando raid takes place on the Channel Island of Sark. They take one German prisoner and execute several others. Hitler is appalled at their action and responds forcefully with orders aimed at future commando allied actions.

* * * * *

- Eastern Front -

Having regrouped, General Paulus starts a new series of attacks within Stalingrad. He has received reinforcements of combat-engineers and police units to help with the street fighting.

* * * * *

- New Guinea -

The Australians pursuing the retreating Japanese forces down the Kokoda Trail take Effogi and advance toward Kagi and Myola.

* * * * *

- October Sixth -

- US -

Roosvelt signs a new Lend-Lease agreement which will deliver to the Russians four million, four hundred thousand tons of supplies between now and July of forty-three.

* * * * *

- Allied Air Operations -

RAF Bomber Command and the US 8th Army Air Force reach agreement on a new bombing strategy. The British will send out their bombers at night and the Americans will fly daylight missions.

* * * * *

- Eastern Front -

The Germans take the oil-producing center of Malgobek located in the Caucuses near Mozdok and push on toward the Terek.

* * * * *

- October Seventh -

- War Crimes -

The US and Britain initiate a United Nations Commission to investigate Axis war crimes. As a condition of any armistice, war criminals are to be handed over for trial.

* * * * *

- Guadalcanal -

The 1st Marine Division breaks free from the American beachhead and is able to overrun the majority of the Japanese artillery emplacements as they take up positions at the mouth of the Matanikau River in support of the troops holding Henderson Field.

* * * * *

- South Africa -

A group of four U-boats operating off the coast sinks a total of one hundred and seventy thousand tons of allied shipping.

* * * * *

- October Eighth -

- Belgium -

The Germans initiate a program to register all males between the ages of eighteen and fifty and all unmarried women between twenty-one and thirty-five for war work, in order to shore up Germany's growing manpower shortages.

* * * * *

- October Ninth -

- Guadalcanal -

The Americans attack west of the Matanikau and destroy a Japanese battalion.

* * * * *

- Madagascar -

British East African forces go on the offensive and begin to move south from the capital at Tananarive in an initiative to link up with troops landed to their south in late September.

* * * * *

- Russia -

Stalin's trust in his new military commanders is demonstrated when command authority of the Commissars in the Red Army have their authority revoked. Commissars will no longer make military decisions, which will now rest entirely with the unit commanding officers. Commissars are also now restricted to responsibility over moral and propaganda only.

* * * * *

- October Eleventh -

- Stalingrad -

Russian reinforcements crossing the Volga in support of

the city are growing and the fighting comes to a standstill on both sides.

* * * * *

- Guadalcanal -

In the battle of Cape Esperance, a naval confrontation off the northwest coast, the Japanese lose a cruiser and a destroyer and sustain damage to two additional cruisers. The Americans lose a destroyer and suffer serious damage to two cruisers and a destroyer. The next day two additional Japanese destroyers are sunk in an air attack by planes from Henderson Field.

* * * * *

- October Twelfth -

- Atlantic -

The first successful sinking of a U-boat in the Atlantic by a long-range bomber, a British Liberator, from the single operational RAF Coastal Command squadron, occurs when U-597 is sunk.

* * * * *

- October Thirteenth -

- Guadalcanal -

Smarting from the effectiveness of the bombers based at Henderson Field in regard to their naval operations, the Japanese bring up the battleships *'Konga'* and *'Haruna'* to bombard the field. The big ship's heavy armament is devastating, destroying more than half the compliment of American planes, approximately fifty aircraft.

While this overnight attack is going on the Japanese take advantage of the disruption in US air support caused by the bombardment to send a group of destroyers and transports to land four thousand, five hundred troops and a huge quantity of supplies at Tassafaronga.

* * * * *

- October Fourteenth -

- Stalingrad -

Hitler orders all offensive action suspended except in Stalingrad and a small area in the Caucuses. Five German Divisions with heavy air support attack the Russian defensive strong point around the Tractor Factory and come to within a hair's breadth of breaking through.

* * * * *

- Canada -

The ferry, *'SS Caribou'* operating between Port aux Basques in Newfoundland and North Sydney, Nova Scotia, is sunk by U-69 in the Cabot Strait, killing one hundred and thirty-seven civilians, including many women and children.

* * * * *

- English Channel -

The German raider *'Komet'* is sunk by the British.

* * * * *

- October Fifteenth -

- Stalingrad -

The reinforced German forces at the Tractor Factory are making ground and reach the Volga a short distance to the north of the massive main complex.

* * * * *

- October Eighteenth -

- Fuhrerhauptquartier Werwolf -

Hitler issues his new *'Commando Order'* in response to the British commando attack against the channel Island of Sark.

* * * * *

- Pacific -

Admiral William *'Bull'* Halsey is given command of the South Pacific naval forces.

* * * * *

- New Guinea -

The US force moving along the Kapa Kapa Trail begins to arrive at Pongani.

* * * * *

- October Twenty-First -

- Eastern Front -

The German forces in Stalingrad make their main thrust

at the Barrikady Factory and housing estate. The battles fought against the defending forces are fierce with a good deal of horrendous street-fighting, but result in little gain.

* * * * *

- New Guinea -

Australian troops on the Kokoda Trail are closing on the min Japanese position at Eora. Momentum has been slowed due to heavy terrain and supply problems.

* * * * *

- October Twenty- Second -

- London -

Conscription is reduce to Eighteen years.

* * * * *

- Guadalcanal -

Japanese forces attack over the Matanikau, supported by tanks. They are repulsed and receive heavy losses from well-positioned US artillery.

* * * * *

- New Guinea -

Australian troops land on Goodenough Island.

* * * * *

- Algeria -

US General Mark Clark lands in great secrecy to confer with Vichy officials and resistance groups in preparation for an impending Allied invasion.

* * * * *

- Stalingrad -

The first winter snow falls.

* * * * *

- October Twenty-Third -

- North Africa -

The Second Battle of El Alamein begins with a massive Allied bombardment of the German defensive positions. Allied forces, mainly Australian, begin to advance while offshore British naval units support their right flank.

The next day, General Stumme, commanding Axis forces while Rommel is absent, suffers a heart attack and dies. Rommel receives orders to return from Germany immediately.

* * * * *

- Burma -

The majority of the British force has advanced to Cox's Bazaar and forward units have reached Buthidaung. Here they meet the Japanese formation which has pushed up from Akyab. The Japanese manage to hold their lines.

* * * * *

- October Twenty-Fourth -

- US -

The US Naval Task Force 34, which is made up of aircraft carriers and a variety of support and troop ships, plus auxiliary vessels, sails from Hampton Roads, Virginia. They carry General Patton's forces slated for *'Operation Torch'* the impending landing in North Africa. Two other task forces destined for *'Torch'*, which will be the first American-led force to fight in the European and African theaters of war, also depart from Britain, headed for Morocco.

* * * * *

- October Twenty-Fifth -

- North Africa -

Rommel begins his return trip from his sick-leave in Germany in order to retake command of the German forces.

Montgomery personally intervenes in the battle at El Alamein ordering X Corps to push forward vigorously. The resulting Allied losses are heavy, approximately two hundred and fifty tanks, but after the attack the defending Germans are left with only forty operational panzers.

* * * * *

- October Twenty-Sixth -

- Guadalcanal -

- Battle of Santa Cruz -

Determined to oust the Marines at Henderson Field, the Japanese send in four battleships and the carriers *'Shokaku'*, *'Zuikaku'*, *'Zuiho'* and *'Junyo'* as well as a fleet of cruisers and destroyers. Their plan is to support their land forces, take the air base, and load it with their own planes from the carriers. As has happened before, this powerful naval presence arrives divided into four different fleets. As a result the aircraft carriers are not accompanied by a battleship and do not therefore have the fierce defensive anti-aircraft firepower of a major ship. The defending US naval forces in the area include two carriers *'Enterprise' and 'Hornet'*, and both of these have a battleship as part of their escort.

When the dust settles the USS *'Hornet'* has been sunk and the *'Enterprise'* is damaged. The Japanese lose a great number of aircraft and two of their carriers are severely damaged.

Both sides withdraw to lick their wounds.

* * * * *

- North Africa -

The British attack against El Alamein is making little progress and Montgomery halts to regroup. When Churchill hears about this, he is furious.

Rommel orders counter-attacks.

* * * * *

- Eastern Front -

In the Caucuses the Germans take Nalchik.

* * * * *

- October Twenty-Seventh -

- North Africa -

British forces are regrouping. Rommel launches a counter-offensive against the defenders at Kidney Ridge but is beaten back by a small but well-entrenched British force.

* * * * *

- Stalingrad -

German forces gain ground in the area between the Red October and Barrikady Factories. With these successes they are now in position to bring the Russian landing stages on the west bank of the Volga under direct machine gun fire. The remaining Russian-held defensive areas are now only about three hundred yards deep. The Russians however, are no longer throwing all their troops into these actions. Instead they are repeatedly blooding new arrivals and then moving them into reserve.

* * * * *

- Guadalcanal -

The Japanese call off their offensive naval forces after suffering thirty-five hundred casualties.

* * * * *

- October Twenty-Eighth-

- North Africa -

The attacking Australians make some progress overnight and Montgomery begins to plan to shift his attack to bring it to bear against the Italian defenders opposite Kidney Ridge.

* * * * *

-Malta -

HMS *'Furious'* delivers a cargo of Spitfires. The city is getting very short of food and armaments, with replacements being brought in by submarine and a fast minelayer. The Axis powers are well aware of the desperate situation currently faced by the defending Allied forces.

* * * * *

- October Twenty-Ninth -

- Guadalcanal -

The Japanese continue to send reinforcing troops.

* * * * *

- New Guinea -

The Australians send in a final attack against Japanese defensive positions at Eora, pushing the Japanese out. General Vasey takes over command of the 7th Australian Division from General Allen, who Churchill sees as insufficiently forceful.

* * * * *

- Madagascar -

East African troops take Fianarantsoa, the strategic town in the south of the island and continue to push toward the final defensive positions held by the Vichy forces.

* * * * *

- British Isles -

The US 1st armoured Division moves from Northern Ireland to England.

* * * * *

- October Thirtieth -

- New Guinea -

The Australians have reach Aloha which is situated about ten miles south of Kokoda. A single brigade is sent toward Kokoda while the other takes a more easterly rout toward Oivi.

* * * * *

- October Thirty-First -

- North Africa -

British forces make a critical advance with armour west of El Alamein. The area has been heavily mined by the Germans but they break through nonetheless.

CHAPTER TWENTY-ONE

- November -

- Hitler -

November can be considered a major turning point in the war for Germany.

On both the Eastern and Western fronts the Allies have begun to score victories against the exhausted and war-worn German troops and armour.

The battle of attrition has begun.

Hitler, still ensconced at *'Fuhrerhauptquartier Werwolf'*, has his full attention concentrated on the Eastern Front, and subsequently, the conquest of Egypt had paid a price.

With the pyramids almost on the horizon, a frustrated Rommel is no longer receiving the supplies and reinforcements he requires for the job and he is forced onto the defensive.

The British forces have been concentrating on and have pierced his southern flank which had been held by Italian troops. He radios for permission to retreat and on the night of November second Hitler sends his predictable reply:

'Do not fall back one inch. The troops must triumph or die.'

Before he receives Hitler's terse message, the Desert Fox has made his own decision to the contrary and has begun to withdraw. He radios to that effect and his message reaches the OKW in the early hours of the morning, shortly after three. When it is received, the duty officer, who has no knowledge of Hitler's earlier message, does not feel that Rommel's second message for the Fuhrer is important enough to pass on to Hitler at that hour.

When Hitler awakes, the message is given to him and he goes ballistic.

He immediately summonses the deputy of operations, Walter Warlimont, but as the man begins down the hallway toward Hitler's office, Keitel shouts at him:

'You, Warlimont, come here! Hitler doesn't want to ever see you again!'

Keitel then informs the astonished man that he is relieved of his post.

On November seventh at the midday briefing conference, the OKW receives a report that a large armada of Allied ships has entered the Mediterranean and is now approaching the north coast of Africa.

These ships had been spotted earlier when just outside Gibraltar and Hitler and the OKW had assumed that they were bound for Sardinia or Sicily. This assumption was based on the sense that their relatively gentile treatment of Vichy France would certainly ensure that no French territory under Vichy control would ever consider turning coat. Now, it appeared very likely that a landing was being made in Vichy territory and that suggested that a plot must have been hatched with the Vichy forces located there.

His senior officers were much alarmed by this turn of events but Hitler brushed it aside. At that point he cut the briefing short and he and his senior officers boarded his private train and headed to Munich for the celebration of the nineteenth anniversary of the Putsch.

Hitler was asleep when the first British and American troops landed on the beaches of Morocco and Algeria.

The initial reports reaching OKW indicated that the French troops were resisting the landings and when the Fuhrer awoke he reproached his advisers for their initial panic over the landings. He then calmly ordered reinforcements sent to Crete at the far end of the Mediterranean and turned his attention to preparation for the address he was to deliver to the party faithful at the *'Lowenbraukeller'* later that evening.

When he spoke Hitler struck out at the defeatists that were questioning his determination to take the city which: *'happens to bear the name of Stalin'*, comparing it to the Great

War battle at Verdun and the cost of that action to the German forces.

He emphasized that he was no Wilhelm II, who he referred to as a weakling, who had surrendered the Reich's vast Eastern conquests because of a few traitors desperate for an accommodation with the West:

'All our enemies may rest assured that while the Germany of that time laid down its arms at a quarter to twelve, I on principle have never finished before five minutes past twelve.'

Despite the strength of conviction he'd delivered in his speech at Munich, Hitler could not ignore the seriousness of the reports from Africa that were reaching the OKW by late evening.

Hitler had von Ribbentrop summon Mussolini for an immediate conference. The Italian Foreign Minister, Glan Galeazzo Ciano, Mussolini's son-in-law, was hauled out of his bed for the second time in twenty-four hours and reluctantly disturbed Il Duce's sleep to pass on the message, but Mussolini, who was ill, refused to make the trip to Bavaria. He had no stomach for a meeting with Hitler under the current circumstances. He ordered Ciano to go in his stead.

By the time Ciano arrived in Munich, Hitler had accepted that the situation in North Africa was dire. Depressed, he said:

'The God of war had now turned from Germany and gone over to the other camp.'

Von Ribbentrop counselled Hitler to approach Stalin through Madame Kollontai, the Russian ambassador in Stockholm, with the proposal that most of the occupied territories in the East be given up, and Hitler leaped to his feet and shouted:

'All I want to discuss is Africa ... nothing else!'

The Japanese took advantage of this change in balance in North Africa by leaping onto the bandwagon, also suggesting that Hitler pursue a peace agreement with Stalin. They went on to formally request that the Germans take up a defensive position in Russia and immediately shift the bulk of their forces to the West.

Hitler politely advised the Japanese ambassador, Oshima, that he was unable to do that due to the fact that it was impossible to dig defensive positions in a country as cold as Russia.

This was purely diplomacy of course. Hitler had two personal missions, the first to destroy Bolshevism and the second to eradicate the Jews from Europe. He had absolutely no intention of backing off from his determination to wipe the Russians off the map.

The rumour mill in Berlin was running with a full head of steam. Hitler was mad, he had to be. No one was prepared to say this to the Fuhrer of course, but among trusted others, and in private, such talk was becoming common.

* * * * *

- Inner Circle -

- Erich Raeder/ Karl Donitz -

By nineteen forty-two Raeder was increasingly being overshadowed by Donitz. The German navy was decidedly separate when it came to oversight under the two Admirals. Although Raeder was technically Donitz's superior, it was Donitz who commanded the U-boats and it was the U-boats that were making the big scores for Germany, not the surface fleet.

The two men disliked each other intensely and Donitz, who made little secret of his contempt for the *'battleship Admiral'*, had started to move independently of his superior in as many ways as he could. He was now going head to head with Raeder over new construction and had gone over his head in dealing directly with Speer in setting construction targets for the U-boats.

In the autumn of forty-two, Raeder moved to limit Donitz's power by taking from him the responsibility for the training of U-boat crews. Donitz responded by informing

Raeder that he was disregarding that order and he continued to train the crews for *'his'* U-boats.

Raeder was furious and longed to replace Donitz, but in view of the fact that Donitz was without doubt the most expert of all the Kriegsmarine Admirals when it came to U-boat warfare and appeared on the verge of winning the Battle of the Atlantic, his chances of having Hitler support such a move was beyond slim.

Donitz was a fanatical National Socialist and without question Hitler's favorite admiral. It was for that reason that Raeder held his nose and always took Donitz with him when he went to see Hitler to lobby for more naval funding. Raeder valued his own position and recognized that he needed Donitz in his current command in order to ensure that the German navy could maintain a viable seat at Hitler's table.

* * * * *

- French Fleet -

A German plan to occupy Vichy France had initially been drawn up in December of nineteen-forty under the codename of *'Operation Attila'* and had evolved. It was now incorporated with the plan to occupy Corsica and considered as a single operation.

This plan was now renamed *'Case Anton'* and envisioned as a joint German/Italian operation.

Following the Allied landing in French North Africa on November eighth of nineteen forty-two in *'Operation Torch,* Hitler could not risk an exposed flank on the French Mediterranean and following a final conversation with puppet French Premier, Pierre Laval, Hitler gave orders for Corsica to be occupied on November eleventh and Vichy France on the following day.

As part of this operation the Germans were to capture the French fleet based at Toulon.

By the evening of November tenth, Axis forces had

completed their preparations for *'Anton'*. The German First Army advanced from the Atlantic coast, parallel to the Spanish border while the German Seventh Army progressed from central France toward Vichy and Toulon. The Italian 4th Army occupied the French Riviera and an Italian division landed on Corsica. By the night of November eleventh, German tanks had reached the Mediterranean coast.

The puppet government of Vichy France limited its active resistance to the invasion to radio broadcasts objecting to this violation of the armistice of nineteen-forty. The Vichy French Army, fifty thousand strong, initially took up defensive positions around Toulon, but when confronted by German demands to disband, they immediately complied.

The German aim was to capture intact the demobilized French Fleet at Toulon. French Naval commanders however, promptly scuttled their ships on November twenty-seventh before the Germans could seize them. Three battleships, seven cruisers, twenty-eight destroyers and twenty submarines went down. The German navy was disappointed with this result, but Hitler held to his original determination that he did not want the fleet and that its destruction meant the success of the operation and had determined that the Free French forces of de Gaulle would never be able to utilize the fleet against him.

* * * * *

- Ghettos -

- Majdan Tatarski -

This ghetto had been established in April of nineteen forty-two and held approximately five thousand. It was shut down and the remaining inmates were sent to Majdanek in November.

* * * * *

- Castle von Stauffer -

All of the immediate family, with the exception of Eric, whose U-boat was en route from Brazil to France, were now happily ensconced at the castle.

Erika, Ursula and Gabriella were working on the new arrangements of family apartments that would now be needed and the organization of the remodelling that involved, as well as overseeing the upgrading of the nursery and the interviewing and hiring of additional staff.

The Count, Wilhelm, Konrad and the Baron were working on the staffing and upgrading for the new genetic research facilities that, thanks to Himmler's support and a massive flow of SS Reichsmarks, were under renovation in the town itself.

CHAPTER TWENTY-TWO

- November -

- Allied Air Operations -

Bomber Command's raids on German soil are reduced over this month. Hamburg and Stutgart are hit and in France, La Pallice, St. Nazaire and Le Havre are targeted. Heavy raids are also sent against Turin and Genoa as well as sorties against Sicily and Sardinia.

The RAF drops twenty-six hundred tons and the American Eighth Air Force in excess of six hundred and fifty.

* * * * *

- Maritime Warfare -

At the beginning of the month the Nazis have approximately one hundred operation U-boats.

Successful U-boat operations in the Atlantic increase with one hundred and nineteen ships being sunk for a total of seven hundred and twenty-nine thousand, one hundred tons.

Overall tonnage sunk reaches eight hundred and seven thousand, seven hundred tons, with one hundred and thirty-one thousand tons sunk in the Pacific and Indian Oceans.

The Germans lose thirteen U-boats and the Italians, four.

* * * * *

- Yugoslav Resistance -

The Yugoslav National Anti-Fascist Liberation Council meets openly in Bihac, Croatia. The Partisan forces are now well enough organized to begin to create the apparatus of government. Courts and other administrative bodies are operating under the protection of the Partisan forces.

* * * * *

- Atomic Research -

At the University of Chicago, under the supervisor of Enrico Fermi, work begins on the first atomic pile.

* * * * *

- November First -

- North Africa -

The Allied breakout from El Alamein, codenamed *'Operation Supercharge'*, begins.

* * * * *

- Eastern Front -

In the Caucasus the German advance grinds on. Alagir, the strategic road junction thirty miles west of Ordzhonikidze is taken by the First Panzer Army.

* * * * *

- Guadalcanal -

Two Marine regiments begin to push west across the Matanikau River, while additional American units start to advance east of the bridgehead toward Koli Point where intelligence indicates a Japanese landing is imminent.

* * * * *

- November Third -

-Guadalcanal -

In the morning a fifteen hundred strong Japanese force land at Koli Point. They are immediately engaged by the Americans and soon forced to pull back.

* * * * *

- North Africa -

The Allies are struggling to make their way through the German-laid minefields and dug in artillery as Rommel gives the order to withdraw his forces. Hitler orders him to hold his ground and some of the Axis units are halted. This makes for a dangerous situation for Rommel but luckily for the Germans, the British seem unable to take immediate advantage.

* * * * *

- November Fourth -

- North Africa -

X Corps reaches open ground. Intense fighting begins and the Ariete, the 90th Light and German Headquarters, all take a battering from the British forces. In short order Rommel's troops are retreating toward Fuka. Montgomery orders pursuit but British forces fail to engage. The Eighth Army has taken thirty thousand prisoners, captured one thousand guns and the shattered remains of four hundred and fifty tanks.

British and Commonwealth troops have taken thirteen

thousand five hundred casualties, lost one hundred and fifty tanks and suffered damage to another three hundred. The Italians can no longer be considered as a fighting force and the German Divisors are now left at no more than Regiment strength.

* * * * *

- Mediterranean -

In response to higher allied shipping sightings off Gibraltar, the Axis have concentrated a group of nineteen German and twenty-one Italian subs which begin active patrols in the area.

* * * * *

- November Fifth -

- New Guinea -

The Australians begin to advance against Oivi and the Japanese begin to fight a rearguard actions as they retreat across the Kumusi River.

* * * * *

- North Africa -

Rommel is forced to retreat from Fuka and his Italian infantry is hammered. The British pursuers are now suffering by a longer supply line as fuel grows low and a minefield blocks their pursuit. In time they come to the realizations that the minefield is a dummy that they fabricated themselves months before.

* * * * *

- Madagascar -

Vichy French forces ask for an armistice and negotiations begin, ending in an agreement which is signed on the sixth.

* * * * *

- Eastern Front -

German forces south of the Terek in the Caucasus fight their way toward Ordzhonikidze but they are rapidly losing momentum.

* * * * *

- Gibraltar -

General Eisenhower arrives and sets up his headquarters. The naval forces are to be commanded by Admiral Cunningham; General Doolittle and Air Marshal Welsh are appointed to command the air forces; and General Anderson will command the British First Army, which is the main contingent of the land force.

* * * * *

- North Africa -

The supply starved Eighth Army is making a disjointed attempt at the pursuit of Rommel's forces. The 7th Armoured Division manages to overtake and destroy the remnants of the 21st Panzer, which finds itself out of fuel and stranded. Towards evening heavy rain begins to fall leaving only the coast road as a viable means of travel, restricting the freedom of movement even further.

* * * * *

- November Seventh -

- North Africa -

Ragged British forces enter Mersa Matruh to find the vast majority of Rommel's remaining battered forces already gone.

* * * * *

- Gibraltar -

The British submarine `Seraph' arrives carrying French General Henri Giraud for talks with Eisenhower. The Allies wish to use the involvement of a more prominent French military officer than de Gaulle for `Operation Torch`, in the hope that it will minimize resistance from any forces who remain loyal to the puppet Vichy French government.

Giraud has somehow been led to believe that he will be taking command of the operation but upon his arrival, Eisenhower quickly disabuses him of any such notion.

* * * * *

- November Eighth -

- French North Africa -

'Operation Torch', the Allied invasion of Vichy-controlled Morocco and Algeria begins. It consists of three main components.

The Western Task Force has sailed directly from the US. General Patton commands the thirty-five thousand troops who make the planned three landings on a two hundred mile front centered on Casablanca. Its naval component consists of a fleet carrier, four escort carriers and a litany of cruisers and destroyers under the command of Admiral Hewitt.

The Centre Task Force, landing at Oran consists of thirty-nine thousand troops under the command of General Fredendall and Commodore Troubridge. Its naval unit consists of two escort carriers and a host of support ships.

The Eastern Task Force lands at Algiers and is led by General Ryder and Admiral Burrough. They command thirty-three thousand soldiers and fifty-two warships.

US troops are being used in the hope that the Vichy defenders will look upon them with less animosity than if they were British. The only large British assault force taking part is the 78h Division which is part of the Eastern Task Force.

Overall naval cover for 'Torch' is supplied by British Force H from Gibraltar under Admiral Syfet and consists of three battleships, three fleet carriers and a considerable screening force of cruisers and destroyers.

The landing at Algiers initially goes very well. The town is quickly captured, as is Admiral Darlan who happens to be visiting.

The landings on Oran include an initial thrust against the harbour which results in the loss of two destroyers. By nightfall progress is good and the troops form an excellent beachhead. The airfield at Tafarai is taken and American-piloted spitfires take up residence. The strongest resistance is in Casablanca where the French battleship *'Jean Bart'*, which is immobile, chooses to take on the USS *'Massachusetts'* in a test of strength, and the French destroyer flotilla also decides to fight. The exchange of fire is soon over as the French destroyers are pushed off or sunk. The other landings of the Western Task Force have varied challenges, Safi going very well but facing strong resistance at Port Lyautey. Eighteen hundred Allied casualties are taken. Pre-planning arrangements have elicited the help of groups of French supporters for the Allied cause. Algiers is the best example of this early work. Here, General Mast does a good deal to hold back the French reaction to the landings, allowing the allied troops to gain a good foothold. His superior, General Juin, does not actively oppose the landings but in the interest of lessening the expected repercussions on the French mainland, moves to make a small show of resistance.

The fact that Admiral Darlan happens to be in the city on a non-official visit and is captured takes both Mast and the Allied leaders by complete surprise. Darlan is one of the principle leaders of the puppet Vichy French government and it is readily understood by all concerned that he could have great influence over the reactions of the defending Vichy forces to the Allied invasion, if he chooses to do so. Upon his capture, immediate negotiations commence.

In Casablanca, General Bethouart is also trying to negotiate with the military leaders of the Vichy defenders. His is an uphill battle as General Nogues isn't particularly sympathetic to the allied cause and the commanding admiral of the strong Vichy French naval force, Admiral Michelier, who is still smarting over the earlier British attack against the French fleet. is strongly anti-British

The Allies are attempting to tightrope walk a razorblade while doing their best to negotiate their victory rather than to have to fight it. They know full well that the Vichy French harbor deep resentment over the British attack against the French Fleet early in the war and they have taken great pains to paint the invasion as an American, not a British action.

While the vast majority of the naval strength for 'Torch' is British, the ground troops and the negotiators are all American. In the prep work for the invasion, it was the Americans who worked at building support in the Vichy territories for the allied cause.

The British, who had better relations with the Spanish and Portuguese had, however, undertaken the pre-invasion negotiations with those countries which were necessary to ensure that a German move, after the launch of the invasion, to send reinforcing troops through Spain to Gibraltar, would not be entertained.

Roosevelt and Eisenhower make broadcasts to the French. The British see to it that the Germans would have to respect Spanish neutrality. The Allies, who had by this point, sidelined de Gaulle as best they could, had not even told him about *'Torch'* and although he is furious, he later swallows his pride and also broadcast his support for the move to the French people.

* * * * *

- Eastern Front -

In the Caucasus the Russians go over to the offensive in an attack on the Terek front and threaten to encircle some units of III Panzer Corps.

* * * * *

- November Ninth -

- Operation Torch -

US forces secure the beachhead at Casablanca. The French bring tanks into play at Port Lyautey. Oran is holding out. French Prime Minister Laval gives the go ahead for the Germans to use airfields in Tunisia and German troops are immediately flown in. General Giraud arrives in Algiers to support the Allied side but by this point US General Clark realizes that of the two, Darlan is likely to hold more support and continues to negotiate for him to turn to the allied side.

In public, Petain is vigorously opposing the invasion, but in private he is encouraging Darlan to negotiate with the Allies.

* * * * *

- November Tenth -

- Operation Troch -

The US forces take Oran, Algeria. The French scuttle seventeen of their ships in the harbor rather than accept an offer for them to join the allied naval forces.

Patton's forces move into Casablanca and Admiral Darlan chooses to turncoat, signs an armistice and broadcasts orders to all defending French land forces to cease fighting. He sends the same message to the powerful French fleet moored at Toulon.

Additional Allied landings are made near the Tunisian border.

$$* * * * *$$

- Munich -

Hitler summons Ciano and Laval to discuss the situation in French North Africa and agreement is reached over Hitler's wish to hold onto as much territory as possible.

Hitler, upon hearing of the armistice signed by Admiral Francois Darlan with the allies in North Africa, breaches the nineteen-forty German/French armistice by ordering his troops to invade Vichy France.

$$* * * * *$$

- North Africa -

Stepping off from Sollum on the Libya/Egyptian border, Montgomery begins a major British offensive. He is promoted to full General and knighted.

$$* * * * *$$

- November Eleventh -

- Algiers -

The British begin to move east from Algiers and take Bougie. They are functioning with little air cover and as a result several of their support ships are lost to the Luftwaffe. The Germans have now deployed in excess of one thousand troops to Tunisia.

* * * * *

- Stalingrad -

The Germans mount a major attack which faces staunch defenders and while some small successes are made, it is relatively uncoordinated and accomplishes little.

* * * * *

- Libya -

Advanced units of the Eighth Army reach Halfaya Pass and move into Libya. They take Bardia unopposed. On the Egyptian border the New Zealand Division halts to reorganize.

* * * * *

- Malta -

Convoys sailing from Alexandria reach the island and an official announcement advises that it has been *'relieved of its siege'*.

* * * * *

- November Twelfth -

- Eastern Front -

German forces relieve the 13th Panzer Division from a

short Russian encirclement south of Terek.

* * * * *

- Guadalcanal -

A major American convoy carying relief supplies and reinforcements is forced to change course due to the approach of a large Japanese naval fleet. The light cruiser, USS *'Juneau'* is sunk.

* * * * *

- Libya -

British advance units enter Tobruk.

* * * * *

- Washington -

The draft age is lowered from twenty to eighteen.

* * * * *

- Tunisia/Algeria -

A combined sea and air operation takes Bone and the nearby airport. German supply ships begin docking in Bizerta despite the fact that local French commanders attempt to block it and prevent them from using it.

* * * * *

- November Thirteenth -

- North Africa -

The British retake Tobruk.

* * * * *

- Algeria -

The Allied forces at Bone receive much needed reinforcements. The British 36th Brigade passes Djidejelli in their advance from Algiers.

A formal agreement between General Clark and Darlan acknowledges the French Admiral as head of the French civil government in North Africa. He will command the French forces which are now joining the Allied side of the conflict.

* * * * *

- Guadalcanal -

A Japanese convoy consisting of eleven transports holding eleven thousand men and escorted by eleven destroyers is headed for another attempt at taking Henderson Field. In support, Japanese Admiral, Hiroaki Abe, commands two battleships, two cruisers and fourteen destroyers and the Japanese carriers lying off to the north are to provide air cover. US Admiral, Daniel Callaghan, commanding five cruisers and eight destroyers, moves to intercept the Japanese naval support formation.

When the dust settles, the Americans have lost two cruisers and four destroyers and the Japanese lose two cruisers and suffer damage to all their other ships. The Japanese convoy turns back.

Later in the day the Japanese battleship *'Hiei'*, which had been badly damaged in the earlier confrontation, is torpedoed by American carrier aircraft from the USS *'Enterprise'* and damaged so severely that it has to be scuttled.

* * * * *

November Fourteenth -

- Guadalcanal -

The Japanese invasion convoy headed for Henderson Field swings about and makes another attempt to land its troops.

It comes under immediate air attack, primarily from aircraft stationed at Henderson and seven of the transports and two warships are sunk. Despite these losses, during the night, the convoy steams towards its target and there is another confrontation off Savo Island.

The Japanese covering force now consists of the battleship *'Kirishima'*, four cruisers and nine destroyers. The Americans now bring in Task Force 64 made up of the battleships USS *'Washington'* and *'South Dakota'* supported by four destroyers. *'South Dakota'* is hit and pulled out of the battle. *'Washington'* sinks the *'Kirishima'*.

While this battle rages the remaining Japanese transports manage to land their troops and supplies, but not without additional losses.

* * * * *

- November Fifteenth -

- Tunisia/Algeria -

The British 36th takes Tabarka on the coast road to Bizerta. US paratroops capture the airfield at Youks les Bains near Tebessa. The Germans have moved quickly to build up their numbers and now have ten thousand men taking up positions in Tunisia.

One hundred Luftwaffe combat ready aircraft have taken over long-established French bases near to the front and these have all-weather runways while the allies are forced to use temporary landing fields located further inland.

* * * * *

- New Guinea -

After construction of temporary bridges, the Australians cross the Kumusi and quickly take Wairopi and Ilimow.

* * * * *

- November Sixteenth -

- Tunisia -

Souk el Arba is taken by a British paratroop battalion and to the north, the 36th Brigade captures Djebel Abiod.

Despite de Gaulle's declaration that he and his Free French supporters cannot accept Darlan's authority and the fact that many British politicians are not particularly interested in the American's decision to make use of the unexpected capture of the French Vichy Admiral, Eisenhower, Nogues and Juin ratify the agreement that Clark has made with him.

They have no hesitancy in accepting the turncoat and placing him in command of the French Vichy troops.

* * * * *

- November Seventeenth -

- Libya -

Forward troops of the Eight Army take Derna on the coast and Mechili as they move inland.

* * * * *

- New Guinea -

The Japanese deliver one thousand troops at Buna. Their positions around Sanananda, Buna and Gona have also been solidly reinforced. All are now well garrisoned.

* * * * *

- November Eighteenth -

- Berlin -

Bomber Command make a very heavy raid on the city and their losses are small.

* * * * *

- November Nineteenth -

- Eastern Front -

The tide has turned as the Russians begin the winter offensive along the Don. Along the battle lines in southern Russia the German defenders are dangerously overextended. The Russians plan a pincer attack and the northern arm now swings into action with five hundred thousand infantry, nine hundred new T-34 tanks, and over one thousand attack aircraft.

In the Caucasus, the Russians also give the Germans a hiding near Ordzhonikidze.

* * * * *

- Tunisia -

French units at Medjez el Bab resist the Germans and are quickly reinforced by British and American troops.

* * * * *

- Libya -

Forward units of the British Eighth Army reach Benghazi.

* * * * *

- New Guinea -

The Australians are nearing Gona and a joint Allied force is moving in on Sanananda. US troops from Pongani reach Buna and begin their attack. The entrenched and reinforced Japanese positions easily throw them back.

* * * * *

- November Twentieth -

- Libya -

The Africa Corps continues its retreat westward as the Eighth Army takes Benghazi.

* * * * *

- Eastern Front -

The southern claw of the Russians pincer movement begins its attacks. The Germans throw in support in the shape of the 29th Panzer Grenadier Division but it is far too little, too late.

* * * * *

- Vichy France -

The Aging Petain, who has recently granted power to Laval, with regard to issuing of decrees on his own authority, takes to the airwaves telling his people that Germany will win the war and that the alternative to that eventuality would be to be ruled by *'Jews and Communists'*.

* * * * *

- New Guinea -

The Australians attack at Gona. They gain entry but are eventually repulsed.

* * * * *

- November Twenty-First -

- Eastern Front -

The Russians have broken though the Rumanian Third Army's lines on a fifty mile front. Other tank units are advancing rapidly toward Kalach. The Russians have advanced so quickly that the German Sixth Army's Headquarters staff has had to move and General Manstein, who has been ordered by Hitler to take command of a new Army Group Don, has just begun his long train journey to take up the post.

* * * * *

- Guadalcanal -

The Americans are in the final planning stages to push the Japanese forces off the extreme western end of Guadalcanal.

* * * * *

- November Twenty-Second -

- Libya -

German troops fall back to El Agheila as Montgomery halts his six hundred mile, fourteen day advance, to reorganize his forces.

* * * * *

- French West Africa -

Darlan publicly announces that he is now in command of the government.

* * * * *

- Eastern Front -

The Russians capture the important bridge over the Don at Kalach. Advance units then cross over the bridge and link up with the tip of the other pincer movement and the three hundred thousand German troops are now encircled within the city. The Russians believe, incorrectly, that there are only eighty-five thousand Germans trapped in the net.

General Paulus telegraphs Hitler to inform him that the German 6th Army is surrounded and under siege.

Five Rumanian divisions surrender around Raspopinskaya.

* * * * *

- November Twenty-Third -

- Eastern Front -

Fighting within Stalingrad is intense. General Paulus receives a reply to his telegram to Hitler. The Fuhrer orders Paulus not to retreat, at any cost.

* * * * *

- November Twenty-Fourth -

- Eastern Front -

Manstein arrives at Army Group 'A' Headquarters. His command now consists of very little. The Sixth Army and most of the Fourth Panzer Army are surrounded by the Russian Pincer movement which the Russians are reinforcing strongly. Five divisions of the Rumanian Third Army have now surrendered. All he has available to him that is of any significance, is a division holding a position at Elista, which he should maintain in position as it is his only link with Army Group 'A' in the Caucuses. He immediately asks for reinforcements from the other German Army Group commanders and the High Command but these are met with reluctance and he receives little, and that in dribs and drabs. Hitler stands firm on his determination to hold Stalingrad and despite the fact that Goering's star within the inner circle has long since shone brightly, he chooses to believe the Reichsmarschall, when Goering boasts to him that the encircled forces in the city need not concern themselves about their situation, in that his Luftwaffe can supply them by air.

* * * * *

- November Twenty-Fifth -

- Stalingrad -

The Russian encirclement of the city continues to firm

up. Hitler again orders General Paulus not to surrender under any circumstances.

* * * * *

- Greece -

In *'Operation Harling'* a team of British SOE agents working with over two hundred Greek guerrillas, blow up the Gorgopotamos railway bridge which had been used to carry reinforcements and supplies for Rommel's Africa Korps.

* * * * *

- November Twenty-Sixth -

- Australia -

In Brisbane fighting breaks out between American and Australian soldiers. There are several fatalities before order can be restored.

* * * * *

- Eastern Front -

Russian unconfirmed reports have it that they have taken Krasnoye, Selo and Generalov. There is a general lull as the Russians concentrate on building up the encirclement of Stalingrad over other concerns.

* * * * *

- Tunisia -

The British drive the Germans out of Medjez Bab and the German-held field at Djedeida comes under attack by a US tank battalion.

* * * * *

- November Twenty-Seventh -

- Vichy France -

The German II SS Panzer Corps occupies Toulon, its intention to take control of the French fleet moored there. The French, who were recently given the opportunity to sail and join the Allies off the shores of North African waters, now choose to scuttle the three battleships, seven cruisers, sixteen submarines and sixty-two smaller craft, rather than turn them over to the Germans.

* * * * *

- Tunisia -

Allied forces take Tebourba, which is fifteen miles west of Tunis, while another column is approaching Bizerta.

* * * * *

- November Twenty-Eighth-

- Tunisia -

British paratroops land at Depienne and begin to move toward Oudna. Allied forces who have taken Djedeida come under heavy fire and begin to fall back.

* * * * *

- London -

Churchill broadcasts to warn the Italian people that they must choose between a full-scale Allied attack and a revolt against Mussolini.

* * * * *

- November Thirtieth -

- Guadalcanal -

Overnight the naval *'Battle of Tassafaronga'* begins. In this action the Japanese forces sink one American cruiser and damage three others.

CHAPTER TWENTY-THREE

- December -

- Hitler -

Field Marshal von Manstein manages to gather his minimal forces together in preparation for the relief of Paulus's encircled Sixth Army at Stalingrad by the twelfth of December.

The push was originally scheduled to begin in early December, but it wasn't until the twelfth that the two armoured divisions were ready to move forward in a single thrust. Two hundred and thirty tanks head northeast toward the city which is some sixty miles away. As they begin to move the frozen ground is melting under sunny skies and soon the slopes become treacherous for the heavy machines.

When Hitler enters the room for the noon conference his first words uttered are:

'Has there been some disaster?'

He was told that the units had met little resistance and that the only Russian attacks so far had been against the sector held by Italian formations.

As he took his position at the map table he grumbled.

'I've had more sleepless night over this business in the south than anything else. One doesn't know what's going on.'

Six days later Paulus and his troops are still waiting for the sight of German armour on the horizon but all they see is Russian formations moving out to take on the anticipated relief columns.

On the eighteenth, a frustrated von Manstein, concerned about the slow progress of his troops, requests of Zeitzler the authorization to order Paulus to break out toward them so that most of his men can be saved.

Zeitzler readily endorses the request as he hands it to

Hitler. The Italian Eighth Army had been routed by the Russians on that day and Hitler has remained adamant that Paulus should hold until relieved by von Manstein. The next afternoon the Field Marshal radios Hitler for permission to order Paulus to break out toward him. Although showing signs of waffling under Zeitzler's repeated urgings, Hitler refuses to grant the request.

Paulus is at the point where he is prepared to disobey Hitler and attempt a breakout but by this time it is too late. He has less than one hundred tanks and only enough fuel to travel less than twenty miles. Added to that is the fact that he has not enough ammunition left for defense purposes, let alone enough to make an offensive drive.

On the twenty third of December von Manstein has no choice but to halt the relief column. In order to hold the front he has to send one of his panzer divisions to plug up the hole left by the now fleeing Italian troops on his flank. In the early evening he sent Paulus a message.

'If worst came to worst - could he break out?'

Paulus responds by asking if that means he has authorization to do so, warning.

'Once it is launched, there will be no turning back.'

Von Manstein responds by telling him that he cannot give that authority today, but hopes to be able to do so the next day. It was wishful thinking. Hitler would not give the order and by this point in time, Paulus no longer has any chance of success at such an attempt, even if Hitler does relent.

The Sixth Army is doomed.

* * * * *

- Berchtesgaden -

- Speer -

In late forty-two, Morell, Hitler's doctor, had advised him to get some rest and surprisingly the Fuhrer had agreed and set off for the Obersalzberg. He asked Speer to join him there.

When in residence at the Berghof, Hitler saw to it that his favoured members of the inner circle surrounded him, trusted faces and good humour to help him forget his problems and improve his mood.

The evening Speer arrived Hitler was morose, spending his time staring listlessly into the flames flickering on the open hearth. The next morning he found the Fuhrer tired and apathetic but toward afternoon Hitler asked Speer to join him for his daily walk.

When they were ready to leave, Hitler told Bormann, who normally accompanied him, to wait with the others and it was just he, Speer and his dog Blondie who set out onto the recently snow-cleared path. They walked together silently for several minutes and then Hitler said.

'I hate the east. Even the snow depresses me. Sometimes I think that I won't come to these mountain in the winter. I don't want to see or smell the snow.'

Hitler continued on in that vein, his voice a monotone and then he paused and turned to face Speer.

'Speer, you are my architect. You know that my wish was always to be an architect. The World War and the criminal revolution of nineteen-eighteen prevented that. And the Jews! November ninth was the result of their systematic, undermining activities.'

As he spoke his voice began to rise and grew hoarse.

'It was the Jews then too. They even organized the strikes in the munitions factories. We lost hundreds of soldiers because of that just in my regiment alone. The Jews forced me into politics.'

Speer was surprised by the vehemence of Hitler's tirade as it expanded and continued. He had expected a portrayal of disappointment over the lost Battle of Stalingrad or Montomery's breakthroughs at Alamein; a host of other things, but not this outflow of bitterness and poisonous resentment against the Jews.

* * * * *

- SS Fighting Units -

Himmler's eternal strides toward empire building knew no bounds and in order to achieve his ends he did everything in his growing influence with Hitler to expand his SS organization. This was reflected by the rapid expansion of the *'Waffen-SS'* (fighting SS troops) since the beginning of the war.

In October of thirty-nine, with Hitler's authorization, its numbers rose from eighteen thousand to over one hundred thousand members. In March of nineteen-forty, at Himmler's urging, Hitler had authorised the creation of four SS-Motorized Artillery battalions, one for each division and the existing units and one for the *'SS Leibstandarte'*.

At that time, the OKW who held the command of the *'Waffen-SS'* was strongly against any expansion of Himmler's supposedly elite *'special fighting units'*, considering them ill-trained, ill-led and generally an affront to the troops of the regular army. This resulted in a determined hesitancy upon their part to deliver the ordered supplies necessary to provide these new battalions with the weapons they required to fulfill their mandate, as they would have to come from their own, jealously held, resources. As a result of this obstructive attitude, only the *'SS Leibstandarte'* battalion had been up to strength in time for the invasion of France.

Himmler continued to push for expansion and personally strived for his own independent High Command for the fighting units of the SS and in August of nineteen-forty, Hitler granted him the right to form the *'Kommandoamt der Waffen-SS'* within the *'SS Fuhrungshauptamt'*. From that date the SS commanded their own formations.

In the same month Himmler, who was doing very well in gleaning recruits from the Hitler Youth programs but wanted a much large pool from which to draw in SS members, got Hitler's approval to begin recruiting volunteers from the conquered territories out of the pool of ethnic German and

Germanic populations found there.

Hitler had been hesitant to use foreigners of whatever ethnic background to flush out his elite *'party fighting units'*, but gave the go ahead for the formation of a new division to be made up from foreign nationals with the proviso that they be led by German officers.

By June of forty-one, the *'SS Regiment Nordland'* made up of Danish and Norwegian volunteers had been formed and the *'SS Division Westland'* had been created from Dutch and Flemish volunteers. These two regiments, together with Germania, which was transferred from the Reich Division were then formed into the *'SS Division Wiking'*.

This endeavour proved so successful, with volunteers coming forth in such numbers, that the SS was forced to open a new training camp at Sennheim in Alsace-Lorraine, just to handle foreign volunteers.

In March of forty-two another new Division, the *'7th SS Volunteer Mountain Division Prinz Eugen'*, was formed. This division was recruited from the *'Volksdeutsche'* (ethnic Germans), who were drafted under threat of punishment by the local German leadership in Croatia, Serbia, Hungry and Romania and used primarily for anti-partisan operations in the Balkans.

Himmler then approved the introduction of formal compulsory service for the *'Volksdeutsche'* in German occupied Serbia. An additional division was formed simultaneously when the SS Cavalry Brigade was used as the cadre in the formation of the *'8th Cavalry Division Florian Geyer'*.

The front line division of the 'Waffen-SS', who had fought through the Russian winter of forty-one and forty-two and the Russia counter-offensive were withdrawn to France to recover and be re-formed as *'Panzergrenadier'* divisions.

Himmler had convinced Hitler that the three divisors, *'Leibstandarte'*, *'Das Reich'* and *'Totenkopf''*, should be re-formed with a full regiment of tanks rather than a simple battalion. This would mean that these divisions were now full-strength Panzer divisions and each would receive nine Tiger tanks which were to be formed into heavy panzer companies. Himmler now arguably commanded elite troops indeed.

* * * * *

- Concentration Camps -

- Birkenau -

Sterilization experiments on women begin.

* * * * *

- Extermination Camps -

- Belzec -

Between March and December of forty-two approximately six hundred thousand individuals had been deported to the camp and given *'Special Treatment'*. Most came from the ghettos of southern Poland. Jews from Germany, Austria and Bohemian and Moravia were also dealt with at this camp, as well as several hundred gypsies. Deportations to Belzec ended in December of forty-two and the remaining prisoners then began to exhume the bodies from the burial pits and cremate them.

* * * * *

- Castle von Stauffer -

Upon docking in Bordeaux, Eric had only waited long enough to see to the organization for resupply and repaints for his U-boat before boarding a train for Friedrichshafen. A car had been sent to pick him up at station in town and bring him up to the castle in time for dinner.

It was the first time that the entire family had been

together for some time and there was light and lively conversation throughout the meal while everyone got caught up on what the others had been doing. After dessert had been served and the table cleared, the tone grew more serious as the Count took precedence over the various conversations and asked everyone to join him in the library.

Once inside the room, tea and brandy had been served and cigars fired up. Gabriella's little one was given over to the care of a nanny and Karl dismissed the servants for the evening.

It was rare for the Count to interfere directly into the activities of his immediate family, but he had every intention of spending a good part of the remainder of the evening by taking advantage of the fact that they were all under one roof, to advise them of his future plans.

Recent developments necessitated a full understanding by all present and that now meant that, the women especially, needed to be given a full understanding of what was to come.

There was a hesitancy to converse and a sense of expectation in the room as he rose from his chair and crossed to stand in front of the brightly burning logs in the big fireplace and all eyes were on him as he turned to face them.

"While it has been wonderful to see you all again, I have to tell you that it was not for that reason that I've arranged for all of us to be together at this time. There have been recent important developments that have taken place outside the control and confines of our family alone. As is my responsibility as head of the family, it has become necessary that I take steps to ensure that the family comes out of the resulting disaster on its feet and prepared to take on the difficulties of a very different world.

The defeat of our forces in Stalingrad, coupled with other developments leave me with little doubt that Germany is going to lose this war...."

Erica, still a very strong party supporter and appalled at the suggestion, opened her mouth to speak and the Count, none too gently, cut her off.

"Hold your tongue for now please Erika. There will be plenty of time for discussion after I finish what I have to say."

The Countess flushed slightly and then nodded her head and Karl shifted his eyes from her as he continued.

"As I was saying, Germany will lose this war because it has dragged on too long. We had the manpower and weapons to win this war if we had waited a little longer to prepare for it and it had been better planned, however, that did not happen and now it has become a war of attrition and that is not a war that Germany can win.

We are already suffering manpower shortages and our expanded enemy base is not. While our weapons are still superior to those of our enemies, we cannot continue to produce sufficient numbers of these to hope to compete with the production levels of the western nations. It is no longer a question of if we can win but has become one of when will we lose. My answer to that is that we can last for perhaps another two years, but not much longer."

He paused to let that statement sink in, letting his eyes flick from face to face to assess their individual reaction.

Erika and Gabriella both registered disbelief, Konrad nodded his head in understanding and Friedrich appeared curious. The Count let out a heavy breath and carried on.

"I foresaw this situation prior to war breaking out and as both Wilhelm and Eric are fully aware of what steps I took at that time and have been kept up to date on developments as they arose, I know they understand what is ahead of us. In order to protect the rest of you, I have only told you on an individual basis what was necessary for you to know as time went on. Under the present circumstances, however, I think it is time that we are all bought up to speed."

Over the next three hours he did exactly that, fully outlining and explaining his plans for the future and answering all their questions.

CHAPTER TWENTY-FOUR

- December -

- Allied Air Operations -

Bomber Command hits German targets in Munich, Duisburg and Frankfurt. The Americans bomb French targets at Abbeville and Rouen. There are additional joint force strikes. RAF bombers from British basis strike the Italian city of Turin on three occasions. Combined RAF and US operations flying out of North Africa hit Naples five times as well as Palermo and Taranto.

The RAF drops a total of three thousand tons and the US Eighth Air Force, based in Britain, drops three hundred and seventy tons.

* * * * *

- Battle of the Atlantic -

Two hundred and twelve U-boats are now on operational patrols.

U-boats sink sixty ships for a total of three hundred and thirty thousand tons. The revamped encoding system being used by Donetz for messaging his U-boats is broken for the first time. The code-breaking is difficult and there are often delays between the receipt of messages and the breaking of the cipher. Experience and time will improve this situation as the month goes on.

* * * * *

- December First -

- US -

Gasoline rationing commences.

* * * * *

- Guadalcanal -

Japanese destroyers sink the cruiser USS *'Northampton'*.

* * * * *

- December Second -

- Atomic Research -

The first manmade self-sustaining reaction is achieved by the research team working under Enrico Femi at the University of Chicago.

* * * * *

- New Guinea -

Australian forces capture part of the Gona defences. A Japanese convoy bringing reinforcements for Buna is forced to reroute by fierce air bombardment but the troops are landed on the coast further to the west.

* * * * *

- December Third -

- Tunisia -

The German 10th Panzer Group takes Djedeida and

Tebourba.

* * * * *

- December Fourth -

The first US bombing of mainland Italy strikes Naples. Two Italian cruisers are sunk and the dock area suffers damage.

* * * * *

- December Sixth -

- Netherlands -

The RAF bombs Eindhoven.

* * * * *

- New Guinea -

Allied troops reach the beach on the east side of Buna.

* * * * *

- Tunisia -

Renewed German attacks push the Allies back near Medjez el Bab.

* * * * *

- December Seventh -

-US -

One year after the Japanese attack on Pearl Harbor the

Americans launch the battleship USS *'New Jersey'*.

* * * * *

- Bordeaux -

British Commandos make a raid, *'Operation Frankton'*, against the shipping in the harbour.

* * * * *

- December Eighth -

-London -

Conscription is lowered to eighteen years.

* * * * *

- Tunisia -

German forces occupy Bizerta, capturing four French destroyers, nine submarines and three additional warships.

* * * * *

- December Ninth -

- Guadalcanal -

The battered marines are relieved by the American army and head for Australia for rest and reorganization.

* * * * *

- December Twelfth -

- Tunisia -

Italian midget submarines sink four ships in Algiers Harbor. There is heavy fighting at Medjez el Bab.

* * * * *

- North Africa -

Rommel abandons El Agheila and retreats toward Tripoli.

* * * * *

- Stalingrad -

Field Marshal Manstein unleashes his forces for the break-though to Stalingrad. The offensive is code named *'Operation Winter Storm'*. He had assembled a total of thirteen divisions for the operation including three Panzer units and initially has armoured superiority.

* * * * *

- December Thirteenth -

- Libya -

Eighth Army captures Mersa Brega.

* * * * *

- Stalingrad -

The Luftwaffe attempts to supply the trapped troops from the air. They achieve little.

* * * * *

- Tunisia -

The Americans send heavy air raids against Bizerta and Tunis.

* * * * *

- December Fourteenth -

- Stalingrad -

Under the command of General Hoth, Manstein's relief column makes good progress. The airlifting Luftwaffe fare better but manage to drop only one hundred and eighty tons of supplies to the marooned troops.

* * * * *

- Madagascar -

Anthony Eden and de Gaulle agree that the administration of the island be handed over to the Free French. General le Gentilhomme is appointed as the High Commissioner.

* * * * *

- Libya -

The 7th Armoured Division commences attacks against the El Agheila line as the New Zealanders try an outflanking maneuver.

* * * * *

- New Guinea -

Just west of Gona, the Japanese land reinforcements and begin to head along the coast toward the Australian's flank. Australian and American forces continue to thrust at Buna, which they manage to take.

* * * * *

- December Fifteenth-

- Solomons -

Japanese landings are made with the aim of constructing an airfield on Munda, which they plan to use to support their operations on Guadalcanal.

* * * * *

- December Sixteenth -

- Eastern Front -

The Russians begin the next phase of their winter offensive. On this occasion they attack the lines held by the Italian Eighth Army on the middle Don and shatter it. There are very few German units left in this area. The Russians are purposely hitting non-German units to disrupt the defensive line. They next hit along the Chir, taking on Army Detachment *'Hollidt'*. The German attempt to breakout the encircled troops at Stalingrad is still progressing well. However, the Russians breaking through in the north threatens encirclement, something that Manstein has worried about for several weeks.

* * * * *

- Guadalcanal -

The Japanese destroyer *'Kagero'* is damaged by American dive bombers and US troops begin their offensive against Mount Austen.

* * * * *

- Burma -

The British have assembled two brigades and are about to attack the Japanese lines between Maungdaw and Buthidaung but before they can begin their offensive, the Japanese pull out and move south to re-form on a shorter line between Gwedauk and Kondan.

* * * * *

- December Seventeenth -

- Stalingrad -

The Volga finally freezes solid. This allows the Russians to send supplies to their troops on the west bank. Hoth's relief column is still advancing and his leading tanks have now reached the Aksai River.

* * * * *

- Tunisia -

The US air force hits Tunis and Gabes and other German air bases.

* * * * *

- December Eighteenth -

- New Guinea -

With the Australians now leading the attack, the Allies take Cape Endiadere, east of Buna. They have now received tank support.

* * * * *

- December Nineteenth -

- Eastern Front -

The Russians take Konemirovka. Hoth's troops are grinding to a halt and are held at the Myshkova River. Manstein orders Paulus to attempt an immediate breakout. The Chief of Staff of the Sixth Army, General Schmidt who is a staunch Nazi and determined to do as Hitler has ordered, convinces Paulus to refuse any breakout attempt and hold his ground.

* * * * *

- December Twenty-Second -

- Eastern Front -

The Germans begin an orderly retreat from the Caucuses. The renewed Russian offensive is gaining speed and they retake Moroszovsk, Fydorovka and Nikolkoe.

Although Hoth had been forced to halt, the encircled troops inside Stalingrad can now hear the raging battle. Manstein pleads for Hitler to order a breakout but his pleas fall on deaf ears.

* * * * *

- Tunisia -

The British begin a renewed attack just north of Medjez el Bab. Heavy rain hampers the fighting centers around Longstop Hill.

* * * * *

- December Twenty-Fourth -

- Algiers -

French Admiral Darlan, the valuable Allied turncoat, is assassinated.

* * * * *

- Tunisia -

A British Guards Battalion takes Longstop Hill.

* * * * *

- December Twenty-Fifth -

- Rabaul -

US bombers launch an air strike from Guadalcanal.

* * * * *

- Libya -

The Axis forces garrisoning Sirte withdraw.

* * * * *

- Tunisia -

German forces retake Longstop Hill.

* * * * *

- December Twenty-Sixth -

- Eastern Front -

Hoth's Stalingrad relief column is now forced to retreat south of the Don as the Russian advance nears Kotelnikovo.

* * * * *

- December Twenty-Eighth -

- Vichy Somaliland -

The governor of the pro-Vichy territory surrenders to invading British and Free French forces.

* * * * *

- Vichy France -

Petain takes to the airwaves and describes the Free French leaders as having betrayed French Africa to the British and the Americans.

* * * * *

- December Twenty-Ninth-

- Eastern Front -

The Russians recapture Kotelnikovo.

* * * * *

- December Thirtieth -

- Eastern Front -

The Russians take Remontnoe.

* * * * *

- December Thirty-First -

Rommel is sidelined in Tunisia, the German Sixth Army is encircled and under siege at Stalingrad and the Japanese appear to be considering the abandonment of Guadalcanal.

As the final day of the year slips past, the Allies can now begin to see the light at the end of the tunnel.

Other Books by Patrick Laughy

Paperbacks

The Little Black Book

Alumni

The 4th Reich Books 1,2 and 3

E-books

The Little Black Book

Alumni

Atlantis-Ship of the Gods

The 4th Reich Book 1 Part 1

The 4th Reich Book 1 Part 2

The 4th Reich Book 2 Part 1

The 4th Reich Book 2 Part 2

The 4th Reich Book 3 Part 1

The 4th Reich Book 3 Part 2

The 4th Reich

The 4th Reich Book 4 Part 1

The 4th Reich Book 4 Part 2

Coming soon

The 4th Reich Book 5 Part 1

www.ingramcontent.com/pod-product-compliance
Lightning Source LLC
Chambersburg PA
CBHW070759180626
46818CB00001B/18